CETAPIENS

S. Amaranthine
1/29/2016

Cetapiens / S. Amaranthine – 1st ed.

978-0-9963229-3-5

Dedication
This book is for Claire and Kate.

ACKNOWLEDGEMENTS

First and foremost I would like to thank David C. Ellerhorst for his support throughout the writing of Cetapiens. Were it not for his backing, these words would never have come to page.

A special note of thanks goes to Laura Geraci for editing the final draft. Her patient and meticulous attention to this project were exactly what was needed. She took the time to read, study and re-read as well as edit. She provided professional, thoughtful feedback based on thorough knowledge of the book contents and her suggestions were wonderful.

A heartfelt thank you goes out to Jenn Stark for reading an early draft of Cetapiens, despite her own hectic writing workload. Thank you Jenn for making the book better by honestly pointing out what absolutely needed to go as well as your favorite bits!

A HUGE thank you goes out to Chris Christensen for reading a final unedited draft for content and suggestions. Chris, your suggested list of terms to add to the Glossary will no doubt be useful to readers.

Thank you to Heather Osborn for providing a professional beta read and early editing. As usual, Heather provided timely, helpful feedback.

Thank you Liz Bemis of Bemis Promotions for your graphic art talent in putting the cover together.

A note of acknowledgement is due to the cetaceans who share this world with us. Their continued plight motivates me to write their character representatives in Cetapiens as I anticipate they would wish them to be. Promising future breakthroughs in communication with dolphins are perhaps only a few short years away. I hope to witness a time when a book such as this one is translated in audio version for them.

Last, but certainly not least, thanks so much to the early readers of The Vencello, the first book of the trilogy, after it was published. Your interest, reviews and kind comments kept me on schedule for Cetapiens, book two of the series!

INTRODUCTION

Who would be interested in this book? I think a reader who wants to sink their literary teeth into thinking outside of the box on time travel, what passes for human achievements, and with the novelty of getting into the mind of a dolphin or whale, would get the most out of this book. Also, those who would like to share an imagined experience outside of our perceived universe, that is explore the multiverse, would get a kick out of it.

What is this book? This is the second in a trilogy. The Vencello was the first of the three. Loosely, that was conception, a new life, a sentient universe emerging from a pre-existing one. This second book, Cetapiens, can be thought of as childhood. It is the result of transition from one universe to another, the subjection to chaos and then making sense of it, the uncertainty of a new way of being, learning what is, how it all works, and what one can and can't do. It is not a traditional book, in the sense that it can be skimmed over quickly. Like childhood, you learn by experience, reflection and repetition. Cetapiens defines new universes and ways of being based on ours because a frame of reference cannot be avoided in order to make sense.

VACATION

In one word, that is what I hope this book will provide the reader. Cetapiens is fiction but I hope the reader will find it a well thought out one. It has been carefully constructed, so I may take a believable albeit surreal extended break, with the reader, from being human, away from this planet, and even apart from this universe.

In the Company of Fictitious Family Members

For a while, exist in a world of human and cetacean species-combined progeny where there is so much more, where we are all hilariously outclassed by Priori – living universes. Universes are characters in this book. From book one; we learn The Vencello is a simple sentient carbon-60 molecule universe. Cetapiens continues; you can visit the ancestral universe, The Vencello, and it might be aware that you are there.

Time is the toy of Priori, and everything in the multiverse has already happened in the past. All suns, within those universes that contain them, have long ago gone nova and all species that depended on them have become extinct. Individuals of those past species are either revisited by Priori or not, as they prefer. As the multiverse and its pasts are accessed by them, events are variables. Time and death are non-sequitur.

For such beings pleasant experiences are paramount. They necessarily avoid pain and discomfort that might be felt as they naturally merge with organic objects within their focus. For Priori, technology is not the prize-winner modern humans believe it should be. Rather, combined sentience and non-technology dependent harmony with nature and the multiverse is favored, such as achieved by cetaceans. That is not to say the vacation is always pleasant. Priori are subject to peril. Their diffusion throughout the multiverse is possible as well as entrapment in the multiverse self-protective reflexes triggered by time paradox.

ACOUSTICS

That is what written words cannot provide. The world of cetaceans is acoustic rich albeit devoid of human language. This book had to be written, so I invite the reader to visit http://cetapiens.com and find the Cetapiens suggested playlist page. Enjoy the acoustic selections I have chosen, but use anything that you know will augment your journey of imagination through word, sound and imagery. Also, listening to recordings of orca vocalization and sperm whale echolocation will enhance the experience of reading the cetacean passages of this book.

TIME

In one word, that's what this book will take. I have endeavored that it be a pleasant extraction. I do not like to have my intelligence insulted when I read and have written my own books with that in mind. Enjoy learning what can only be visited by imagination; multiverse realms, mental landscapes, intriguing believable beings and their advanced long lost culture. Cetapiens is meant to be challenging. Creating and defining new universes and fictional human history, should not be easy. It has not been for me. A glossary of fictional Cetapiens terminology is provided at the end of this book and I believe it will help the reader greatly. I enjoy having my mind expanded and playing with ideas opened to me. So, I aspire to offer what I love best in books to my reader.

TIME-SAVER

Each chapter includes subheadings that help the reader switch perspective at each transition between universes and character groups.

Who or what did I write this book for?

- *Humans* – I love science fiction and time travel and I have enjoyed many of those related products of human entertainment. But I would not have done it that way. This is my way, 180 degrees in the opposite direction of most, for the record.
  - o Especially for my children, my beloved Claire and Kate.
  - o And my grandchildren (who, by the way, are not born yet at the time I write these words.)

These are the times and places I would love to have *really* gone myself, but could not, because they are outside the realm of human limitations. They exist only in my mind, where I long to bring you. This is a family vacation to be had by reading in your own time and then closing your eyes and going there. Hopefully you will imagine me there too.

- *Cetaceans* – They are a footnote if mentioned at all in the majority of science fiction and fantasy of my time and for that I am writing this trilogy, a tribute and an apology to them. They are not only included, they are central to the themes. Maybe one day we can translate books so they can enjoy them. I hope they like my trilogy.

- o Note to all cetaceans in general: I get it, you guys rock.

- **Orca** – If I could choose what I can come back to live as, in another life, it would be an orca. Or a sperm whale. But orcas are way prettier and I am that shallow. I believe we are all one and that they are the best part of me.
  - o Note to orca matriarchs: If I could have saved your children and grandchildren from our slavery, I would have. Their plight makes me ashamed to be human.

- **Sperm Whales** – Their brains are so massive and communication so different, it leaves me worlds apart even though we share the same planet.
  - o Note to sperm whales: More than any other species on my planet, I regret I could not know yours as you do. It is not possible that I accurately imagine the amazing intelligence and true nature you possess. I hope I have done some small justice to your kind. You deserve more than just this trilogy that puts you on the pedestal you deserve. I humbly offer this to you.

- **Cephalopods** – Our fellow non-mammalian sentient Earthlings. If we ever send astronauts to Europa, I suspect they'll be present, albeit unwillingly. They can go where humans can't, and we humans need to know. If I am right, I hope those individuals survive whatever is in store for them and if they don't, I hope the end is quick and merciful.
  - o Note to Cephalopods: You guys rock too.

- **Our Planet and our Universe** – I'm stuck like a fly on sticky paper in/on it. I *love* it.
  - o (Note to God: Remember when I said I wanted to know everything and you answered it would break my heart and I said I wanted to know anyway? Well, you were right. I don't even know near everything and already my heart is permanently broken. I'll keep going though. After all these decades and no matter what, I still really do want to know everything, even though I know my brain can't handle it.)

- ***All Other Universes and the Multiverse*** – I can only imagine, and do. (See bullet note above)

What is next? Since The Vencello was conception, and Cetapiens is childhood, it follows that the third of the trilogy, entitled Orcasekai, will be adulthood. I will have written three different books, each different in style from each other. While they are continuation of the same story, they are from vastly different perspectives, from molecules to universe, from ancestors to progeny. It seemed fitting to do it that way. The universe is set in motion in book one. The early lessons are learned in book two and now I can move on and write the third volume introducing the universe of Orcasekai, the world of the Orca, my imaginary grown up vacation world.

CHAPTER 1 – ITERATION

Universe: Vencello

Human

The moment Alvar first came to, rather than rejoice he had survived yet another birth, he agonized. Everything hurt as if his body had been blown to bits. His sensitive skin, rebuilt tight around him, holding him together, simultaneously itched and stung. He wanted to scratch everywhere but couldn't.

He opened his eyes and made out the silhouette of a face looking down at him from off to his side. Its identifying features were shadowed by a brilliant quasar-like sun, the sole light source for the open-roof operating arena in which Alvar now lay. It took a surge of determined effort to lift his head just barely enough to see that he was reclined prone on his own bed in its center. It felt as if his whole body was wrapped tight in bandages. He looked down at one arm to make sure it was still there. Just as he had imagined, he saw the bandages. Just as he had hoped, his still had his arm. His shoulder and what he could see of his torso were wrapped tight. He looked like a mummy.

He focused on his other arm and then each leg, taking inventory. Everything that should be there was present and looked real enough.

"Well, look who's finally awake". The shadow moved to his other side as it spoke and Alvar's gaze followed.

From there he recognized the face all right. It belonged to his classmate, a potential friend turned nemesis, the same one that had stood watch while two others beat him, the last face he had seen before…

Alvar couldn't move his body below his neck. Too bad. He so

wanted to grab Johnny by the throat but nothing was moving.

"How do you feel?"

Alvar just barely managed a flinch and head jerk in place of a punch.

"Here." Johnny misinterpreted and in doing so reached down and lifted Alvar's head so he could get a better view of his body, or what was present of it. "Not fabulous is my guess. Discomfort is indisputable evidence of living. Better?"

Alvar rolled his eyes and saw that both of his hands were also covered in tight binding and then his stomach lurched. Both of his thumbs were missing.

Johnny followed Alvar's eyes. "Yeah, about those…it's the *only* rule around here, really. No thumbs." He shook his head in sympathetic disbelief. "But don't you worry, we're working on it."

Alvar began to lose consciousness.

"Good man. You go right ahead. I'm not done yet anyway." Johnny's voice faded in Alvar's ear as he babbled on to himself. "There's more to you than meets the eye Alvar. I've had a hell of a time chasing down your…"

The pain was greatly diminished the second time Alvar came to, enough to permit him to have linear, coherent thoughts. He could hear Johnny talking to someone. He was just outside the room and the door was shut. Some time had obviously passed. The sun was no longer visible overhead but daylight still lit the room from above. Alvar thought to yell for help but the mere idea of doing so was enough to exhaust him. He had to fight to remain conscious.

Johnny answered to the visitor, "He just saw me the one time…No, he couldn't speak…I can't detect any critical omissions or rogue markers and believe me I've searched, but if you really want…Great, because I'm done…wake him up if it's time, he'll be all right."

"Well, *that* took long enough. I thought he'd *never* wake up again." A second voice complained. She sounded *very* familiar.

"I promised you, because I broke it, that I would fix it. And I did." That was Johnny.

A third voice mumbled, but Alvar heard it "Will you just give him one break? He worked hard."

The woman said something that Alvar couldn't hear to which the man responded. "No. Wrong *again*."

Alvar strained to keep focused. He desperately wanted confirmation that the familiar voice belonged to his mother. Want did him no good. He passed out.

When he woke up the third time his mother was standing bedside, smiling down at him. "Alvar honey, wake up. It's momma. Wake up baby."

Relieved, he found he could finally move. He sprung up and felt his feet hit a warm, soft floor. He gave her kisses and a huge hug from which she was reluctant to release even as he finally pulled back a bit. He looked down to view the source of warmth and found the floor was either completely transparent or not even really there. He feared for a split nanosecond that he had dreamt her.

He was awake, no doubt. He had not dreamed the room or his pain. He was still there, although the bandages were gone and had been replaced with his favorite jeans and T-shirt. To his horror, his thumbs were still gone.

"Momma…" Alvar was confused and panicking as he examined the absence of scar tissue or evidence of wound. It was if he had been born that way. Nothing hurt anymore.

Delora hurried over to a window that Alvar was certain had not been there before and awkwardly pulled a cord attached to drapes. Her thumbs were missing as well. The fabric parted to showcase binary suns; the smaller had been in orbit behind the larger when Alvar had seen it earlier. Now both were on glorious display framed on each side of the opening by a rich burgundy felt curtain and a parent. The suns danced their do-si-do on their path of descent beyond a glassy calm ocean horizon. Just beyond the window, exhibiting its own dance of shadows on the water from each sun, was a dock and at the end of that, their boat.

Alvar stumbled back.

"Alvar, look at it." She nodded toward the two setting suns. They were orbiting each other so fast that he could perceive they had already changed positions.

"Who *are* you?" Now that he looked at her, she was *different*. She looked like his mother, only younger than he had ever known her and she had paddle-like appendages in place of her hands.

"You'll remember soon enough, it's me, and I love you and I am *so* glad you're finally awake, but we are out of time. We can't linger long enough to explain it all now. We need to go. I know it hurts; we'll be as gentle as possible. It's near the end. You see those suns?" She motioned to the view, "Do you know what they are?"

Alvar took a moment but it came to him. "Brough…and…*Akenehi*?"

"Exactly. Good. Can you walk? How about swim? Can you dive?" She didn't leave much time for an answer.

"Yeah…but…" His memory was coming back fast and he had a lot of questions.

They were in the Vencello. A tsunami of recollection washed through his mind.

He had had visitors other than Johnny and his mother. He remembered them now.

"Where is Amaranth? She was here…and she was with…"

Delora ignored his question and moved toward him. As soon as she touched him they were no longer in the sick room. They were in the boat with his father, Liam, whom he had never met. Liam offered his paddle appendage in handshake greeting then waved it instead as Alvar recoiled in reflex. "You'll get used to it" he smiled.

Johnny, who had only hours ago, it seemed, participated in his fatal beating, was there too.

For Johnny temporal sequences were non sequitur. He could not have accomplished his task otherwise.

Not so for Alvar. His perception of the passage of time, since he was pummeled senseless, had made it home alone, bleeding internally was that none had. Had he been conscious, he would have lost count of the years as they accelerated incrementally with each passing until he came to that boat. They were untold hundreds.

Johnny waved at Alvar too, playfully imitating his Uncle Liam. Curiously, he *did* have his thumbs. Johnny gave him 'thumbs up' with both of them and then apologized, "Not rubbing it in, I promise. I'm just passing through, visiting family." He winked at Alvar and didn't wait for a response. "I'm not from these parts. I get to keep mine so long as I don't use them here. Other than to put you back together again, that is."

Delora and Liam chattered between themselves as if they were the only two on the vessel. Their whirlwind of banter detailed with amusement the mysterious affliction that had slowly overcome the Vencello and had grown so that it now necessitated their evacuation. Delora insisted playfully they had an infection or parasite. Liam stood his ground, lightly retorting that it was a tumorous growth, a cancer.

They both cheerfully agreed the Vencello had been losing energy as a direct result of it and there was nothing any of them could do to halt the coming undesirable transformation, the death, or something analogous, of a universe.

Alvar carefully noted it all and mused it was very unlike his mother to take such grim news so very lightly. She had obviously been genetically altered. Perhaps her personality had been affected. He had nothing to compare Liam with but didn't think his mother could normally be attracted to someone who was so...*Liam*.

Without the help of wind or motor, they were transported. The binary sunset was seamlessly replaced by a single radiating sun-like orb of another realm. It felt more like his planet of origin at last, but not exactly.

"Well, you guys are home!" Johnny clapped his hands together to signal his work was complete. "Love you Uncle Liam, Aunt Delora." Johnny gave them both a quick hug, although Delora had obviously held back a bit. "And you" he smiled pointing to Alvar, "I'll be seeing you later Alvar, or should I call you Alvar-G?"

Alvar blinked at him and said nothing. *Aunt* Delora? Then he remembered some of it and was none too happy.

And with a second clap, Johnny was gone.

*****

Brough was not alone at the end. The tiny binary human orbs that had distinguished them as a rare quad-system had vanished. The remaining massive brilliance of Akenehi, the orca matriarch, reduced them to a short lived binary. Eventually she had gone too. The ambiguous growth, that Akenehi had so loved and fiercely protected as family, and that Delora and Liam had feared was a deadly disease and had wished to destroy, was still there. It was more massive than ever. Brough scanned it as he frequently did and learned it was even more complex, exhibiting increasingly purposeful behavior and it was definitely a part of them. Its expansion required energy and it had already consumed so much of their realm there was nothing left for it to do but devour him as well.

He was good with that.

The bright lights that were the apex points of his cherished sacred bit, encapsulated him. However, without Akenehi's effort in producing the required complex song, if and when the membrane was disturbed, in one snap of broken harmonic, he was certain he and the growing mass would be no more.

He was good with that too.

In his final solitary moments he had hoped to float in the center of his own private universe and enjoy peaceful reflection. The detail of the memories of his life on his planet of origin and throughout the entire existence of the Vencello was a gorgeous multi-dimensional mental map, a virtual cosmic wonderland fixed in his formidable mind. He imagined himself swimming through his favorite memories as his own light faded.

But his privacy was violated by a visit from a familiar Aware Master of the Ocean, Param. For their cetacean species, known to the humans as sperm whales, and to Akenehi as Long Jaws, they were the oldest two in existence. Param was his senior by a multiverse nano-moment but he still revered her with all of the awe and respect of an Aware elder. They exchanged formal traditional and then their affectionate familial greetings.

When he recognized it was her, he didn't mind at all. In fact it was a relief. It was better that he would pass on the data clicks that chronicled their existence and she, in turn, would pass it on to other living cetaceans. The affirmation of so many lives would be preserved in the mighty vault of Master of the Ocean community memory.

She had come to congratulate him on yet another iteration of an unprecedented long life spectacularly lived. She shared the vivid echo-details of Master lives, long separated from Brough. All of whom he so loved and who dearly loved him. He especially enjoyed learning of the new additions to their super-pod, young he knew only as echo-data representations she shared with him. He was serenely content in the knowing. She, in turn, received his updated precious mind-sculpture of memory mapped to include events since they had last met, detailing two universes and then broke the news to him.

This was not to be the end of Brough.

He was confused. Then he was frustrated.

No, no. He protested. It was his time. He had done all he could and lived more than any Aware Master could have hoped. He was tired and looked forward to recycling his energy. He yearned to be diffused into the multiverse, to exist unaware he had ever lived a prior form, to be naive, innocent and ready for a new adventure, to see things new and fresh with newborn eyes.

Had he a place to go he would have fled her and found a quiet spot in the multiverse to diffuse in peace, but he could only float in the center of his carbon-60 molecule realm and accept his fate.

Iteration was unavoidable.

Param swiveled to one side, gracefully avoiding Brough's catalyst;

a minuscule sailfish-like form as it zip-transitioned into the fluid of his universe. Brough mistook that familiar being as a sailfish simply because he was too tired to track its dizzying speed to get an accurate read of its structure and energy flow. So many of those had fluttered around him in the Vencello in times past, showing him and Akenehi particular curious attention and exhibiting the most interesting and chaotic behaviors. Here was one last delicate visitor, pulling into an increasingly tighter orbit around him. It was harmless. It increased speed and he lost track of it altogether. He was sure that had Akenehi been present, she could have translated the song it was obviously performing, honoring him and so on. Then there erupted a blaze of light such was its nature that he was reminded of nothing except how wonderful it would be to breathe one last time at the surface of his beloved ocean under the warm, yellow sun.

CHAPTER 2 – RITE OF PASSAGE

Universe: Multiverse

Priori

Family began to arrive. As they did, they easily took their place in loose colonial pre-formation. Grandmother circled the mass, carefully scanning and evaluating. She acted as if she was indecisive, but I knew her and this was pure ritual.

"Cetapiens!"

At that, shared memory was triggered. It rearranged us by pulses and waves of common purpose. All shifted, positioning me in the center. I was then the sole object of Grandmother's intensifying scrutiny. Everyone else but me seemed to comprehend. Congratulatory whistles, "Ah, wonderful!" and similar exclamations were made all around.

Grandmother continued the rite. She announced with skilled ceremony and complex polyphonic song that I was approaching an important developmental stage during which my unique characteristics, many of which had already begun to manifest, would become fixed. The future of the entire clan depended on my imminent transition.

I was unsettled. I hadn't anticipated *that* announcement. I had expected her to acknowledge that I had been *accepted* into the clan, just as I was, in their loving company, forever.

My grandmother explained that we were Masters of O-O. O-O was the absolute Omni-spatial-temporal essence of the multiverse in which we existed and through which, once initiated, we could time travel at will.

Each Master achieved their place in the multiverse by perfecting an idiosyncratic acoustic O-_U_-O. The result was a _U_nique particle-like universe stabilized within a protective resonance compatible with O-O; a self-similar progeny of the Vencello. This was their own realm, each one of them a universe in and of themselves. As long as the harmonic was maintained it prevented their dissolution throughout the multiverse or in organic terms: death. For our clan, once O-U-O had been achieved we would have a fixed place in the colonial formation on those occasions when we became one body. Something different appeared to be in store for us through my transition, however.

Once an attempt at a definitive O-U-O began, Masters only had one try. Do or dissolve. They had to literally sing for their very existence; that is produce and hold the perfect harmonic resonance, somehow time travel back to _themselves_ at the very instant when they _began_ the song and negate the time differential through the creation of a closed harmonic sphere; encapsulating themselves within.

So, the achievement of O-U-O required, among other abilities, non-linear time travel. The first successful solo time travel was like a newborn cetacean taking its first breath. It was an innate ability and it either worked or we dissolved. To prevent my own death, I would begin a time travel journey with an experienced guide, in my case, my Grandmother. At some point during the journey, the O-U-O would be initiated but then I had to end it myself, with help of none other than my corresponding time-differentiated self.

No trial and error. I only got one go, same as the others.

Everyone in my clan had obviously succeeded and they didn't seem extraordinary or special. My mother had achieved hers and she was the most unstable singer I had ever heard. Of course, Grandmother, before her, had succeeded and that was no surprise to anyone. She was a _fabulous_ singer. Surrounded by examples of unlikely varieties to have survived it, I thought that meant a guarantee of success. Had it been that simple there would have been no concern among my clan either.

Unfortunately, singing had nothing to do with our dilemma.

I had a grievous throwback; hands with fully opposable, human thumbs. It was a very rare but extremely serious problem. Fortunately, a prior 100 percent correction rate had been achieved for those who had manifested the trait, including my own mother. So, my thumbs had been removed at their emergence but for the first time in the history of my kind, they had spontaneously grown back. A second, more aggressive, technique had been employed to remove the new thumbs and that had seemingly worked, for a while. Regrettably, a third auto-regeneration of my original thumbs was beginning to emerge.

Now, they pressed their consensus that the repeated extraction of my debilitating deformity caused cruel continued suffering, not only to me, but also to the entire family. It just hadn't worked. A third attempt was unacceptable. All agreed that Cetapiens seemed our only hope.

The ritual ended. The mass that was my clan began to relax the colonial formation, preparing for the next phase, each in their individual way.

I thought I knew, before Cetapiens, what I *wanted* to be. I willingly accepted the pain of my thumb removal because I believed, as even my own mother did, that I had a dangerous deformity. Thumbs were one of many that had been demonstrated irrefutably through time travel alternate pathway exploration as incompatible to sustaining mutualistic harmony. Multiple alternate all-human histories were examined. In each line the mere presence of thumbs culminated in the unnatural and far-too-soon destruction of far too many beloved sentient species and even multiple worlds. Worse, the thumbs stunted the highly prized uniquely human cognitive abilities that would have eventually emerged otherwise. Human thumbs were decidedly a threat to not only me but to *everything*. I too wanted them gone. I wanted to remain a part of my own kind, to be accepted. I wanted to learn about the multiverse and time travel to experience it all directly, just like my Grandmother.

…Cetapiens…

"Relax, little one." Grandmother soothed so only I perceived it, "I will always be with you."

"What does Cetapiens mean? Are you going to take away my thumbs?" I asked with deepening concern.

"No. Never again."

Then she explained that foremost for our kind, it was an important and very pleasant destination in time. It was home and culture to interesting ancient organic beings; many with thumbs just like mine. Her melodic verses told how the Cetapiens existed within the Vencello's universe of origin for a short period in their planet's history. Beautiful refrains celebrated that despite being organic, mortal and frail, they were also compassionate, adaptive and humble in unprecedented breadth. The finale celebrated that their tiny combined culture, cetaceans (those ancestral cousins *without* thumbs), humans (those ancestral cousins *with* thumbs), and something so vast, mysterious and sacred, had united within the membrane of a stabilized time travel haven.

That haven served as a model to certain young of our kind who had precariously struggled for survival and balance between cetaceans and humans, ocean and land, flippers and digits.

The critical moment was upon us. My early transition had already begun and so our journey began immediately.

Of course I was thrilled. Something fun! My first extended time travel! If she believed I was ready, I knew that it absolutely must be so. She was our matriarch. I felt so honored and lucky.

As we glided together, she sang that the multiverse was mine to discover. During that process I would make my own world from what I found there, as I desired and was able. She promised she would help as much as she possibly could. And most of all, she loved me.

Universe: Sponge

Human

Johnny fingered the dials of the recording equipment but he wasn't paying attention to it. His focus was on the orca pod that had surrounded their boat. They had submerged in unison and had not resurfaced. His Uncle Liam and Delora were geared up and ready. As soon as the orcas dove, they did too.

When he saw nothing at the surface but water, he glanced back over the array of electronics, notebooks and other water-sensitive materials and checked the seals making sure they were all wrapped tight. He shifted his weight, balancing on the floorboards in rhythm with the boat's rise and fall.

He was eager to prove himself indispensable. They needed a research assistant and he knew it. It was unlikely Delora would agree. Her son, Alvar had been her assistant and since Johnny had played a role in his death…well, it just didn't seem realistic to expect his dream would come true anytime soon. Nevertheless, he was going to give them his very best.

Equipment worked fine, he recorded dive start time, number of orcas and their last known proximity to the vessel, and stayed sharp for events of particular note. At first nothing unusual seemed to be happening; at least not from his vantage point. He figured perhaps that is exactly what was expected. He started to record the fact that nothing was going on when something certainly was.

A localized violent turbulence pitched the boat so erratically and unexpectedly he was thrown off balance. He held on to the nearest grab rail and crouched low. He didn't dare loosen his hold for fear of stumbling overboard. Sudden turbulence under clear sky couldn't be good. His instinct was that something had gone terribly wrong and he started to take cover in the cuddy but he stopped. His Uncle Liam and Delora were out there and likely needed his help. Desperate to see them safely back on the boat and head to safer water, or better yet, home, he searched port and starboard. Nothing.

Just as suddenly, the water recovered and he could balance again without holding on to the grab rail. Still flustered, he picked up a boat hook and then put it right back down again. He did the same with a life ring. He called out their names and listened and strained his eyes. Nothing but brine, multitudes of tiny peaks with sparkling sunshine as far his human eyes could see. When he searched directly down into the water, only distorted Johnny faces scattered among the surface waves looked back up at him.

Finally, Orca fins broke tall above the surface with loud chuffing and explosive breaths spewed a fast expanding fine mist into the air. They dove just as quickly as they had come up. Johnny remembered what Uncle Liam would expect of him. He jumped to the equipment to make sure it hadn't been fouled and recorded the number and proximity of the orcas.

The sea maintained its relative calm, but Johnny was under the full effect of an adrenaline dump. He held a semi-crouched position and listened intently to the speakers, hoping to hear impossible words from underwater that they were ok. Instead he heard heavy echolocation clicks and a cacophony of whistles. Liam and Delora still had not returned to the surface. He began to fear the worst.

The sick feeling in his gut reminded him of a day long ago, shortly after the death of his identical twin brother, Miles. Johnny was devastated. He had withdrawn from the world. He stopped going out to play after school, was not talking or even eating as a normal boy of nine should have.

Uncle Liam had taken him out on a fishing trip to get him out of the house and into some fresh air. After a while, his uncle had cut off the engine and rather than proceed to fish, he picked up his binoculars. He stood searching the ocean for a long while. Johnny had remained sitting, uninterested, sullen and quiet throughout.

Johnny finally spoke up, "What are you looking for?"

"I'll know it when I see it."

Johnny looked away and mumbled, deliberately, "That's dumb."

"That's how it works sometimes though." Liam did not get upset in the least. He knew his nephew was having a rough recovery and he was glad the boy had at least started to talk to him.

Johnny challenged him further, "How can you find something if you don't even know what you're looking for?"

Liam simply shrugged and kept the dialogue going, "Gotta be in the right place, I guess. Don't know where that is yet. Gotta keep moving."

"That's dumb. We aren't moving. We're just sitting here... I want to go back home..."

He had dreamt of that conversation later that same night. But that vision expanded into a surreal, emotional dreamscape.

No sooner had Johnny said he wanted to go back home, than the water around the boat had become violently turbulent. He saw the surrounding ocean beyond was strangely calm and unaffected. A low rumbling sound intensified as its source approached until he shook violently. The ocean splashed up around the side of the boat and became immobilized in mid-air.

He had looked up with apprehension at his uncle's face for guidance in how he should be reacting. Was this what his uncle had been seeking? Was it expected and safe? His uncle's countenance was serene. Johnny recalled how his uncle's unaffected, direct gaze had guided his emotions in the dream, instantly transforming them from fear to calm.

His serenity coincided with the cessation of shaking. The water that had been suspended, released back to the ocean in a series of tingling splashes like fine glass shattering on cement. As if that music had triggered an environmental event, the water resumed its prior calm and the breeze stopped. His uncle spoke no word out loud, yet by silent command an unusual looking whale appeared, strange in that it had short stubby arms with hands, lifted half of its body out of the sea and came within Johnny's reach. The whale extended one of those alien arms toward Johnny as it transformed into his deceased brother, Miles.

As Johnny pulled himself out of that memory he also recalled he had wanted to reach out to take his brother's hand, but it didn't happen.

He never told anyone about that dream but it had grieved him terribly. He felt he should have touched his brother's hand. In doing so, something vital would have been accomplished, rescuing him from the ocean perhaps, but he awoke too soon and had left it undone. It was like learning his brother was dead all over again.

Johnny had obviously been struck by his uncle's words all those years ago and the dream that followed. His uncle and Delora might need his help and if so he wanted more than anything to rescue them, to be their hero. To find them safe and bring them back under his protection. He decided to attempt one last surface search and then it would be time to dive in and search below it.

This time, when Johnny peered directly down into the depth, something hovered there, beneath the scattering of reflections, looking directly up at him with one eye. As it slowly rose closer he determined that it was not an orca or even the sperm whale they had seen earlier. It was smaller than the sperm whale but it was large, definitely some species of whale he had never seen before. And it continued to watch him as part of the head and eye surfaced from the water.

Johnny reached down cautiously, very slowly, to touch the glistening grey flesh, fully expecting the whale to shy away and submerge. Quite the opposite happened. The whale lifted further out of the water, encouraging his touch. Johnny anticipated a rubbery, slick feel as his fingertips made first contact.

What he perceived instead was a pleasant tingling of nerves as the multiverse O-O connected to his single universe physiology.

Instead of meeting resistance, his fingertips entered smoothly and painlessly into the side of the whale. The molecules of Johnny's hand and the whale slid unhindered right past each other. The whale-G was of the Vencello and O-O. Johnny was not, so something quite wonderful was able to occur.

To Johnny's eyes, simultaneously as he touched the skin, an identical fingertip began to emerge and progress outward at an angle. It was as if the whale skin was a penetrable mirror and visually, his fingertips were reflected back out in 3D at an equal and opposite angle. It looked strange but it felt…good, really GREAT!

Johnny did not break the bond. He had absolutely no desire to do so.

*****

This was no ordinary whale; it was a Gemini, or G, a human nickname that playfully described an *exact* reproduction of organic life that had served as substrate of a Metavoli-2. All Metavoli were universases; multiverse enzymatic beings that sometimes colonized in a self-similar manner to slime molds. This meant that while they were indeed distinct individuals they could alternatively join to become one being as simple or complex as needed and possible. As an enzyme-type sentient it read, copied and transferred organic substance and energy between universes through O-O.

The Metavoli manifested types characterized by how many copies of an original it could produce at once. A -2 indicated two, a -4 indicated four and so on. The Metavoli threw out the viable-adapted copies into suitable universes. Until the whale-G bonded with Johnny, no Metavoli found anywhere in the Sponge had achieved anything viable higher than a 32.

The particular Metavoli-2 that had reproduced the whale was a progeny of the Vencello. The Vencello was a C-60 molecule universe. The C-60 harmonic membrane encapsulated those within. The whale, the orca, the humans and all its other constituents provided the initial conditions and fodder for genetic variation and viable lifeform generation. The Vencello was a power source for genetic variation, but it was not the only one.

Throughout the multiverse there were, of course, so many others. The Vencello, with the contributions of those multitudes of similar mutualistic universes, incubated lifeforms and enzymes that eventually coalesced into a unique Metavoli-2. Without the help of those other universes, that were of the most ancient multiverse organic beings, all of which had achieved adaptations and wonderful universases of their own that enabled them to lead fabulously complex existences throughout O-O, the Vencello could not have evolved.

The Vencello adapted in kind with their fellows and achieved the ability to reproduce constituent components of their universe asexually, seeming to replicate at will, which then self-organized in synchrony with the O-O. Their singular C-60 molecule universe accomplished viable adaptation through its interaction with what was already successful and suitable throughout the O-O.

When an organic being came in contact with and was then accepted by a Metavoli, such as a whale had done in Johnny's case, the source physiology was worked on and transformed into two compatible multiverse partners; twins of sorts. Both became a G. Each shared all detail right down to memory and idiosyncratic behaviors of the original.

The balancing matter and energy was obtained through the multiverse during the process. Hopefully, no one was already using it.

Gs could not occupy the same universe at the same time. Multiverse biomatter reproduction was so complex and energy intensive that it necessarily mandated the G's would annihilate very soon after emergence if they were to try to occupy the same universe. To an observer in the Sponge for example, it would have appeared that only one had ever existed as the other twin would transition at the very moment of reproduction, to a suitable, unobservable universe.

The whale G was entangled across O-O to its origin, the Vencello. So at the slightest touch Johnny was in contact with them. His Uncle Liam was there. Delora was there. Inasmuch as those two human elements of that universe were aware and could translate into language all knowledge they shared with Brough and Akenehi and the others, Johnny was also cognizant of what would happen if he continued.

*****

Physical contact between Johnny and the whale-G included access to the instantaneous and comprehensive communication between source (whale) and the Vencello. Through his interface with the whale he knew, should he so chose, he could also become G right there and then. Once he had been reproduced, essentially he would exist in two universes at once. One G would be transitioned through O-O to any place in the survivable multiverse, and the other identical Johnny-G would reemerge in his home universe, the Sponge.

Alternatively, before completion, he could withdraw the part of himself that had already duplicated in the G back to the unduplicated original and remain as he was in one universe. It was mutually up to him and the G.

The Metavoli-2 created and expelled a complete viable reproduction of whatever lifeform entered it. In its current form, a whale, its range was limited to the sea, and only those parts of the sea that the whale could survive.

As a G he could learn to time travel. Although the whale-G was capable of time traveling and could go anywhere it could survive in time and even the multiverse, it would go there as *whale*. Thus, to access the places on *land* it desired, it required a human form, specifically Johnny's.

Johnny-G as a time traveler in human form could easily find Alvar within the Sponge's time and space, utilizing the innate G ability. That was to recognize easy-to-locate marked objects and then subsequently jump instantaneously from one to the other without traveling through the space and time between them. Such easy-to-locate marks included near identical large scale entangled objects and one required innate ability to perceive the congruency between them. Although everything in the multiverse was entangled, the arrangement of matter and distribution of energy throughout was so impossibly complex that it was simply too risky to just randomly pick two points to link and jump between.

The C-cage (a nickname given by Alvar to his spherical carbon-60 molecule model) resting on Alvar's nightstand on the night he died, for example—was an easy-to-identify mark for even the most novice multiverse time traveler.

Johnny could save Alvar.

But…once the G process was complete and the twins were thrown out to survive in a distinct universe their adaptations became fixed and adaptive metabolic changes concurrent with living in their respective realms began immediately. *Absolute* identicals could reintegrate in O-O, but for *organic* prior identicals to reintegrate after living for a length of time in their separate universes was virtually impossible. Therefore it was going to be a permanent change for Johnny for many complex physical reasons. For those same reasons, Johnny couldn't have just remained with one arm in the side of the whale-G for very long; the exchange had to happen very quickly.

Both Johnny-Gs would be Johnny in every aspect, personality and memories included, but as a living product of the Vencello, they would be more. Upon full body duplication, the Johnny-G that remained in the Sponge would live out a lifetime as a human, albeit a multiverse-connected one. In other words, Johnny didn't have to worry that he would be discovered. Even his mother would never know. Johnny-G would love her, every bit as much as he did before the process, and *could* tell her of the exchange, but he wouldn't. He would live the rest of his life, in full knowledge of the Vencello and the multiverse and also knowing his counterpart Johnny, was living his life in a viable universe.

Johnny trusted the Gemini as he trusted his Uncle Liam. He also trusted the bond he still felt to one who had died years ago. He could, with time travel in his arsenal, fight his way back against a current of improbability, to his beloved *living* identical twin brother.

As he observed his fingertips bending unnaturally back toward him, he pulled back his hand, to verify that he could. The connection was indeed broken. He was still only Johnny. The Johnny-G duplicate anatomy had simultaneously been pulled back and was gone. The whale-G looked up at him without a flinch; it now seemed to Johnny to possess his uncle's eyes, and it remained still, ready to resume the precise duplication. Johnny knew there was no threat. He was being given time to consider. He held his hand up to his face and examined it for a few seconds. That's all it took.

He was ready. He reached solidly and deeply into the whale-G, at which he instantly regained the link and observed the perfectly duplicated forearm and flesh that protruded back out.

*****

There was no question in Johnny's mind. The choice made itself. Johnny rolled easily over the side of the boat and merged comfortably and painlessly into the whale-G. Had there been a human observer close by, to that person it would have appeared that he simply reemerged seamlessly, every detail perfect, right down to the clothing and scars. Although it would have looked very strange, the speed and flawlessness would have erased any concern and the memory would have been dismissed as bizarre hallucination or misperception of the mind.

Johnny-G emerged as coolly as if he were emerging from the door to his room, a living human Gemini hybrid with comprehension and abilities he would never dared dream of possessing. He easily got himself back inside the boat. Dripping wet, he found a towel. Then he found the C-60 molecule model and grinned. It all came together. When his uncle said he would be helping with their research that day he could not have hoped it would have turned into such an incredibly awesome experience. He was, without a doubt, having the *best* day of his life.

He had Vencello connection and therefore had no problem working out that he could and should play the recorded orca calls. He got right on it and called Akenehi's clan to the boat. Needing only a few minutes to await their return as they were still in the area, he plopped into the water as soon he could see their approach. Clutching the model in one hand he swam toward them. Johnny-G was able to reproduce, to the best of his closed human mouth ability, compliments of Akenehi's memory, the orca name call of her eldest daughter, Seasnán.

Seasnán instantly came forward. He held out the model to her and swam directly at her, arm extended. He repeated her name call and she responded by uncharacteristically coming in so close that they touched. At the instant of contact, the orca was connected, through Johnny-G, to the Vencello, and most importantly to her mother Akenehi.

Rather than initiate a Gemini reproduction, Johnny-G had simply conveyed information to her. He allowed his body to be the conduit-only to deliver Akenehi's *message* to her clan. Running out of air, he withdrew his touch, terminating her G-specific bond with the Vencello, but not erasing her memory of it, and returned to the surface.

Next: Alvar. For Johnny-G, it was only a matter of physically possessing the C-60 molecule model and learning how and where to focus his newly acquired innate G perception. As a novice, he floundered through a few miss-stops where C-60 models of similar size existed. Soon enough, he found Alvar where and when he needed to, just at the moment before brain death, all with relative ease. Through him, the Vencello, including Delora of course, was there.

Delora, an ordinary human female, had accomplished the amazing. She made it back across universes and time to her son, albeit not entirely by her own power or even in her own body. A complex and improbable path led to him but she had found him. Alvar was still alive, but just barely. Johnny-G, and the Vencello within him, stood beside.

Through the dark he saw that Alvar's eyes were open and looking up, directly at him. Before Alvar could make a move, he reached down to touch him. By then, Johnny-G was already an initiated time traveler but he most certainly did not have all the time in the multiverse. He would most likely have just drawn attention of other time travelers as he had already marked a few clumsy time disturbances to get to Alvar. If that were the case then outcomes would become increasingly uncertain. He paused as he perceived, for the first time, temporal travel by something else was occurring. But he relaxed. It seemed the orca's distraction may have worked. He perceived another not precisely in his current time although it was undeniably close. He had to move carefully and quickly. *Now.*

Orca

Akenehi's clan was elated at first, but then worried when she did not instantly reappear. They ceased all harmonics. That did not bring her back. In haste, they spread out to examine a wider area around the boat and above the long jaw below, echolocating in the hope she was somehow nearby but unable to call out to them. Then a cacophony of overlapping confused whistles proclaiming she would return somehow, call out to them, so shouldn't they remain quiet, and be vigilant for her, as she would surely rejoin them.

Their noisy exchange was interrupted when they recognized a familiar recording emanating from the boat; a call they all knew as Delora's greeting. Wisely, the older members of the family approached the boat, explaining to the apprehensive younger ones that meaning relevant to their plight might be gleaned, however unlikely. When they detected a human unexpectedly swimming right for them with a familiar object in his possession and obviously seeking physical contact, they decided to permit a much closer approach.

The youngest orca, still very naive to the superior abilities of orcas compared to other ocean creatures, suggested they attempt a sleep song to determine what was known from this other witness. This would have seemed preposterous to the adults before the event they had just witnessed, but now they deeply considered the possibility.

Seasnán, Akenehi's eldest daughter, who would be next in line if Akenehi did not return to them, approached him. The clan encircled and echo scanned the scene as it unfolded.

No sooner did Johnny-G's fingers touch Seasnán, a necessary gesture, not to create a G but to establish the direct link to the Vencello, than she jerked in surprise. An alarm call went out among the family. They feared she might have been injured. Seasnán immediately calmed them; she sang out to them that she was in no pain or danger. In fact, she could hear the distinctive acoustic perfection of her mother's singing, and required their silence and restraint. The clan scanned Seasnán physically, carefully noting her heartrate and emotional indicators. All was calm and seemingly normal within her and so they quieted, hung back and waited.

Within moments, Johnny-G swam back to the boat.

Seasnán scanned him as he kicked and reached awkwardly through the water as any human had ever done, comparing it to cetacean skill, amazed that she could not determine by any natural method she possessed that he was anything other than a land squid. However, Akenehi and the multiverse had informed her otherwise.

As a result of their interaction Seasnán was in possession of important information on unforeseeable threats and increased hardship to their clan in the not too distant future. Akenehi had conveyed precise instructions that they were to strictly adhere to that would ensure their survival. Through that strange land squid, Akenehi assured her of the communications authenticity and of her absolute, unaltered and undying love for all of them.

Before Seasnán would answer any of the cacophony of inquiring whistles from her anxious clan, she needed to perform an unusual behavior. Akenehi had assured her that it was imperative she do this, immediately. She had called it a 'distraction' and orcas certainly understood what that meant in hunting terms. Obviously, there was no

24

hunt in progress but there was no questioning Akenehi when she issued a stern command.

Seasnán called her family back out of her way. She rose to the surface and inhaled/exhaled deeply, as they did for emergency deeper dives. Upon the last plosive, mist-ejecting breath she tucked her head in tight to her underside and straightened immediately as she dove fast and directly downward, pumping her lower body with all the strength she could muster. Thrusting mightily and mentally rehearsing the strange song her mother had commanded, she descended. The daylight diminished and soon she continued in darkness, silent except for minimal echolocation meant to warn creatures out of her path. Despite it, she still smacked into more than a few startled fish on her way down. When at last she felt her tolerance for the pressure reach its limit, warning her from all sides that she was reaching the end to her dive, she suddenly sharply turned and twist rolled according to Akenehi's very specific sequence of movements. Then, as her matriarch had instructed, at the end of the last roll, Seasnán loudly emitted a new harsh cry and held it long, surely heard over a great distance and alerting any prey to her presence, as she turned straight upward, never losing power of her thrusting lower body. She rolled, turned, straightened in successions faster and tighter than she had ever done in her life.

Seasnán considered: perhaps her mother had gone minnows during the transition. Perhaps *she* was blindly irrational to follow these instructions so willingly. It really was a bit dangerous at those speeds and at that depth, but she continued because her mother depended on her. During her rapid ascent she emitted and held the polyphonic harmonic, as precisely as Akenehi had sung, for as long as she could despite the discomfort of her body.

Unknowingly Seasnán had produced an imperfect yet unmistakable rendition of an O-O song for the first time by any species on her planet of origin. It was an effective distraction that would pull time travelers to it within centuries, as a shark would be compelled to follow a bleeding hemorrhage.

In one graceful move she broke the surface with powerful force, coming body lengths clear of its tension before she blew her used breath in one hard pulse and then took in a rejuvenating deep fresh one and lazily arched her back. She turned her nose downward to the pull of her home planet for minimal impact at surface reentry.

Seasnán had no way of knowing if the distraction had worked, but she was certain she had followed Akenehi's detailed commands to the last breath.

Now that that was accomplished, Seasnán was on to her next urgent assignment. What Akenehi instructed, they were to achieve as a family and in such short order was unprecedented. Somehow Seasnán would have to teach them new concepts related to 'other worlds' and 'time travel'. Even their sophisticated use of clicks of whistles would be insufficient in those respects. Sleep song would certainly have to be utilized for absolute clarity and successful execution. There would be no more moments passed idly in their beloved ocean. She declared herself the matriarch, also by Akenehi's direct request.

Sperm Whale

Param scanned the event in amazement. When advanced wave zero had passed, Brough, along with the grandmother Orca, two confounding humans, their immediate surrounding ocean including all of its tinier inhabitants had...*vanished*. She quick-scanned the wider area and determined no catastrophic damage to ocean floor, remaining cetaceans or the nearby human boat had occurred.

She and Brough had planned that his first objective would be to reestablish clear communication with her, if at all possible. She stayed at a safe depth, near ocean bottom even after the remaining Orcas left, alternating periods of alert silence with intense scans upward for evidence of his communications, or an unexpected but highly anticipated return.

It was during this scan she perceived a connected reaction had occurred, precisely at advanced wave zero, elsewhere on the ocean floor. She calculated it had happened a relatively easy swim distance away, within the surface of the ocean floor but at a depth no Master could survive.

She was also amused to feel the unusual tickle, not unpleasant, in her long, sensitive jaw that had initiated when Brough vanished, was persisting. It was not random, but was clearly rhythmic with distinct features, rather like Brough's coda. In fact, it *was* Brough, she was sure of it. He was communicating. The data was rudimentary and she could not locate the source of his message. It seemed to be emanating from *within* her entire jaw, which was perceived by her to mean *everywhere*. That made no sense to her at the time, but from the pulses she clearly understood phrases of information that corresponded to *four* and *Deepers*.

Her attention was abruptly drawn to a most unusual orca vocalization. Param was several decades old and through her long and eventful life she had amassed and processed more than enough data regarding her ocean and all of its inhabitants to recognize this sound as unprecedented. From the organic characteristics, its proximity and source of the call, it was very likely coming from one of the same orcas that had participated in the advanced wave zero event. Perhaps the grandmother orca had reappeared. Perhaps one of the others had been mortally wounded. With no frame of reference for this particular call, Param could not understand if the call was one of pain, joy or something else. Whatever it meant, it was loud, long and obviously meant to be heard over a great distance.

Param turned immediately toward the sound which had originated at a depth that nearly matched her present one and indicated the orca was in rapid ascent. Param intensified her echo-scan and followed the call to the surface.

Her returning echoes, including those of water itself and the orca that swam erratically through it, constructed a new and exciting mental model for her consideration. The turbulence created by the orca, (who even at that distance was easily determined by Param's expert scans to be one of the remaining orcas and NOT the grandmother), her speed and rolling, then her graceful execution of the most improbable physical movements returned echo data that made Param's massive heart pound with awe and appreciation.

The trajectory of the turbulence cut a path that Param read easily. She followed it, scanning as she swam. She realized the orca had emitted bubbles during part of the call and so she paused a moment to mentally integrate her freshly gathered data of those images. She pulled her mind back and put all the pieces together. She took in the whole dynamic sequence from beginning to end. To her amazement, when she mentally slowed it down to reveal split moment detail, an unmistakable combination of bubbles, turbulence and tiny sea creatures combined to reveal the tremendously scaled-up arrangement of a sacred bit, the same representation that Alvar would have recognized as a spherical carbon-60 molecule. It completely encircled the orca for a perfect moment, at its center. It was clear. There was no mistake.

Param divided the data seared in her mind into two parts; one physical and the other acoustic. The acoustic vocalization was pure orca and she was not predisposed to understand that form of communication. So, the song of O-O, did not offer her any hint as to as to its purpose or meaning. What she did comprehend of the physical part was this. The orca had apparently communicated through movement that she had knowledge of something of which Param believed she could not have been aware. The creation of an unmistakable structure and subsequent positioning herself impossibly in the center of the sacred bit was a deliberate act, one that only an Aware Master of the Ocean could have perceived in sufficient detail, mentally put together and correctly understand. It worked mightily on her.

Just when Param believed she had pretty much scanned and swam through everything that her beloved familiar ocean had to offer, this day passed into her experience. Everything she thought she knew about the ocean was still sound but the events of the day, especially the behavior she had just witnessed and the construct it had created, apparently for her own private knowledge, awakened her. She came to realize there was a great unknown, wondrous and *completely* unexpected ocean of events yet to be experienced.

The orca had breached the surface. The Aware Master followed within dangerous proximity to the remainder of the pod.

Param silenced her clicks and descended.

She worked out very quickly that Brough's clicks indicated that the four of them had survived the advanced wave zero event and possibly the orca's choreography had provided some information as to how that was so. Further, she must get as close as possible to the site of the deep ocean advanced wave zero event. Once there she would have to appeal to yet another species, one that would be essential to establishing a much clearer communication link to him. She knew where she had to go, and that she would not be able to succeed without the assistance of that long disdained species—Deepers. This wasn't going to be easy, even for her.

CHAPTER 4 – A TOUR OF UNIVERSES

Universe: Multiverse

Priori

I experienced my first *puffs* before we even arrived at Cetapiens. Grandmother clicked we were approaching our first stop. Oh, and that I should prepare for the unexpected. Also, it would be instructive and...*different*. In retrospect I called it the cockroach test; several quick swats and stomps in succession. If I hadn't known she loved me and would always protect me I would have thought these were intended to either mercifully and quickly finish me off or determine that I could survive what most others of our kind couldn't. I had no idea what to expect or what I should do so I hung back, keeping physical contact with her and watching every nuance in her movement, which resembled tremors and twitches more than propulsion of any sort. I listened intently as her song dropped octaves and echo-clicks slowed.

Universe: Sponge

Priori

Without warning or explanation, Grandmother pulled us into a realm quite different from ours; the Vencello's universe of origin. My first impression amazed me beyond explanation as I had little to compare it to. Later, at Cetapiens, I would come to call it the Sponge Universe or 'Sponge' for short. Grandmother took only a fraction of a nanosecond to orient then she honed in. At that, we slipped through to a magnificent blue giant specimen of spinning, pulsing energy. The radiance was almost unbearably intense even at a far distance and only increased exponentially as we zoom-glided straight toward it.

We approached so close that it scanned as a flat infinite wall of blue blaze before us. My scans suggested absolutely nothing of its spherical geometry. Grandmother navigated by click alone and I could sense she was struggling with the giant's gravitational pull.

Suddenly we lurched and began to lose cohesion. She had obviously miscalculated and pulled us out of the glide late and we were way too close. We were in serious trouble. Simply put, we were going to permanently diffuse in a few nanoseconds. I zip-scanned her and sure enough she exhibited unmistakable indicators of stress and fear. The unbelievable was happening. Grandmother had made a horrible mistake.

Without a conscious thought, I puffed myself out (didn't know I could do *that* until then), sucked in a portion of my midsection, creating a pocket of sorts just big enough for her to fit into (didn't know I do *that* either), cut her off mid-glide and caught her in it. I enveloped her instinctively while holding our position at just the right orbit. It was one I alone could tolerate. Grandmother would have been vaporized and her energy absorbed into the blue giant had she not been in my pocket.

And yet I was to keep us in a stable orbit and we didn't diffuse. As we circled I began to really enjoy the experience. I discovered that I had sensors that I did not know I had, simply because they had never been directly exposed and thereby switched on before. The puffing instinct resulted in more than an increase to my outer surface area and the envelopment of my beloved matriarch in a safe pouch. It had pushed internal sensors, developing since my emergence, close enough to my outer surface. Experiencing even the most extreme frequencies of my blue beauty as entirely comfortable, I marveled at its complex color and shade play.

The indescribable beauty was observed by me alone. Grandmother was enveloped and could detect none of it, except what she could scan. She didn't seem interested in the blue giant at all, though. She was scanning *me*, focusing her clicks on the sensory spots and then a sweep through the new configuration that my body had assumed.

Holding that form came naturally as if light and gravity had triggered it. I was not threatened by our proximity to the blazing orb but I was increasingly concerned for my beloved passenger. I had no idea how we were going to break away from the giant's powerful pull. I wanted desperately to return to distance that was safe for her, fearing she might be dying. I pleaded with her to get us away from it. By then she was not at all afraid or annoyed with me for my inabilities but was willing to stay as long as necessary.

I learned just how fearless and risk taking she was from that first celestial orbit. I thought she had made a mistake but then I suspected it was intentional, she had seemingly put us in harm's way to trigger any inert ability I possessed that would come in handy. I had always thought she had a scary, even brutal essence about her. But she had discovered that I had incredible unknown potential. For that, I admired her and wanted to be like her more than ever. Now, I scared myself too.

She was learning from me as I was in turn learning from her. She stated that what we had just discovered was entirely unexpected but immensely invaluable. As she had suspected, I was highly adaptable, virtually indestructible, regenerative and plastic. Changing shape, when appropriate, was not unheard off. But what she had just witnessed was truly exceptional, even for one of our kind. She suggested two ideas about my development that I had not, *cephalopod* and *tardigrade*.

When the Vencello, consisting predominantly of two cetaceans combined with two Homo sapiens, was first pulled into its own new universe, several genetic contributors were also included. Fresh remains of a just-swallowed giant squid (the contents of one of the cetacean's stomach) that was not yet completely brain dead, and a living tardigrade both made the transition. They were one with Vencello and every now and then, in varying ways, they manifested in its progeny. There was a lot to consider.

She knew I would survive lesser Sponge extremes and soon we were on our way to a celestial tour of the Sponge. I was so sad at leaving my giant friend that as we broke easily away it didn't occur to me to realize that she could have pulled us out at any time.

Together, we glided into and out of orbits, as easily as if I were in a slipstream. Learning had little to do with finding my tolerance limits. My body adjusted instinctively to gravity, temperature, radiation, etc. I saw everything through my original eyes as well as alternate views with my newly discovered sensors. When I got too close to a star I felt a distinctive tingling which triggered an adjustment; I *puffed*. I felt fine.

For most radiant orbs we remained at a distance Grandmother could comfortably tolerate. I resumed my original form for most, but when triggered, my pocket cradled her safely as I pulled her in to introduce us to those spectacular stellar lovelies I just couldn't resist.

Grandmother guided me to many of her favorites, huge blue beauties, magnificent reds, yellow and whites. Some pulsed; some were in the process of merging with companion orbs. Some were new, some ancient, others in the various stages of supernova. Some were even rouge, without companion or reason to stay put. Those were especially so much fun to tease as we followed and looped simultaneously, singing to the loner that they were never truly alone.

All glowing spheres looked unremarkable from afar but when scanned up close, an array of individual features marked each as fascinating and unique. Appreciating the individual complex beauty of each while whipping and orbiting around was the most exhilaration I had experienced to that point.

There were no other like-kind travelers emitting time-chatter or interfering in my lesson in any of the orbits we selected, at least none that I could detect. My whole world at that moment was our beautifully radiant friends, their darker companion orbs, Grandmother and me. I wished to form permanently right there and then, just as we were. I could have star-looped for all of my remaining existence. Grandmother had taught her lesson well and she jerked me instantly away to the Vencello universe while she still could.

Cetapiens
Universe: Vencello

Priori

I was in the presence of the very early Vencello; a new universe, our ancestor.

To my eyes and sensors they manifested as four distinct orbs, spinning and pulsating, enclosed in a translucent soup of organic matter and fluid, filling what in the Sponge was space. Grandmother invited me to scan them. That revealed further details of the complex dynamic within and between them, each spinning itself but also maintaining a stable orbit with the other three. She pointed out that their system's configuration was very rare in *any* universe. The most common was one single orb, followed closely by two, a binary. Sometimes three could survive but that was very unlikely. In those cases the smallest of the three would be absorbed into one of the larger two. Four, as in the Vencello's configuration, was *extremely* rare and typically short lived.

Now with many of the Sponge's celestial examples to compare it to, The Vencello universe resembled a conjoined quad-pulsar of sorts; a blazing, improbable, precarious dilemma it seemed to me. Grandmother explained they were prevented by diffusing instantly throughout the multiverse by the very carbon-60 molecule outer resonance that had snapped them inward from the Sponge. Each of the four emitted their own distinct patterns and range of bioluminescent light; thoughts resulted in dancing flows and flashing bolts of multi-colored beauty. To her, they presented a vision of the wondrous complexity of pure newborn sentient energy. To me they seemed poised to collide in chaos at any instant. But they didn't.

Everything within their C-60 universe was connected by the organic fluid that made up a sustaining field they shared. The result was analogous to distinct areas of a mammalian brain, existing in an internal brine-like environment, connected by neural bridges. We had inherited some of that structure. We understood them.

Grandmother and I synchronized trajectories, then spiraling in turn to each of the four Vencello orbs, Brough, Akenehi, Delora and Liam, until we reached that sweet spot distance that allowed optimal connection.

There was Brough, formerly a Master of the Ocean, as impressive as he was in organic form. Then, he was called a "Long Jaw" by orcas and "sperm whale" by the humans. Now, Brough was the most massive and brightest sentient energy by far of the four. His awareness, care and kindness were omnipresent. He emitted powerful clicks which I understood as en element of our native communication. He perceived us as we did him. He extended his welcome and protection to us while simultaneously orienting himself. Brough had breached his new universe awake and swimming. Even as he adjusted his orbit so as to remain stable in relative position to the other three, he was already processing newly accessible multiverse data.

At just the right moment, we propelled away from Brough and glided instead toward Akenehi. Akenehi was the orca matriarch, acoustic genius and possessor of a gorgeous polyphonic singing ability second to none. She too perceived the multiverse and recognized some common harmonics suggestive of her own song resonating there.

Akenehi, the maestro of the Vencello harmonic, had stopped singing as she lost consciousness during the transition. Thus she had inadvertently caused much to become trapped within the C-60 molecule, transitioned as if inside an air bubble, through O-O. Their joining and entrapment defined their own C-60 universe. Carried by her initial momentum she involuntarily orbited Brough, as he provided a much higher percentage of the new universe's total mass. She had only stopped vocalizing for a moment but that had been enough. Although she resumed the perfect harmonic immediately upon awakening, she remained bound to the others in the Vencello.

She spun much faster than Brough, pulsing with bursts of energy, formidable intelligence and determination. As we flung around her orbit, we were awash in her impossibly radiant intent and it was as the *fiercest* turbulence. Grandmother and I could think of little else when in her presence other than her awesome calculating resolve.

And we knew something more; her love; so much *love*. She broke our hearts as she sang in acoustic perfection, incessantly of her family and their importance to her, the necessity of their survival and her desire that they be reunited with her. She took care of her family first, foremost and for all time. She recognized Grandmother's own song as we orbited her. We were *family* and so those sentiments were naturally extended to us. We were protected by her maternal devotion. I understood at that moment why we called her our First Grandmother.

A synchronized tuck and spin and we were far from Akenehi and Brough yet still within the Vencello membrane. We approached the two small barely radiant spheres of light. I almost mistook those pure humans, Delora and Liam, as one entity at first. They were so tiny compared to the other two and they orbited so quickly and tightly around each other in such a way that if you *looked* at them they would have appeared as one. Upon an easy *scan*, however, their distinct individuality popped into perception. Their collective power was somewhat weaker than the orca or the whale as they contributed much less mass than either of them.

Liam was swept up in his new perceptions, exhilarated by his expanded awareness. He had transcended his prior existence and was completely satisfied with himself. He chattered, giggled and laughed to himself. He couldn't have been happier.

At this first scan, Delora was still preoccupied with memories of her son's death to notice her ability to do exactly what she had desired; get to him in time.

I stopped scanning her almost as quickly as I had started, for fear of being sucked into her sadness.

I was already forming opinions and preferences for our ancestors. I was proud of the cetaceans and always had been. They had reinforced my pride in them. They were aware of us, communicative, affectionate. But given a choice at that moment, I would have judged the human aspect, both unable to perceive much beyond their own tiny orbits, altogether as irrelevant. *There* was part of my own dilemma.

So, we beheld the unique marvel that was our ancestor, a newborn organic based universe, its hypnotic swirls of radiant energy, and the paths of each orbit that respected the space and distinctiveness of its counterparts. We looped around them each in dancing turn assisted by the gravity of their mass. We scanned and perceived with fascination as Brough continued clicking, with amazement as Akenehi sang, and with amusement as Delora and Liam chattered away, providing me with the only lesson I needed to master their simple human language.

The Vencello had already made their transition and all were conscious. Grandmother and I were there with them, but we were not the only Priori visitors.

The Vencello was not a private experience, like the peaceful star-loops had been, by any means. This was a flurry of so many that I could not easily determine individuals. On the edge of perception I thought I detected a familiar form within the chaotic time disturbances. Just before I could turn to scan...

Grandmother caught herself, she seemed almost *embarrassed*. The Vencello energy dynamic indicated the linear progression toward consciousness were obvious. Yet we had emerged into the Vencello just slightly later than she had calculated. I had missed important details elsetime that she wanted me to experience. She really *did* make a mistake and it bothered her. She sang her apology to me, laughing that she had only made an error one other time in her travels and that was when she had erroneously *thought* she had miscalculated.

Her discomfort at flubbing the timing was actually *cute*. I was so surprised at her confession that I laughed. Now that I had a distinct frame of reference I recognized for the first time that my laughter was rather *Liamesque*. I couldn't place the characteristic of hers. It had features of both human and cetacean but there was something else. Before I had time to ask, she made her adjustment in time-focus. She mentally calibrated, emitting no clicks but I saw a barely perceptible twitch, and back the correct span of moments we went, nudged precisely at the Vencello's instant of emergence.

At that instant of transition from the universe of origin to the new infant universe, all but Brough were temporarily spun into unconsciousness.

Brough, the sperm whale, Aware Master of the Ocean, remained cognizant throughout. His massive brain had instantly transitioned to a state that was now capable of voluntarily inhibiting much of its prior organic filtering function. Rather than resulting in a disoriented and confused whale, he became a hyperaware multiverse-infused sentient hybrid. Knowledge of the multiverse and his accompanying ability in his new realm became instantly apparent to him. He easily accessed information he had been surrounded by in organic life but had been unable to perceive there due to necessary limits inherent to the mammalian brain. He was so much more aware as part of the Vencello than he could ever have hoped to have become as an individual whale.

In their universe of origin the mighty brain of a sperm whale detected and processed much more detail than either the human or even the formidable orca. Yet sperm whale ability alone was not sufficient for the creation of the Vencello. Their universe could have come into being only through the contribution of all three species.

His prior existence had instantly become as a single krill in an infinitely expansive ocean. He was well aware that there were limits. His new realm was by no means permanent or omnipotent. Nor was it empty. The nanosecond after the Vencello slipped through O-O the time travelers were drawn to it and they never stopped coming and going.

Most of the Vencello's visitors were of a loose community of universe-phase beings that our kind generally conceptualized as Priori. The Vencello was a variety of those. None were God, nevertheless as Priori, the Vencello absolutely possessed a universe's powerful innate ability to create, transform, and most importantly, progress.

The Vencello was a unique universe. All are. The *method* of their emergence was *not* unique to them. Untold numbers of similar Priori had preceded him to the multiverse. Brough innately recognized many;

specifically, those that were also formed by process of multiple organic beings having combined into their own connected realms.

The Vencello was distinctive within the multiverse as an individual color frequency was to white light. A prism revealed constituent colors of its spectrum. Analogously, Priori perceived with innate ability a select *range* of other universes in the multiverse. Each Priori possessed its own distinct color by analogy. The Vencello had its own, was recognizable and accepted. They blended in with their new community.

Brough benefited immediately from those Priori, like-color multiverse connections, in that most had originated from larger brained beings from many realms with vastly differing experiences from his own. He accessed a tsunami of fascinating histories and varying abilities of those others and became powerful new creative force. Yet he was and would always be Brough.

He had not forgotten Param, his ocean or his obligation to detail events as best he could. He fluidly click-scanned the entire transition event; from one universe to another, before, during, and after. He knew they had, all four, survived.

While some characteristics of Sponge such as energy and mass were brought with them, the fact that they constituted their whole universe created an entirely new unique set of self-similar physical laws. They were made up of analogous energy, had mass and their orbits around each other gave off gravity-like waves that transcended universes. The gravity-like waves emitted by their own orbits were perceptible to those in similar universes including the Sponge, assuming they possessed the sensitivity.

Back in his home ocean, Param, a most revered Aware Master of the Ocean, was a very rare individual in that she could perceptibly detect gravity waves naturally. Fortunately for Brough, and the future of cetaceans in his home ocean, Param read and comprehended his gravity-like wave messages.

Param's and Brough's potentials were astounding. Such shared caring for their ocean and everything that lived in it, coexisting with raw, brilliant problem solving; such hope for the progression of sentience!

*****

Grandmother nudged us forward again. By this time, the mammalian brains were in the very early stages of adapting to their new configuration. The first of their memory bonding was in progress. Our trajectories adjusted into to a tight whirlpool of human thought, most intensely shared between Delora and Liam.

Strong emotions were dominant driving forces for mammals. And so it was for the Vencello. They exchanged the neural energy of their original brains. That meant sharing emotion and corresponding memories. Despite her small relative mass, Delora's initial grief and the memory of the loss of her son Alvar were powerful—creating strong currents as winding rivers of memory through the Sponge—enough to move them all.

The Priori and Brough's presence contributed expanded processing and natural echo skills to her own memory of the scene. Delora listened with a heightened acoustic perception, thanks to Akenehi's presence. Never before had she been able to perceive so many sounds in such an incredible range. She remembered the human visual details, but now a whole universe of echo-scan detail, resonances and harmonics revealed themselves to her. Had she been only Delora, she knew the complexity and constancy of those frequencies and amplitudes would have driven her quickly to distraction. Now her brain shared connection and therefore pre-understanding and Priori perspective. They were natural, familiar and comfortable. Her sensory abilities were likewise now theirs.

They shared, with hyper clarity, the last moment when Delora leaned over to kiss her son goodbye.

The cool tactile sensation of Alvar's skin, as she pressed her touch receptor-dense lips, shocked the cetacean elements of the Vencello to attention. This was memory from anatomy they did not share in their prior lives. Her home planet's worldwide resonance was now audible to Delora. As a human she could not have possibly detected such a low frequency. The orca contributed perception of the omnipresent planet resonance, essential to sleep-song communication; an extraordinary prior-life gift they all now shared. She could hear its song gently massage her with low, slow, deep and ever-soothing vibrations, as it coaxed her to calm. The morning sunlight beaming in through the window had always vibrated and filled the room, a symphony which she could not appreciate at the time, but through the Priori it was now obvious and pleasing to her. This was quite a different experience from the horror-filled room she remembered.

Then the identity of the body became clearer. It struck her that the energy that was ebbing out of the body was her own. Not just hers. It was also Liam, Brough, and Akenehi. A part of all of them was going to sleep with Alvar and would eventually return to them. An idiosyncratic trade had occurred. It made no logical sense to her original human memory but it was truth, plain and simple. Alvar was more than the body. The body was more than her son. It was a physical memory of Alvar, made perfect with the help of the multiverse, Brough and Akenehi; made deliberately indistinguishable from her son by the help of an ability far surpassing the Vencello's. As soon as she woke up into the Vencello, she had visited that scene and she now she knew it plainly. They all did.

Alvar had preceded her to the multiverse. He was also there, along with the multitude of time travelers but the humans were not experienced in their new capacity to single him out yet. So Delora remembered her son's lifeless body instead and it continued to hold her.

That memory was the moment they first experienced together what it is to no longer be an organic individual but rather a Priori, albeit a new one. Who or what small piece had she been that she could not perceive at that moment, the now obvious—that *Alvar* was not *dead*?

Her sad reverie was suppressed for a nanosecond, and they were able to explore other individual memories, to mentally drift, as distinct and apart from their collective thoughts.

Delora, Liam and Brough turned their attention to the Orca. "Take the wheel." They all understood exactly what this meant. Akenehi was the next to set the flow of the river of recollection. She took them back to one of her most cherished moments.

Her beloved children, grandchildren, sisters and their progeny, and a visiting male from a friendly pod were experiencing the very best hunt Akenehi could ever remember.

It was a beautiful day at the surface and even better under it. The water was clear and bracing, the submerged ice was a spectacular labyrinth of varying translucent blue tones, the full acoustic orca perception of the groaning of the creaking 'bergs, the appetite-whetting call of nervous sea lions, the pod's own calls in excited anticipation and clever strategic planning. They had traveled far toward much colder waters but despite the chill they felt in their fins, they had a sufficient protective layer of fat and were comfortable. As they increased speed, weaving, stroking, confirming position with calls and distinct markings, they alternated slipstreams saving strength for the hunt. The water was as yielding as air. They were totally free in the three dimensional realm of their ocean home.

Her beloved daughter Arva'Anati was there. She had not yet been plucked from the sea and pulled mercilessly from her family. There she swam, singing as beautifully as Akenehi herself. Alive. Healthy. Free. About to be very well fed. The whole clan enjoyed the physical movement of their powerful bodies. Their hunger only spurred them on and was welcomed for its help. They gracefully dodged ice in easy passage through the water toward their prey. There had been neither recent illnesses nor deaths. All the clan felt the immense joy, power, energy and privilege of being an Orca.

They had located a huge colony of sea lions and their tender offspring; it was the peak of pup season. They perceived the alluring frenzied fear of their prey; the hunt was on. The pod members each had a role to play and they spread out to collect and share data. The ice floats were in just the right positions so even the prey out of water could easily be tipped off and taken with very little effort. Some of the younger orcas had suffered a bite or slash from their prey but nothing serious and took it well. It had been one of the more satisfying feasts that Akenehi could recall. The very small young pups were melt-in-the-throat delicious, the finest and tastiest fat to be found in the ocean world. None of their stomachs could have taken in one more pup.

Brough refrained from adding the full force of his naturally repulsed counter-perspective, and other than a noticeable spray of super-detail including krill and several varieties of small fish, his gift was not contributed to this memory. Rather than feel horror for the prey, Delora, Liam and even Brough were *Orca* in the recollection, pure and simple. As such, they shared in the subjective intense pleasure of the hunger relieving feast and Akenehi's long term happy recollection that in correlation with the grand feasting that year they had suffered no deaths among the clan.

In turn, the subject of celebratory feasting drew Liam's memory easily to his favorite winter holiday, as his family enjoyed the morning breakfast at his grandparent's house.

He remembered clearly his ninth year. The Vencello were carried along in the current of his vision. He felt he was more present in the collective remembering than he had been at the time. Now he enjoyed the added gifts and perspective of Akenehi and Brough. The human family was seated in a grand orangery while just outside beautiful snow was softly accumulating on the surrounding pines and bare branches. Liam individually viewed snowflake after snowflake; pleasingly consistent in possession of six radiating arms, yet each simultaneously unique. All of this detail thanks to Brough and the Priori. He heard the rapid breathing and heartbeats coming from outside the window and at Grandma's bird feeder were a few female brown-red birds and one spectacular red male, all watching those inside carefully with one eye as they enjoyed their own feast of seeds. The superior acoustic processing of an orca missed none of their soft whistles and chirps, otherwise muffled to human ears by a layer of glass.

His grandmother, long since deceased, was still living at that time, and he could clearly hear she had a slower, louder, heartbeat than the birds. She was casually making room on the table with her left hand, for the ceramic plate full of warm cinnamon rolls, just out of the oven and dripping with her own recipe icing. He saw through and into her hand—her joints were swollen and inflamed. With her left hand she moved a favorite dish of Liam's closer to him. She turned her back to them and he perceived with new ability the wince of pain she had concealed from those at the table at the time. Such secrets could not have been kept from a cetacean.

The low rhythm of multiple heartbeats and slow respiration drew his attention and he felt a new intimacy with his family he had not known then. The black, robust aromatic coffee was being poured by grandpa into the eagerly outstretched mugs of his happy parents. He heard empty stomachs grumbling low and digestive juices being quietly excreted and realized it was his own as well as everyone else's. He saw through things that would have embarrassed him or been an invasion of privacy then, but now were natural and comfortable. He perceived skeletal structure, intestine contents and even the presence of microscopic mites on the dog. He felt happy at the perception of his friend, lying patiently near his feet, waiting in hopes of a covert offering; a tasty morsel under the table. Liam was completely known in this new version, as well as knowing. Liam and his two siblings were antsy in their chairs—not for cinnamon rolls and not because they were seated on hard metal folding chairs, but to open their gifts.

Brough and the Akenehi were spellbound. The cetaceans had never experienced smell, so these memories, with the distinct and pleasant details, which they now also knew provoked strong emotions from humans, was a beautiful universal awakening in and of itself. Also, completely new to them was the importance of so many *things* with no function other than ornament or sentiment, to be treasured and kept over so much time. Nothing in this scene required effort to keep itself in a fixed position and nothing fell into a cold dark crushing abyss. The human realm was a shallow stable plane containing a plethora of *things* within their reach and manipulation.

Brough did not wish to share a favorite memory. He believed his finest memory was not yet available to him, as it would occur in the future. He tried to swim against that current but he was too weak and many of his wonderful observations during his long travels were re-lived by the others.

They exchanged memories, perceptions, and knowledge, and were quickly growing accustomed to their individual parts of the whole. As soon as they remembered an event in their past, they were all seemingly instantly transported there to witness from any vantage point, as much as they desired. At first Liam suggested it was enhanced memory, but now as he noted detail, there was no way he could have held in memory. He started to believe they were actually going back to that place in time. Perhaps Delora was right; maybe they *were* able to time travel.

Brough knew whatever was going on, they were still in the center of what Aware Masters knew as the sacred bit. The humans called it a carbon-60 molecule or buckminsterfullerene.

Delora and Liam agreed that Brough might be correct, in that they had somehow become entrapped within a molecule because it aligned with their perception of their prior experience. What was not easily understood was where this new place was, exactly. Delora and Liam both had often pondered their own mortality, a possible afterlife, and began to wonder if they were merely dead and this was such a place.

No. Brough was still cognizant of their universe of origin, the Sponge, and reviewed his mental map with them. They all therefore agreed they were not dead yet, but had retained memory, identity and purposes from home.

Before the Vencello, Delora and Liam had wanted to exit their first sphere where they were unknowingly enveloped within a molecule. At that time, they were drawn out, thanks to Akenehi's presence on the outside. Their next question, since Akenehi was *inside* with them, was collectively pondered. Could any of them leave now? None of them wished to, yet. That was immediate and clear.

Time in their bubble universe was non-sequitur. Delora and Liam's son, Alvar had preceded them to the multiverse. That was so because they had traded part of themselves, as the Vencello, for Alvar's sake. Delora had requested it. They all loved Alvar as their own and had consented. Although for them in a linear sense, it hadn't played out yet.

For Priori, and likewise the Vencello, events of any perceptible universe, the Sponge and their individual realms, were non-linear. Yet everything about time made perfect sense to *them*.

Most newborn Priori experienced ambiguous and ever moving points of past, present and future, typically chaotic and confused at first. There was only one indescribable tense for a Priori, and so for convenience, our kind sang in only one, the past.

The Vencello was rare in that as soon as they opened their temporal eyes, at once, their perception of time travel was unusually mature.

*****

Again, Delora commanded their collective memory to Alvar right before the tragic fight that resulted in his death. She could not help herself from thinking of him and that lead to her strongest, most recent memory, his death. She could not stop the natural progression of her thoughts any more than an apple could stop itself from falling once its stem had detached from the branch. Her memory of his death started a loop. Desire to save him took her to a specific memory and the time leading up to and after. Delora would approach him, ready to intervene and save his precious life. She wanted him with her and did not even stop to consider whether he could or would wish to join her. She was determined. She ran to him, calling to him as she did so, tried to throw her arms around him, but to their collective and utter despair Alvar could not perceive them. Delora was unable to alter that event or even to interact with him or other participants, and certainly could not pull him into their universe that way.

Delora tried thousands of attempts, revisiting earlier in the day, then earlier in the week, again and again. She even tried communicating to him while he was asleep the night before, hoping, through Akenehi's talent, some subliminal message—even sleep song—might get through.

She took them as far back to a clear night where she and Alvar, as they frequently did, headed out to sea, cut off the engine and gazed up into the galaxy filled sky. In addition to the science of cetaceans, they also shared a deep love of astronomy. Alvar knew all of the constellations and was easily reciting names and facts as Delora pointed them out, identifying individual stars and their light distance from their home planet.

Through this particular memory, Akenehi and Brough shared the human's limited knowledge and fascination with the cosmos that filled the Sponge. They had, in their prior lives, experienced their nighttime ocean world, beautiful from their cetacean perspective But from a new human vantage point the sea became as a floor, near glass in its calmness, and their dark sky view of their home galaxy was reflected upon it. The cetaceans comprehended and agreed as Alvar sighed. "Beautiful. I love the universe. I feel like I belong out there, momma. It calms me. Like home." And then they were instantly on to Delora's next heartrending reflection.

They had been learning at that very time, as they carried each other by their thoughts, they could not alter past events, but observe only, and by revisiting them in the past as a whole, obtain clearer detail, perhaps even expanded understanding. Delora's repeated failures gave them no hope whatsoever that in their *present* form they could modify any part of the Sponge. That ability to alter had been theirs in organic life, with many limits. Those realizations weakened her resolve and finally came an ability to pull away from Delora's feedback loop.

As soon as he perceived his chance, Brough propelled them mightily out of her quandary and directly and firmly to where and when they had already achieved success. Brough demonstrated that he was, among many things, a Master of non-linear time navigation.

* * * * *

As the Vencello, they perceived that crucial moment with combined perspectives.

Alvar tightened his breathing against the pain in his gut. An ironic smile widened his lips as he relived the lesson he had learned that day; no good deed goes unpunished. Defending a female classmate from sexual assault earlier in the day had somehow brought him to this moment; the end of his life. He had waited too long to get help and now he couldn't even move. He didn't want to be weak or defeated and didn't need medical attention of any sort. But he was sure changing his mind now. He could feel it coming; it was the end, no doubt.

His facial muscles relaxed but he widened his eyes and took in the faint outline of his C-60 molecule model. It was close by his head, right on his nightstand. He pondered its secrets he would never get an opportunity to seriously investigate. He thought about his mother and how freaked out she would be when she came home and found him…he wondered what Akenehi and the orca pod were up to at that very moment… he imagined an emotional and affectionate introduction to the father he had never met.

This was too sad. In defensive reflex my attention drifted back to the calm and wonder of star looping. Grandmother put this, Alvar's experience, into perspective for the moment. For Priori, death came as a painless process of losing cohesion. Energy would then disperse and be formed elsewhere in the multiverse. We knew of change only from one phase to another. For organic beings such as Alvar, it *seemed* final. He experienced physical pain and discomfort. It was a big deal. Grandmother focused in. She would not let me avoid it and I felt it…

The final surge of endorphins in Alvar's dying neuroanatomy kicked in, not unlike star looping. His brain's information filter was also reduced from its normal functioning. Alvar became aware of more information than he had in life. His eyes opened wide, taking in their final image of the carbon-60 model on his nightstand and then…

Alvar wondered, why was Johnny suddenly there, crouching right at his bedside in the dark, studying his face? Johnny was one of those who had participated in his beating, albeit as a lookout only, and was partially responsible for his imminent death. He stared hard trying to clear the hallucination, if it was one, from his mind. Johnny was still there, almost as motionless as Alvar. Alvar had enough sense to reason that Johnny hadn't come with medics.

"Come to watch me die?" he solved the puzzle with a query but couldn't speak it. Johnny wasn't talking either. Alvar tried so hard to jump up, to fight to his last breath, but didn't have the strength. He focused, in paralyzed frustration, on a taunting finger Johnny moved slowly and silently to his face.

"This wasn't the way I thought this day would end" Alvar mused. He wanted to shout out his second to last word in defiance but the bio-mechanics to express his plosive curse refused to respond. Then he heard himself think, for the first time, the last word he would ever form clearly in his mind: amaranth.

Johnny's fingertip finally made the slightest of contact with flesh. Alvar had his first epiphany. Despite the external appearance, Johnny was also his mother and Alvar was no longer angry.

Everything in the universe was idiosyncratic in some way; complex organic beings, such as humans and cetaceans, even more so. Alvar, at this instant was now unique in yet another sense. He was in the Sponge lying on his bed but through that light touch he was also connected to a part of a bubble universe, a Priori, specifically the Vencello. Brain death was imminent and Brough had brought them to the critical moment.

Alvar knew buoyant relief as he began the pleasant diffusion of his organically focused neural energy. The natural process of human brain death progressed.

His mother was unmistakably horrified. She feared she would lose him forever, again. She reached out, from the Vencello directly through to the Sponge, pulled him back from that brink and gave him a precious essential moment to reverse his drift.

Alvar, the Vencello and even Johnny shared it.

How very refreshing and full of possibility, to completely be free of one's human past, one's memory of its pain, shed completely the knowledge of individual and collective death and its corresponding suffering, Alvar realized in unison with the Vencello, and yet, at the same time, how universally very sad at the loss of each identity that was so unique and essential at the time.

The consternation of Delora stormed their reverie. She had improbably but undoubtedly avoided death thus far. She did not consider Alvar's phase change as something he might desire. Following her maternal instincts, which Akenehi also shared, she perceived his pull away as avoidable and it would be against her nature to let it happen if she could save him.

A series of pushes and pulls then resulted. The physics, chemistry, thermodynamics and free will of two universes had a party and everybody came. It was a chaotic, unpredictable moment where many possibilities could have happened.

The overpowering realization that hit the cetaceans as soon as Alvar came closer to them, aside from experiencing Delora's and Liam's corresponding elation, was the familiar mammal instinctive bond they all carried from their prior individuality. They were moved with recognition and welcome for this human whom they now and forever after felt was as beloved as one of their own.

Love was a very powerful attractant all its own and Alvar felt its pull.

In these, his last moments as Alvar, it seemed he would have to finally and permanently detach from his individual particle-like human life and rejoin, as wave-like, his eternal mother, the Sponge, *or* enlist with his human mother in the unique and fortunate collective of the Vencello, *or* follow one of infinite currents flowing between the Sponge and the multiverse. He still possessed free will and it was his choice. It was going to be a tough decision. But he had to think fast. He loved them all so very much.

CHAPTER 5 – THUMB LESSONS

Universe: Multiverse

Priori

In retrospect, Grandmother taught me why opposable thumbs were more dangerous than advantageous. There were many similar variations on the functional theme throughout the multiverse. Tentacles manifested that were capable of the finest manipulations, tongue like protrusions that split at the ends and organisms that could spontaneous join together as one to manifest super-abilities that put the human digits to shame. The thumbs that plagued me were among the most simple but dexterous enough and pervasive to my entire being to threaten the continued existence of my clan. Why?

Grandmother enabled my understanding of specific outcomes through direct time traveling examples. Meticulously following each of those lines, in all their variation, the end result was the same; humans distracted by the products of their thumbs ended up with freakishly stunted sentience. Those lessons hurt more than any physical severing I had already endured but there is no other method that would have taught me better.

Humans were no different than orcas in their desire to feed to their family, sometimes at any cost, to hunt, to kill for sport and sometimes even for fun. And they were ok, right?

In every single timeline we followed, humans not only halted their natural progression toward unaided time travel, which could have been achieved had they not been distracted by artificial methods, they eventually inadvertently enclosed themselves within an inescapable bubble universe; an isolated realm within that was devoid of everything except themselves. A long and miserable existence followed where costly attempts were desperately made to enforce and continuously adapt to, again through thumb-centered artificial methods, a complete independence from other species. Without the infinite complexity of their home world and all its parts, which were all interdependent and contributed to the survival of the whole in their own way, they became sick and miserable, mutating within just a few generations to something so repugnant that most outside time travelers could not bear their presence, even for a nanosecond.

For those that did attempt intervention…well…it didn't take a time traveler exploring alternate timelines or the calculation ability of Akenehi to work out that the humans would ultimately exploit, consume and subsequently explain away all that possessed non-human sentience. In essence, in all possible realities, the end result of thumb-centric humanity was that they entrapped themselves in their self-made eternal universe of ironic misery.

I despaired to myself, "Why not just dissipate me *now*?" as Grandmother continued with the history lesson.

We found ourselves amid the most horrific of human experiences. War. These were historical events held in high regard and of great value, promoted and pushed by Liam, our Homo sapiens male ancestor. He was a self-professed human war buff. He knew statistics on battles, names of commanders, famous deeds, ships, weapons. He had never been in a battle personally; however during his organic existence he had found it instructive and even fascinating to study these events from afar, as a safe third person. His knowledge and memory were more than sufficient guides.

However, he had not experience it as we, multiverse time travelers, would.

We, unfortunately, got all of it, directly, completely, from each life's beginning to death and beyond...one direction, forward, linear experiences of each individual as well as the collective whole. Hundreds of thousands of variations on the theme including the repetition of hope of victory, belief in righteousness, the obscure mutated desire for thumb-products: possessions, physical and emotional agony, loss of family and loved ones, humiliations and unbearable defeat. Our experiences were not mere memory or theatre. Grandmother and I were *reliving* it...all of it.

This also meant we didn't just get the worst, that wouldn't be fair. The Priori were nothing, if not *fair*. Following the complete timeline of every detail of every war meant the associated tribal warfare, family feuds, and lovers' spats and so on. War was considered the most efficient way to learn the *thumb* lesson because we experienced an all-inclusive human behavior odyssey of everything experienced during that time. It was rare to experience any *thumbness* that was not in some stage of war.

That explained the dearth of other time travelers among humans in general. Human war was a mandatory lesson for me because I was manifesting the appendage-in-common, but not one that time travelers wished to experience or repeat. It served, among other things, as a testimony to the toxic effect of thumbs that humans *did* repeat these experiences, seemingly inescapably.

It seemed ironic to me that those who could have helped, that are time travelers, were by their very nature repulsed by the pervasive unpleasantness of those events that they could have perhaps altered. I then supposed since humans themselves did not avoid it, in some way it must have gratified.

Thumbs in common or not, I was certain I didn't share in any of that tendency. So, at first I wondered why Grandmother did not hurry us away from these excruciating sensations. Then I entertained the thought that perhaps she was not able to, did not possess the knowledge of how to pull us away. Just as quickly I pondered whether she wanted to. Was she trying to expose us to as much pain as possible? Was this a mandatory lesson in thumb-enabled weaponry and physical suffering that I had to learn by experiencing these horrific, traumatic moments? I calculated many other possibilities. I did not know I had it in me but I did something I had never done before, I took the lead from Grandmother.

I had sufficiently *lived* as a human and absolutely refused to proceed any further along those war-tainted timelines. To my surprise, we were then underway, by my own navigation, and Grandmother was with me, silent. I sang to her as I carried us, reasoning that those humans experienced what they did, in their own time, for whatever reasons or lack thereof. But it was not going to trap or consume me, nor would I be present and watch her suffering either. I wanted no part of it. No memory of it. Whatever my future held, I would make sure it did not include any of *that*.

I didn't really know where to go next, and then Grandmother gently resumed control and guided us once more. She took me away from human war and instead to one specific individual, an orca. And it made me just as furious and heartbroken. Again, I wanted to leave immediately but since this would be a single experience I decided to endure it, taking any lesson that Grandmother intended.

*****

Quite frankly, the cetaceans found Delora's desire to eliminate death pathetic. They truly loved their human element but it was replete with backward thinking. Akenehi reminded Delora and Liam of the knowledge that cetaceans have of the natural cycle of the ocean and the necessity to return one's body to it. They came from the ocean, they lived their whole lives in it and they returned to it when they passed. In fact, Akenehi knew that her own beloved son, Hototo, had made his choice and had been at peace with his species' destiny, which was to be recycled back to the ocean. His death had resulted from an injury inflicted during a great white shark hunt. He died that day and was escorted by his family in solemn ritual to an appropriate point of release. It was what he wanted and it was natural and right. She did not desire to trouble his dying moments with confusion. She was definitely terribly sad at his loss, but it was the way of things and the whole clan knew it. While Delora found this harsh and unloving, Akenehi knew it was not only loving in a comprehensive sense, but also healthy and in keeping with the oceans need to be full and in balance.

Then Akenehi had an inspiration. Unlike Hototo's death, she had never found peace with the unknown fate of her daughter, who had been captured and removed entirely from their ocean world, never to return. This created a hole, an imbalance, and she had never been right with it. That, Akenehi pressed, would be something she must change, if possible. They all agreed with more than the sum of their joined hearts.

Greatly facilitated by Akenehi's maternal connection and sympathetic Priori, they easily honed in on the space-time coordinates that contained the living, breathing, captive orca, Akenehi's beloved daughter, and in one collective heartbreaking memory they were there. The orca was cruelly imprisoned by a small inescapable enclosure and had been for decades. Her body was severely atrophied. Her mind was an unbearable torment of despair and hopelessness.

*****

Once a physical object was scanned it was a simple action, inherent in my kind, to follow its history back in a smooth sequence of time-memory. Grandmother lead by example scanning the enclosure and then I followed the related harmonics and the strand of time, forward and back in relation to physical markers, events that lead to its existence and her long-term imprisonment. The lesson I absorbed from that song was painful but essential. Had there been no opposable thumbs in the history of human kind, there would have been no prison. I examined and followed time-strands of every object in and near the enclosure and there was the same conclusion: complex fitting and altering, measuring, carrying and placing. All of the intelligence in the multiverse alone could not think it into existence, but opposable thumbs with a limited intelligence could make it so.

I knew from here on out it would ultimately be my choice to stay or go in any time travel destination. I mustered my emotional courage and we stayed until the scene played out and Grandmother indicated our departure.

*****

From the Vencello, Akenehi found her daughter, Arva'Anati, in the Sponge, still alive after so many long seasons, in human captivity. Her daughter's song was weak and much altered, but the essence was unmistakable, she was not beyond her mother's recognition. Akenehi's precious orca child had been ripped from her family very young and had lived her entire life from that point forward entertaining Homo sapiens through bizarre, skewed concepts collectively known to their human parts as corporate profit. The cetaceans struggled with it; mostly it just made them sad for the humans who were also captives in their own way. Still, Arva'Anati lived deprived of her mother and family, emotional needs cruelly underestimated, severely intellectually under-stimulated, physically restrained and torturously confined.

Delora and Liam were mortified with shame for their species and had to acknowledge that they shared blame. Any sentient being with a shred of compassionate awareness would have been appalled at the existence of any captive orca, and they had been. Yet, somehow Arva'Anati survived decades of it, albeit in a weakened spirit and body.

Brough was in disbelief that the orca was able to survive at all in such a restrictive, small space. He worked out as soon as they arrived on the scene that if humans had been able to keep a Master in such a place, they would have. A quick check with the multiverse, his own method of following strands, and he knew humans had indeed attempted it, on more than one horrific occasion, and those unfortunate Masters had died en route or soon after arrival in their captivity. He easily followed related human-infested strands and discovered so much more that sickened him. He could do nothing to save his fellows. The only thing he could do was remember what he had clicked. As much as he disliked orcas in his past, that had also grievously harmed his kind, he felt full empathy with Akenehi's love for her wronged family member and righteous grief.

As the Vencello was easily able to examine in detail the entire enclosure and surroundings Akenehi carefully observed every confining aspect of it. Her daughter was alone in the tank and floated, suspended aimlessly in its center. To Akenehi it was as if she was dazed and injured. Arva'Anati sang nothing. Akenehi understood the acoustic effect of those walls. The sound of any song bouncing right back to her unanswered would be too much. Akenehi wondered in a mothers agony how long it had been since she last sang with her clan.

A human approached Arva'Anati with an object, lazily dropping it with a low thud and metallic clank near the water. The Vencello scanned it, and contents, easily. To Akenehi's horror, her daughter responded hungrily. The human casually walked away and came back with another object in his hand.

I observed every detail, while Grandmother observed me. The human deftly pinched his thumb to forefinger, which enabled him to grasp and then loop the new object around his neck. Each object entailed a manual nuance and each of those movements required agreement of intention. He knew exactly what he was doing and why he was doing so.

Akenehi's soul sickened as she realized the dead fish were her daughter's meal. *Dead.* There was no exhilaration or challenge of the hunt. There was no live prey to surprise her daughter with clever defensive behaviors or to evoke the physical exercise of pursuit. She would not be able to hunt in any event. She was confined in a tiny space, isolated from the assistance, company and family bond of her clan, alone, and made to eat dead—as Akenehi supposed it passed somehow for—food. And then it got worse. This had obviously become routine for her beloved child. Her cherished Arva'Anati was compelled to perform various stupid, human-amusing, repetitive behaviors on cue and, for each, received a limp, dead carcass.

The Homo sapiens element of the Vencello recognized the very essence of slavery. Arva'Anati was fiercely intelligent and aware of her tortured emotions, she was held in perpetual confinement, forced to behave and thereby produce for the 'master' and in return receive only conditional-upon-compliance meager existence. Akenehi eventually comprehended the situation somewhat through the human perspective. The sad rehearsal continued until the bucket was empty.

Akenehi was desperate to swim alongside her daughter to offer comfort and company. She imagined an orca heart still within herself and it pounded violently in preparation for an attack on the trainer, for sheer hatred and revenge and little else. Akenehi, in her own interpretation, now felt she understood Delora's inability to accept Alvar's fate. Alvar was alone in his room when he died. This was 'alone'. A concept so foreign and so horrible, it was hell itself. Akenehi too wanted to save her child, get her the hell out of that unbearable isolation and back to her clan.

The Vencello and the Priori followed all associated timelines to the creation and maintenance of that prison. They learned more than they expected or wanted to know.

The orca matriarch's grief combined with rage that was neither concealed nor containable. So many human individuals, who benefited, promoted, participated or just didn't give a damn and so there it was. Her righteous disdain seared its mark in the essence of the multiverse and through them. The shared sensibilities of Priori, cetacean and human disturbed her previous orca serene acceptance of finality, and she would never be the same.

Akenehi became even more influential. Her powerfully evolved emotional intelligence filled the Vencello with a determination to be righteous. The two orbiting humans had to think forward immediately and give some context to ease their own consciences and soothe their shame. Delora and Liam, as cetacean researchers, were well aware of guidelines for housing cetaceans and wanted to assure Akenehi that her daughter was treated well, her food was high quality, albeit dead, and she received medical care and attention from her human 'caregivers'. Also, there were other cetaceans in other tanks nearby, although she was the only orca in this place. Then they regretted their thoughts. What good could that possibly do? They were sorry they were even thinking at that point. They all shared the mother's overwhelming love for the captive orca, also perceiving Akenehi's undiluted revulsion, and knew there was simply no excuse to be made. It was wrong.

Akenehi's desire for hands of her own was resolved. She never again envied those human appendages but rather thought of them as hideous, cruel, malformed tentacles.

Delora and Liam spontaneous and gladly forfeited the repugnant genetic distinction and sought the assistance of Metavoli. As Vencello, their opposable thumbs were of no benefit and served as a genetic relic of a horrific, shameful, primitive history. They modified their hands to reduce the thumb so that they were virtually unnoticeable and webbed all digits mimicking cetacean genetic code.

I realized that mine were the only thumbs in the Vencello. I felt Akenehi loved me despite them, but then again, I reasoned, I was not pure human.

Arva'Anati was Akenehi's beloved daughter. Now that she was found, her mother could not leave. Just as Delora had compelled the others to endure her continuous attempts to save Alvar, the Vencello had to stay with Arva'Anati. Akenehi was adamant they do that. They could stay with her, even if they could not be detected by the captive for the entire duration of her confinement. To watch her suffer, feel with her in her own painfully slow passage of time the bored existence, would be horrible but to leave her alone would be far worse.

Akenehi focused intently on her daughter as if she could convey with sheer will to her over and again that she was not alone, that she was loved, and her mother was close by and they were going to help her. Arva'Anati just had to find the strength to endure until they could figure out a way to get her out or somehow convince her captors to return her to her clan.

Until then, maybe at some level, their presence might be detected or at least some comfort could be offered.

Yes, Akenehi agreed she might be able to reach her daughter through orca sleep-song. Orcas possessed superior acoustic sensitivity and brains that could only sleep one hemisphere at a time. The combination resulted in an ability to communicate in half-sleep, or sleep-song. The resonance of their new universe had physical properties inherited from the Sponge. Perhaps sleep-song could be communicated between both realms. She would try to reach her.

Akenehi recalled how she was unable to perceive her daughter's dreams after she was taken and therefore thought her dead. Now she despaired and worried that perhaps her daughter had given up and had "gone silent" out of hopelessness.

A sharp clang echoed through the tank as the empty bucket was inadvertently dropped, causing the captive orca to jerk. Arva'Anati's ears rang. As the familiar pain diminished she watched near the surface with one eye as the trainer picked up a few large items and finally exited the enclosures visual area. Arva'Anati could still hear the human as he tinkered and bumped, conveying heavy footsteps to her sensitive ears that became increasingly dim until she knew at last he was gone.

The Vencello stayed. Still unaware of them, Akenehi's daughter sometimes floated still on the surface, chewing masochistically on surfaces that she knew very well held her captive. Watching an occasional bird land beside her tank, imitating its whistle, listened to the mumbling chatter of the outside human world and sometimes she just swam slowly in a circle. Time did not pass quickly for her. Finally she dozed off.

Because it was natural that orcas did not allow both halves of their brain to sleep at the same time, they possessed an easy ability to fall into a power nap at will. When she saw her daughter had dozed, Akenehi fell into a lucid dream state. Akenehi intended to prevent her daughter from succumbing to grief upon seeing her mother again. She was very fearful her daughter would despair when she awoke again, still very much alone, in captivity. Of all the maternal emotions she had experienced as an orca, this was by far the most powerful and loving and she was lost to it as she awakened into her daughter's dream.

Akenehi, as all orcas did, sang even in dreams, using her unique and perfectly tuned acoustic voice to call her daughter's name. It took experimentation with the changes her new realm evoked but Akenehi was a quick acoustic study. She adjusted her frequencies, added some harmonics that were likely to be recognized as belonging to her clan and was recognized quickly by her now-adult child. Akenehi recognized her daughter's dreamscape, they were no longer in the prison but rather in nature and freedom; a shallow-watered and familiar location of home, and though they were in half-sleep. Her daughter knew this was a communication and her mother had somehow found her and was at least partially there with her.

They rushed together, Akenehi singing, stroking each other with their pectoral fins, mother pressed her child along the length of her body, soothing and comforting her as when she was an infant all the while repeating her lullaby in refrain: "My daughter, I am here with you."

"Mama!"

Delora had always wondered if orcas cried. They did.

*****

What made me want to stay? I wanted to take care of Arva'Anati, Akenehi and all of them and keep them company. Grandmother and I both did, caregiving was in our very essence. So we stayed with them, following the time-strand of Arva'Anati's entire captivity to its end.

During this whole visit, I longed to return Arva'Anati to her family and her ocean. I proposed many solutions. I asked Grandmother if somehow we could give her my hands. Maybe the captive could figure out a way to use them and escape, such a bad idea. It was obvious upon next thought that the humans would surely notice *that* and then…

No.

Was there a way we could take her place? I would do that in an instant if I could. Her entire captivity was as a mere second to me. I had experienced so much human suffering in our war lesson, how bad could *this* be? We would endure Arva'Anati's suffering relatively easily and it was not final for us by any means.

No perceptible affirmation *that* idea would work. But Grandmother flinched and I thought something passed through me, like a wave. My mind felt like it was floating elsewhere by her side, with something else too, and I mused that giving Arva'Anati my hands, which I didn't like or want, even to help her, had been self-serving regardless of whether I had not intentioned that. Self-sacrifice on the other hand, taking her place in her suffering, even if it was easily done on my part…well…the wave pulsed through me again.

I asked Grandmother, did she feel that too? I perceived her emotional response only as a blank and I could not describe it to her as anything other than *pleasure*.

Once I had actually experienced how our kind transitioned the multiverse it would only be a matter of acutely focused thought to begin an independent journey. I knew rescuing Arva'Anati was definitely something I *wanted* to do, for no self-serving purpose, only to release her from suffering and reunite her with her family. Once I was fully formed I would be free to explore any number of solutions within my ability that could be utilized that would help the captive.

There was her hope, and mine.

As Brough, our ancestor from the Vencello was a Master of the Ocean, our kind were Masters of O-O. Humans, save those two who were part of the Vencello, were usually not capable of non-linear time travel. They grappled with analog or whole picture in their perception range, as if analog were nonsensical and incomprehensible. Human brains bottlenecked and filtered so much information as to create a constant stream of digital processing and their pieced-together perception of reality. However, not every species was as weak in this respect. Brough's kind possessed massive brains that easily and quite naturally put 'whole pictures' together using echolocation, and particularly *Aware* Masters readily handled information as detailed as the molecular level.

Fortunately, our ancestry was cetacean as well as human. So like Brough, we processed information in analog, or wave as we also call it. Through him, we inherited the ability to know the most delicate detail, take it in with the whole, and process it as one, and even project highly accurate outcomes along multiple hypothetical alternative timelines. We were fluent in both human and cetacean thought which provided distinctiveness and defined our limited ability to navigate the multiverse once we perceived it.

Grandmother utilized an unmistakable orca technique intermixed with observable Broughesque nuances as she chose what to focus on. She possessed the skills of a highly experienced navigator. I was honored to be in the presence of, let alone be a descendent of, one of the finest.

I anticipated many future journeys I could undertake completely on my own. I didn't have to anticipate long. Grandmother was satisfied right then that I could take my first solo journey.

So soon? Wasn't *she* taking me to Cetapiens? I wanted to stay with her. I was learning so much. I still had no clue how I would begin and then subsequently close an unbroken song; *once*, on my first try no less, and ensure my survival.

I was stunned at her complete confidence in me, thumbs and all.

Further lessons at her side were no longer needed, she informed me. She would remain within call range. She urged me on to Cetapiens, providing me with specific markers to scan for, there were so many there, that would ensure I hone in safely and within the desired temporal range. She had other times and or places to be, preparations to make, none of which required both of us.

No sooner had I begun to phase-shift and hone in on Cetapiens, exactly where she indicated I would find it in Sponge space and time, than she was gone from my side, abrupt and seemingly unemotional. Her only parting assurance was that she would remain aware of me and I would be safe. She would be at my side again when I was ready.

Whatever *that* meant.

CHAPTER 6 – METAVOLI AND THEIR GS

Universe: Multiverse

Priori

On the planet of origin, humans never *intentionally* accomplished a reproduction of even a single particle of matter that paralleled the function of Metavoli. Only cetaceans, namely Akenehi and her clan, had come so close. And it is a Priori-celebrated credit to her that those orcas reproduced fish with no less than a Metavoli-8 result. The humans outside of the Vencello simply never attained the sensory capability inherent to success.

However, they did inadvertently at times, borrow energy or matter pulled from a similar universe. The Priori and others perceived those events and managed to limit the devastation it had caused in all universes. It was also noted that, as typical, it was human thumb related and the corresponding neuroanatomy rendered them insensitive if not downright oblivious of the damage in their wake.

Metavoli were of countless varieties, all incredibly dynamic and at any cross-section-moment existed in a range of multiple universe colors. Like a much simpler human enzyme, they worked on originals without being changed in the process. However, like a slime-mold they could transition from existing as constituent essential universases to one complex colony and back again. Miniscule parts could pinch off or transition away leaving a whole behind, to rejoin when called or homesick. Like the Vencello from which it came, they were alive and intelligent.

Their most distinguishing feature however was their sense of humor. Because they were necessarily meticulous, they noticed quirks and unexpected flaws. That was inherent in order to function as a universase. Each genetic flaw broke up the monotony of its lengthy whole organism reproducing task and was most times considered more hilarious than tragic and seriously debilitating. Depending on whether the Metavoli were alert, and in a good mood, they would fix it. If not, they would let it be or even worsen it. Just because they had a sense of humor didn't meant it was always a nice one.

Suitable organic matter that penetrated its membrane was safe but immediately subject to replication and subsequent expulsion back into suitable universes. The enveloped organism experienced time as non-sequitur and virtually non-existent. Within the Metavoli, as many sequences as needed, to adapt to each universe, occurred that would otherwise have taken way too much time and been virtually impossible outside of its membrane.

Metavoli replication was therefore a method of trans-universal travel achieved by organic beings such as humans and whales, as long as they had been duplicated and successfully ejected into a viable similar universe.

*****

A whale or human, even after Gemini processing, could not just go anywhere and everywhere. They required appropriate density and temperature of water, gas composition of air and so on. Similar rules of survival applied to Priori. Some destinations, rare but in existence, were believed to be toxic to our kind. Those were the dark and featureless quiet realms which emitted no attractive beacon or marked invitation to explore. So, it was likely travel to tried and true destinations was safe and the vast unexperienced multiverse was left to itself. Once traveled and favored, an attraction to that destination pulled in other travelers and then at a critical point a *puffing* phenomenon, self-similar to my survival reflex, occurred.

The effect of time travelers coming and going to a highly popular destination in non-linear progression, meeting one's self, changing one's own past and that of others…well…it follows that common history was non-sequitur and there was only one tense, the now which we did not distinguish from the past. The result was that we time travelers lived in, each in our own *now* time-frame, or shade, and everything in the multiverse had already occurred, in the *past*. The interaction and connectedness of so much chaos in space and time within a small area stabilized into a puff.

It was not always achieved safely but if a time-buffering puff existed it did so in a stabilized state. Within its membrane everything that could happen, might happen; yet there were no paradoxes. All possibilities played out without threat to the existence of the puff.

But what if the effect of the time travelers did *not* stabilize? Laments were sung of how all within would merge color in a multi-spectrum burst of puff membrane failure, spewing out the travelers into the multiverse leaving a time-void where the travel activity had occurred. The effect was there would remain no evidence of any of the non-linear overlapping temporal variables; only the linear constants would remain. So rocks, or even long standing human built structures, might be in evidence to those outside the temporal puff but no remains of any organic that remotely had a part in the time-flux would have ever existed.

Each successful highly favored destination created its own dynamic time-balanced system, within a membrane, a *puff*, protecting all within and preventing the effects from interacting with and being detected by anything outside of its sheath.

Destinations such as Cetapiens had become puff-systems. In fact, Cetapiens was a rare model of a puff that successfully included a very pleasant human experience.

The instant the Vencello emerged, Brough attracted a lot of Priori friends, a welcoming committee of esoteric sorts. Instantly, they clicked, informing the Aware Master of the entire history of his planet of origin in all its possible alternatives and in each version they despaired right along with him at its sad end, its complete annihilation of so many wonderful sentients.

Just as quickly, a solution that would salvage some of these wonderful beings was offered.

C-60 Metavoli were initiated and began to self-modify to their maximum ability within the limitations of Vencello conditions at the time. Brough had thus received an extremely useful welcome gift from neighbors and time traveling progeny. The Metavoli-2 colony that eventually evolved was not merely transportation or an entrance/exit to another universe, once activated it accomplished just about *anything* the Vencello required.

*****

It was possible, if one possessed the means of detection, to locate the Vencello's Metavoli-2 while it was in the Sponge. When it embedded around an unremarkable C-60 molecule, an equal and opposite reaction to the Vencello's exit occurred. It displaced surrounding matter and a small shock wave followed and many cetaceans and sea life felt that. The location of the Metavoli was not random. It had been deliberately anchored where Param would be able calculate access to it, albeit indirectly, yet away from humans and orcas. Thereby, Brough and his friends throughout the multiverse had managed to limit access to it away from those two species; both decidedly dangerous and treacherous by Master terms. Param would completely approve.

The waves from the seafloor tremor reached Param and she

calculated that its time of origin corresponded to Brough's disappearance. However, she was greatly discouraged by the depth of the source. She would not be able to dive to it and survive. It was too deep and the pressure would surely be lethal. Deepers, on the other hand, distasteful and annoying vermin to her mind, could reach it.

Entanglement explained instantaneous communication between the sperm whales in differing universes. Everything in the multiverse was already connected to, entangled with, every other universe and all within. There was no such thing as empty nothingness, O-O manifested across the multiverse in continuous shades and there were no holes or voids. Everything came from something else, albeit often transformed. The unifying effect of the connection/entanglement was that communication through multiverse-in-common O-O was possible. Communication was possible but infrequent because one needed to know where and how and be in possession of the physiology to perceive and comprehend. It was of course possible between the Vencello and loved ones back in the Sponge. The Metavoli-2, and to a limited extent the Gemini duplicates, served as communication conduits.

*****

Markers were essential to my early survival.

It helped to know where safe transition coordinates were to increase chance of survival while transitioning around the multiverse. In order for a novice to go unassisted from point to point, the most basic color, space, time and a plethora of universe specific variables were involved. Markers were commonly therefore created and utilized.

Once embedded in the ocean floor, the Metavoli -2 served as an obvious marker for instantaneous and safe transition directly from the Vencello to the Brough's home ocean and back again. The Vencello and the Metavoli-2, entangled by default, shared so many characteristics, that they were very easy to follow markers. The easier the link, the more it was illuminated or understood by those lacking the advanced skills of time travelers such as Grandmother.

Carbon-60 molecule *models* in existence, at the time of Alvar's death and the Vencello's creation, were also easy to follow markers. They were very unusual similar objects, yet easily identified to a C-60 based time traveler such a Grandmother and me. Identical human and cetacean twins were also such highly complex yet very similar objects. Those were duplicates of sorts and could serve as very easy to follow markers.

The Metavoli-2 was a very busy youngster right from its inception. During its very first day on the planet of origin several G reproductions were accomplished. The first occurred with an Orion—known by Masters of the Ocean as Deepers. The second was with Johnny. The third was with Alvar and so on.

The first communication link occurred between Johnny and Seasnán, Akenehi's daughter, who in turn communicated her new knowledge efficiently to her family members through their own natural vocalizations and sleep song. The second occurred between the Orion and Param, who in turn conveyed what she learned to the super pod. In short order, Gemini reproduction and communication accomplished its objectives.

The Vencello was by no means stable in its early form and therefore its existence was not guaranteed. If the Vencello *died,* destabilized, so to speak, so that its energy was dissipated to the multiverse, so would its Metavoli-2, in equal and opposite reaction, in obedience to multiverse energy conservation. The importance of not wasting time was profoundly understood.

The potential of the Metavoli was ready to be released, but first it had to be accessed by a willing sentient being in the planet of origin.

CHAPTER 7 – PARAM AND THE ORION-G

Universe: Sponge

Sperm Whale

Masters called them Deepers. As far as Brough, Param and the super-pod were concerned they were little more than obnoxious vermin. Deepers ate their squid, confounded their hunts. They were mildly interesting in that they could dive deeper than Masters, hence their designation, but that was considered one of their very few respectable qualities. Respectable, because it meant Deepers knew things in close up detail about their ocean world that Masters detected only through weaker returning echoes. To understand the ocean in every detail was the ultimate state of being to Masters.

Param thought about the demeaning jokes, lessons she had been taught by her own family and every experience with Deepers she could recall. She was involuntarily repulsed that she would have to come into close contact with one of those vermin. She realized how exceedingly difficult it would be to even locate one, let alone communicate with it. The disdain between species was mutual. Few things stumped her and this problem of how they could communicate in any sophisticated way, did so *completely*.

Continuing with undeterred purpose toward the source of the advanced wave zero deep sea tremors, her returning echoes alerted her to the distant approach of a large object. It was coming from behind her. She turned, focused and intensified her clicks and worked out her plan of escape if it turned out to be one of a few possible predators. She easily determined as it came a bit closer that it was a large cetacean, moving directly at her at its top speed. As it moved closer, her detailed scans revealed it was neither an orca nor pilot whale. She would be in no danger. She remained intrigued and scanned its continued steady approach. It was emitting an awkward pulse uncharacteristic of any cetacean. There were four distinct grunts in succession between longer periods of silence. It mimicked the rhythm of the tickle she was detecting through her jaw from Brough.

No doubt about it, it was accelerating even as it approached her. She calculated with growing alarm that it would collide with her if it didn't slow down or veer off. Alarm transformed to amusement as she realized the problem was apparently about to solve itself. It was a *Deeper*!

*****

They did not call themselves Deepers, of course. They were known amongst themselves as the Orion—the privileged. The beauties and wonders of what humans thought was merely the cold, dark, pressing deepest ocean world were available for their appreciative minds alone. No other species of cetacean could dive as deep as they could. Although the surface was easier to endure and provided essential air, it was not where they felt safest or most content. Their preferred domain consisted of pockets of peaceful havens deep and beyond the presence of many potential predators and bullies. Only at the most extreme depths could the Orion live hours of their days and nights in unfettered bliss.

Their realm was a gift. They loved it, took care of it and were so very proud of it. They felt special and loved themselves as its most essential part. They were self-sufficient and would remain so as long as their private world continued, and they believed it would always be.

The deep realm of the Orion was bejeweled with bio-luminescent beauty and variety. During their long lives they learned to identify the unique dances, flashes and patterns of glowing creatures and used that information for their own utility. Those uses included the obvious such as hunting, courtship displaying and entertainment. Adult males possessed special boney structures on the ends of their rostrums that they used to collect and stir up tiny bioluminescent creatures, creating temporary glowing beards and head frames that were especially appealing to Orion females. At depth, where Orion lived most of their hours each day, males gave considerable thought to creating the most imaginative and beautiful bioluminescent displays for females. They also gleaned information from the lights to read the presence of prey and their population numbers, seasonal changes, tectonic movement indicators and evidence of human machinery.

Light itself was sacred to the Orion. The twinkling stars that floated above the limits of the water surface were beloved by the Orion as much as the bioluminescence of the oceans depth. Stars were well integrated in Orion experience and culture. Among other stories, stars were said to be fortunate Orion high above the surface membrane, separated by a distance that could never be crossed by a surface jump. Held at a height no Orion could possibly go in life, they nonetheless believed that those lights were alive and content and a part of a single world, to which Orion alone had always had access to its most privileged realms. The obvious chasm which separated them from stars permitted their distant admiration only. The heights reminded them of the limits of their living bodies. The chasm was nonetheless in unity with the ocean with those places beyond the surface where their bodies could not reach. Transparent on a clear night from the surface, they contemplated the sky full of Orion in that other realm.

At death, the deceased Orion sank into an abyss the living could not endure, and were lost to the survivors' echolocation. Nonetheless, those who could still swim understood a great journey would continue beyond their living ability. Thus, like all cetaceans they were witnesses to nature's cycle of consumption and production. Orion did not believe in endings or nothingness. When an Orion died it was desirable to release the body to an area over an unreachable depth. It was believed that the dead would transform and then reemerge, alive again, above the surface, to exist in that unified unreachable realm. They even observed, on fortunate occasions, what they believed was the journey of a deceased Orion to that lofty destination—a shooting star or even a fireball.

Although *above* them, the sky was the realm of the same deceased that sank. The concept, that their world *looped,* like an eel grasping its own tail in its mouth, and their beloved dead had *sunk* to far *above* them over the surface, was passed from generation to generation. Each finite life was believed to be intricately bound in the loop.

Very deep diving was of course a most prized skill. Competition was ongoing to bring back the rarest glowing living jewels up where others in their small family groups could enjoy and admire them. Spontaneous flurries of deep underwater activity were continuously sought and when one commenced it was an object of entertainment. One of the sought after skills was putting on a light show to Orion song. They were so good at it that even the squid and octopi were sometimes compelled by fascination to participate. This of course often resulted in an easy meal which was then presented as a gift of courtship.

A healthy adult Orion who had mastered the deep dive had few dangers from which to be on the alert. Their most despised enemies were the Orcas, who possessed skills of amazing stealth and cunning. They could detect Orion calves with disturbing accuracy. If given the opportunity, orcas mercilessly fatigued Orion mothers protecting new calves with unrelenting chase from below. Even though a calf only a few months old was not as capable of deep dive for escape, they were very fast. If they could get under the orca, they could speed straight down and avoid capture. Fortunately, Orcas could not follow a hasty straight down decent for long. Successful Orion mothers are by necessity expert at teaching even a newborn how to out maneuver orcas. It was fortunate indeed that orcas were, in comparison to even a newborn Orion, slower swimmers and poor, pitiful divers.

Despite their few predators, the deep ocean realms were their sanctuary. Orion history stood firm on that truth, but more recently things were changing. Eventually humans had developed thumb-tactics for invading their realm. They regarded humans as predators as well. They knew enough about those strange creatures and their rude machines to always avoid them if at all possible. The Orion endured their clumsy but lethal company during encounters where humans exhibited the utmost disrespect with their extremely damaging blasts of sounds. Humans were the only unwelcome invaders to their deepest realm.

Masters were enemies of the Orion but they were not predators. Masters and Orion had always been at odds. Masters were frequent and omnipresent invaders to the most upper part of their private realm but they could avoid them by deeper dive. They ate the same food and that was the main problem. Masters brilliant strategic cheats in disorienting and confusing them mid-hunt, even at great depth, and then luring away and eating their squid were legendary. Masters, like orcas and humans, were to be summarily avoided.

Far beyond the reach of even Masters, their private world was far from featureless and dull. The Orion were very much like Masters in that they were students of oceanography. They were fascinated by the contents of varying floor layers, from the soft, fresh, constantly blanketed topmost layer to the deeper, more solid strata.

The Orion were also interested in comparative marine biology, identifying specific remains to living counterparts. They always shared information they gleaned happily with others. When an interesting fresh carcass arrived still largely unconsumed it provided an urgent and rare opportunity to study comparative anatomy. Of course, bodies did not come to rest on their isolated realm for long. During the sinking many creatures fed off of it and it was especially true for bottom dwelling scavengers. Often times an arrival was announced by a spectacular light show stirred up by frenzied glowing cloud of turbulence.

Two very special Orion in particular were fascinated by anatomical differences of various light-producing species, specifically those that produced steady glows and flashes of bioluminescent special effects that intensified when disturbed. Their meticulous study resulted in their unparalleled mastery of bioluminescent display.

The two were identical twins, Auden and Jomei. Twin births for Orion were *extremely* rare. Finding twins that survived past birth was even more so. As deep diving was essential, it was almost impossible for an underdeveloped newborn Orion to survive the harsh physical requirements.

Once an Orion reached adulthood, they commonly lived for many decades. However, infant mortality was high among their species. Their older sister had very recently lost her own calf, her first childbirth, just before the twins' arrival. Even though she knew her young was very likely to die soon after emergence, as most first births did, she and her mother tried desperately to save it. They could not. The young mother had managed to keep her dead calf with her for days, protecting it from being eaten and sinking beyond her touch. Very soon the small lifeless body became increasingly ripe and scavengers were overwhelming their efforts. Her mother gently encouraged her to release the body so her beloved grandchild could her take her place among the stars.

Their grief was still raw when the twins emerged, sooner than expected, it was feared they too would die before their first breath. Even if they did breathe, normally a choice would be made. One would be permitted to nurse and the other would not. It was a horrible fact of Orion physiology; only one could be adequately nursed by its mother.

These twins were in luck. They were happily accepted and nurtured by their grieving sister, who was still lactating, and therefore both managed to survive. With essentially two mothers, they were nursed adequately, protected properly with the cooperative efforts of the mothers, and granted the time to develop the anatomy required for deep dives. Their sister, who they would have grown to love in any event as a cherished family member, was therefore even dearer to them as she was as a mother and had literally kept them alive as infants. As a result of the very protective and intense cooperative care between the two mothers, the twins carried an unfaltering devotion and deep attachment to both equally. Another benefit of their family structure was that they were not at all competitive between themselves, as twins they shared an even stronger unique bond which also reinforced family cohesion which included intuitive unique communication and unprecedented sharing.

Upon reaching adulthood they both became attached to a single female, Monifa. It didn't bother them at all that the other wanted the same mate. Normally, had they not had an identical twin with such a singular family history, they would have fought and perhaps even injured each other to show their strength and health to her.

The twins instead celebrated yet another bond they had in common, their love for Monifa. She accepted them both and remained with them for her remaining life. They became a unique Orion family unit that consisted of the twins, their mothers', Monifa and their offspring. Occasionally the sister and mother attracted temporary mates that joined the family unit, as was the norm for Orion.

The twins mating and family arrangement were unprecedented among the Orion. For one thing, none were mated for life to any individual. Paternity was irrelevant as a female would mate with several males to ensure fertilization. For another, for the sons to stay with their mothers was also uncommon. Usually, the males would mature and begin a more nomadic existence, forming small transient groups that might last an entire mating season but then move on. This family's unique arrangement turned out to be very beneficial. *All* of Monifa's offspring survived birth and the delicate dangerous period of early childhood. This was due to having two caring, experienced grandmothers and a mother who had the devoted attention of two vested fathers.

It was their characteristic Orion spiritual attachment to their deep ocean realm combined with their individual circumstances that evoked an unprecedented generous, sharing nature between these twin brothers which marked them as suitable to become Gemini.

The Metavoli-2's appearance and the twins' subsequent reproduction happened within seconds of each other. The Auden and

Jomei family were teaching their youngest son some important male-bioluminescence collecting strategies. They were in Deep Ocean, well beyond Master dive range. They had experienced some recent human sonar rudeness which turned out to be very fortunate as the youngster had accomplished the necessary desensitization to the surprise. Within a meter of their lesson, a sudden tremor and earth displacement occurred. The loud rumble and accompanying shock wave was not as startling as it would have been otherwise and none panicked. They recovered quickly and positioned themselves again at the site of the disturbance. Before they could commence with the seismic geographical teaching opportunity that had just presented itself, all were transfixed to the Metavoli-2.

The area was suddenly a kaleidoscope of brilliant seductive bioluminescence. It resembled octopus dermal visual signals in pulses, variety and intelligent direction of movement, but appeared to hold great numbers or indistinguishable organisms and unprecedented intensity. The whole Orion family moved in joyfully for the gorgeous unprecedented spontaneous entertainment.

Auden and Jomei, utilizing their unique twin communication coordinated their rostrum touch to occur simultaneously with the glowing matter. They planned to drag and spread it outward, twisting it into flashing swirls that would further delight the youngster. However, upon mere touch, they were in connection to the Vencello and through them the multiverse.

The young Orion was spellbound. He peered across at his fathers' faces, close to each other and both gently illuminated by pulses of organic brightness. The light faded darkening their lengths to black so that all he could visually see were Orion heads floating in soft shades before him.

As the adults remained in contact with the Metavoli, metachrosis betrayed the presence of a large octopus that had also been attracted to the light display. The youngster startled but was not afraid. This was no predator and it was far too large to be considered prey. None had been aware of its presence but there is was, one eye directed at the Metavoli and those Orion surrounding it, several long tentacles gently reaching out to touch the glowing membrane.

Within mere moments, enough Gemini-time to be educated, consider and decide, Auden and Jomei accepted duplication. With sudden synchronized thrusts, Auden and Jomei swam headfirst and smoothly through the Metavoli membrane. They were adapted and expelled as G instantly into the congruent depth of a wonderfully clean and quiet new ocean of a similar but newborn universe. They rose together to its surface, took their breaths and dove again as soon they were able. The surface looked unremarkable but beneath it they had a lot of bioluminescent fun to get to.

The remaining two of the four, Auden-G and Jomei-G, glided instantaneously right back out into their home Sponge. A few quick touches and their family members, who were startled but were not given the time to process their surprise, all understood through the communication conduit direct to the Vencello, exactly what had transpired and why.

Auden and Jomei were now four instead of two. One set of twins were safe and preparing a multiverse marker for the transition of many to their new home. The other pair, there with them in the Sponge, was tasked, among other things, to extend the Metavoli-2 marker on their end and modify it to populate the ocean in that pristine other realm. Every one of the Orion family had important work to do and they knew they were privileged to be a part of it.

*****

The appearance of the Orion-Gs, which was perceived simultaneously as Auden and Jomei entered, completely startled the octopus and she jerked back, tentacles following the direction of her body's pull. Her species mechanisms of metachrosis inherently included her awareness of chemical and light variations in living beings. She recognized a change in the physiology of the Orion had occurred when they emerged from the membrane, they were no longer the same. She did not retreat however. She again flowed forward, this time she gingerly touched the Metavoli-2 and established a connection of her own. Message received, with one thrust she slipped back into dark, away from the Orion family and toward an unpreceded sharing of knowledge with many more of her own kind, cephalopods.

Jomei-G left his family and proceeded to communicate the coming evacuation with as many Orion as possible. Jomei-G had an urgent invitation to extend to his kind and their species-saving task to begin.

Auden-G also left them immediately and hastened to Johnny, at the surface advanced wave zero area. He offered him an opportunity, met no resistance and then proceeded to Param. He connected her directly to Brough. All tasks were successfully completed with amazing ease. He was the first twin to rejoin his family.

Monifa, her children and her children's grandmothers remained near the column of the Metavoli, surfacing only long enough for air and then returning to it. Others, Orion and many cetacean and non-cetacean species as well, were attracted to the tremor source. Humans detected the tremor via machine. The Orion family unnecessarily charged themselves with staying around the Metavoli and making sure it remained undisturbed at its depth.

Until the Orion-G returned, no attempts to urge it into reactivation would have worked. It remained dormant. It had gone completely dark and assumed the appearance of the surroundings.

CHAPTER 8 – JOHNNY AND ALVAR MEET AGAIN

Universe: Sponge

Human

The Gemini time traveled via marked entangled objects. As the Sponge manifested omnipresent *wave* properties, everything in that universe was connected in its way to everything else in it. The more similar two objects were, the easier it was for the Gemini to bridge the connection between them. One C-60 model was likewise entangled on a relatively easily followed strand to all others.

Johnny-G scrutinized the surrounding ocean surface once again. Delora and Liam were gone. It was really happening. He balanced easily on the floorboards as the boat rocked under his feet. He grasped his marking C-60 model tight.

"Marker, right. Set....focus." He spoke out loud and it helped. "Alvar, the fight...*marker*." He looked down at the molecule model and then he heard it, a sustained but barely perceptible high pitch violinesque screeching tone. It amplified and it seemed to him it was an orca call, or many, perhaps hundreds. He thought they must have been right under him because there were no direction cues of right, left, front or back from the sound. He looked out over the water but there were no fins breaking. It continued, louder and became so shrill he clenched his eyes shut in protective reflex and braced for the glass covering the boats instrumentation to shatter. Then the echo-pulses, whale-like and powerful, came from nowhere, vibrating throughout his whole body so that he almost lost his balance and grip on the model.

The orca song and whale echo-scan simultaneously ceased. Johnny-G fell through a distance that was short enough that he did not break bones or lose his grip on his marker. It was long enough that he did not catch his balance with eyes closed as he hit the ground. He landed humbled but safe on his backside in a small one-window office, on the floor between a closed door and a desk. He examined himself; he was fully clothed and uninjured except for a possible bruised bottom and short suffering dignity.

It was dark outside but a street lamp striped the room in bands of light through narrow blind slats. His eyes adjusted quickly and he got up and found the light switch. He looked around and wondered if this was Alvar's study. Sure enough there was a C-60 molecule model on the desk. It had served as the end marker and explained how he had gotten there. But after a moment of examining documents and books it became clear he had landed in a university physics department a good distance away from their seaside home town. Alvar would not be there. He figured he must have been close, the marker was correct and perhaps even the time was right, but the place was certainly wrong.

He saw a small refrigerator tucked under a table and opened it up without hesitation. He was so hungry. He wondered if he had left his contents of his GI tract back on the boat. He was thirsty too. He took out one of the only two bottles of water, opened it and guzzled it empty without taking a breath. He wiped his mouth and chin on his shirt and promised himself he would take food and water on future time travels. He threw the empty bottle in the bin and grabbed another for the road, but then thought the better of it. He put the bottle on the desk. He needed a free hand to stabilize against in case he should stumble on landing.

He went again, not thinking to turn off the light or return the full water bottle to the refrigerator. Instead he thought only of the sensations to come. He was certain he would fight to keep his eyes open during all future goes, despite the instinct to the contrary that the intense sound evoked. He modified this start in a semi-crouched stance with his empty hand extended down, ready to catch himself and land in a tri-pod balanced position should he free-fall again. He held the model.

He was certain too that the talking out loud had really helped and so he began, "Marker, focus, set...Alvar...his room, still alive...C-60 marker, focus."

The second go had become old hat already. The same sound and vibration did not startle him and he kept his eyes easily open. Although he was vigilant, he did not determine the exact moment of transition, it had happened imperceptibly. He was just suddenly in Alvar's room. Johnny fell the same short distance from mid-air to floor this time in broad daylight and Alvar was not there. Johnny landed like a pro. He stood up and looked around. He had seen Alvar's effects arranged shrine-like in the room Delora kept in her home. He knew he was getting close. Alvar was still alive and in evidence had left his room a fresh adolescent mess.

Johnny examined the electronic date and time display and saw it was the day Alvar died but it obviously hadn't happened yet. Johnny-G felt ill at what his past self was about to do, somewhere close, outside of the walls of that house. He knew there was no point trying to stop an event in the past. The Vencello had taught him that. He was there for another purpose and he was determined to succeed.

He looked at the bedside table and there it was: Alvar's spherical Carbon-60 model. Again, the marker had illuminated a path to yet another near duplicate of itself, to the right day, but wrong the moment. Johnny-G wondered if he should just hide and wait or try time travel again. It would be hours with nothing to do. Johnny wondered if he would have to wait for anything ever again. He wanted to hone his skill and he was obviously making huge strides so the decision was easily made.

The third time was truly the charm. He assumed his position and spoke his words out loud, "Marker, set, focus". The rest was intense concentration of thought in conjunction with the orca and whale acoustic phenomenon and it worked with accuracy and precision.

*****

Alvar was beginning to lose consciousness. He looked up and saw a figure near his bed. He recognized the face as it came closer through the dark. It belonged to Johnny.

It was actually Johnny-G, who was already reaching down to make light physical contact with Alvar as he began to struggle to get up.

With his last breath, Alvar managed two syllables, a defiant curse to his enemy.

Johnny-G chuckled. This guy was a fighter to the end. He respected that. Alvar was also his cousin. Neither had been aware of that fact but Johnny knew it now and Alvar would know as soon as he touched him.

Even through the dark Johnny-G could see that Alvar's eyes followed his hand, as it approached Alvar's head Johnny mused over how and where he should touch Alvar as they would both always recall this moment as their first *true* meeting.

Johnny-G bent further over Alvar so he could see the detail in his eyes and expression. He supported his weight on his left hand, enabling a steady gaze, and reached out to his dying cousin using his right. Johnny-G carefully curled his middle, ring and baby fingers under to the palm of his raised hand and gently held them in place with his thumb. Keeping his eyes fixed on Alvar's, whose in turn were fixed on the approaching hand, Johnny-G extended the remaining free index finger straight. Alvar's eyes were wide and increasingly crossed as they followed the distal phalanx of that digit, until it softly came to slightly depress the very tip of his nose.

At that touch Alvar was instantly connected to the Vencello, therefore his mother and father, and through them, the multiverse. His first shared thought communicated a clearly understood curse, again meant for his cousin and followed by familiar, friendly laughter, not all of it his own.

Alvar closed his eyes to his bedroom for the last time.

Cetapiens

He thought he must be experiencing delirium. In his mind's eye he saw what he thought were stars but were the points of the C-60 enclosure of the Vencello and the radiant orbs at its center. He heard a pleasingly syncopated blend of deep echo clicks which suggested a full detailed scene of his bedroom in his mind, a beautiful harmony of orca song which he understood as a joyful greeting and urgent familiar human language chatter he recognized as his mother and even his father. Either the room was spinning or his bed was. In fact, he was star looping, carried and protected within a membrane, around the Vencello pulsars in turn and he could hear them in his mind as he orbited.

The knowledge of the Vencello filled his mind. Their love emanated from the central orbs and welcomed him. Johnny-G had come to present him with an opportunity. The G touch could progress to a full G-reproduction if he so desired. Alvar would be in two places at once, each existing in a separate universe, or he could choose to remain as he was and die, as was natural and otherwise mandated to his species by the physics of his native universe. At least he would have the comfort of the loving presence of his parents at the moment of his passing.

The communication link with the Vencello also taught him that both Alvar-Gs would always be entangled in the multiverse sense. Both would be completely the same as Alvar in all detail, including fatal injury but only one would remain in his room and die. Upon leaving, the surviving Alvar-G had further choices. He could choose to join the Vencello in their universe or select a destination in any similar universe where his organic form could survive.

Alvar definitely did not want to die. However, the promise of immortality and existence within the Vencello, sentience at the level of an entire universe, really held no appeal for him. At 16, he *already* believed in his own immortality. He really wanted to live out his life, as Alvar, what he was convinced was the best of all possible lives. He was looking forward to getting *away* from his mother and having his own space. He liked who he was becoming. He had things he wanted to do, lots of human, cool, fun things. Things that involved activities his mother would probably not approve of, certainly things he didn't want her to witness. Omnipresent parents were not an attractive option at that moment.

He absolutely didn't want to leave the other as a sentient sacrifice; no matter how willing it was, especially being his own duplicate to die in his place. Certainly, he wanted his life to continue and his physical suffering to end, but not at the expense of another. He understood plainly that G was a part of the Vencello and they went to all that trouble to find him in space and time and then sacrificed part of their own living essence gladly for his sake. That was unacceptable to him nonetheless.

Then Alvar asked two questions to Brough and through him made a direct desperate appeal to the associated Priori. The second question would shape the nature of his appeal and was conditional on the answer to the first. If the G must die in his place, wouldn't he simply die from his wounds in the other universe as well? The answer was a clear no. As a universase, the Metavoli was a genetic reader and molecular manipulator. Alvar's undamaged genetic code would be adhered to. The physical damage of that day was not genetic and so it would be repaired. Alvar-G could and would be healed completely. That was what he was hoping to learn. Alvar's next question flowed naturally.

If that was the case, could the other Alvar-G somehow be cured as well? Relieved of its obligation to die at that place in time? Could some wonderful enzymatic process be undergone for him too, perhaps keep the G in a stasis of sorts that would return to the Vencello, all harm undone?

He understood from the Priori the unacceptable chaos that would ensue if bodies suddenly healed miraculously, vanished or sprang to life. Organic and physical laws of the multiverse were unbreakable, their *appearance* of being adhered to even more important. Anyway, a timeline centered on his death had been followed to a certain sequence of events, a whole universe had come into being and others would follow from it. Did he wish to undo all of that?

No.

Cetapiens

Alvar had won Brough and Akenehi over completely upon his decision that their new existence was more important than any of his own selfish desires. Both cetaceans shared the human parents protective instinct toward him. Brough noted Alvar had the making of a fine caretaker and so consulted with Priori for best fit solutions that would make use of this gift.

Yes, there were attractive options. These included existence on other planets within the Sponge. Those would require some change in Alvar's personality as his physiology would have to be altered to adapt to those conditions. If the body changed, the mind would necessarily follow.

No, that was not what Alvar or his parents wanted.

Ok, so that limited the suitable planets significantly; to his own home world, specifically. Only a very few destinations could be considered and they involved time travel but at least he would keep his original physiology and suffer minimal alteration. Those fulfilled the requirement of extreme isolation, where no long-term record of Alvar's existence could possibly carry forward to confuse his own timeline, ancestors, and progeny and so on. There could be no mummification or special burial that would call attention at any point to his life there.

Pre-human eras were the safest in that regard, but Alvar and his parents in the Vencello agreed; those times were too psychologically harsh. His parents wanted him to have human companionship, even if it couldn't be theirs. For their son they wanted love and a family and the ease of a thriving human community. It was a luxurious demand but they were successful in their appeal.

With those conditions in mind, there was a suitable destination, popular among multiverse time travelers who sought a pleasant extended visit to the Sponge. It so happened, this particular one was on his own planets deep distant past. Alvar could carry out his remaining human lifetime, healed and whole there.

Alvar already had an idea where in the past he wanted to live, long before this option had ever been possible. He had studied an ancient enigmatic culture in school that, he had imagined, practiced sophisticated spirituality, enjoyed centuries of non-warring, generally peaceful coexistence with its surrounding pristine nature. Alvar happily recognized that what the Priori offered was to live out a full lifetime as a member of that very same long-vanished culture.

That was *it. Perfect.*

If Alvar remained in that distant past he would be sufficiently and permanently separated by huge expanse of time from his remaining entangled G. Although in the same universe, the bond between the duplicates would be so severely strained and reduced it would render any conflicting *energy* effect as negligible. However there would be a *time* differential to be reckoned with. Alvar would be adapted by the time travel transition process to that past culture, to perception rate suitable for his survival there. Time would pass normally and naturally for him.

Because they were entangled, the remaining G would be thrown off in a time-linked compensating reaction, which made their energy existing in the same universe balanced and possible. In essence that G would be thrust into a time rate entirely different from what he would find himself in. In effect, he would move *very* slowly in relation to events around him. The passage of a thousand years would seem to him as a mere nanosecond in a sort of unconscious stasis.

Any decomposition the seemingly lifeless body underwent, no matter how altered or how spread out, over those hundreds of years by nature and normal moving humans, Alvar-G would not be aware of, would feel no pain, nor would he be *dead*. Alvar-G would look like a lifeless corpse to all who observed him in the Sponge. To human eyes the transition would be as slow as to be unnoticeable, his body unchanging.

Every atom of each of Alvar's G-bodies would be thereafter marked as different from those around it. Through multiverse reverse-diffusion, anything thus marked could be recalled with the help of the right universase. With the right reader, again a universase, each atom could function as a sort of quantum computer. Those marked atom-computers, containing their entire history of multiverse activity, could be switched on as such. They then could be induced to self-organize, assuming their former organic structure, neither instantaneously nor commonly, but it could be done. When a Metavoli solution to matching viability had been achieved, the body would be adapted to a suitable universe. As an original and not a mere copy, the only remaining detail was mental continuity.

And with a little luck thrown in for good measure, there you have Alvar-G, alive, back with his parents in the Vencello, none the wiser and happy as a baby orca.

Simplicity itself. Not fast, but simple.

From Alvar-G's perspective, he would be instantly reabsorbed in less time than it would take for a pain receptor to send its message of alarm to his nervous system, reunited in entirety, unharmed to the Vencello. Theoretically.

The other G was also Alvar yet was to be adapted as mandated by multiverse nature in order to survive so far in his planet's past, where space and time was not congruent to his own. He would undergo a one-way Metavoli process; one which would permanently temporally alter his body for viability in that different time albeit within the same universe. Mentally, he would undergo a concomitant transition which included a dizzying absorption of his planet's deep human history, especially this particular culture, to arrive and integrate relatively seamlessly into the time and place he would call home to the end of his days. The terms were clear: it was a one-way trip and there would be no coming back.

He would be able to satisfy his grieving mother who wanted him with her in the Vencello. The G she had found that morning would eventually be with her. At the same time he would be living out his human life and that would have to suffice. He provided her the immense comfort of knowing that through the multiverse there would always be a connection between them and he was never lost to her, no matter what.

Alvar really was happy to live on his home planet *and* deep in its past, specifically *this* one. It was his dream-come-true. He loved studying with his mother and he loved the orcas. He thought he loved theoretical physics most of all. But experiencing near death he learned he loved relaxing and just enjoying life more than anything. The life he believed was being offered to him, that is one of very little work and a lot of play, was one that he never dared to hope for, one that he believed would have been frowned upon as lazy and underachieving by his academic and success driven culture.

Even better, completing his life there would provide an '*everyone lives*' solution with inherent balance in physical laws and compassion. It was Alvar's choice that it was so, and that was fortunate, because there was no time to consider another alternative.

He made his choice final. His desire to break away on his own was not entirely unexpected and his parents in the Vencello were sad but they understood. He would emerge in his new life as a young human adult, after all. His protection of them and his G made the Vencello so very proud.

The Gemini duplication went forward. Alvar entered the multiverse and became G.

The remaining Alvar-G lay still and seemingly lifeless on his bed; rendered motionless and unaware that his mother was just then entering their home and unable to awaken even when she anguished over him in the morning.

"Marker, set, *focus*." Delora might have heard these words if she had paused and strained to as she opened the door, but she did not. The change in pressure throughout the house as she did so had signaled Johnny-G it was time to jump to his next time travel destination. He was gone before she had even stepped inside.

*****

Through the multiverse Alvar hyper-studied. Because time was non sequitur he studied for a moment and he had studied for all time. He was mentally and physically prepared. He emerged genetically into an ancient culture as Alvar, although aged by the transition process to the equivalent of a fully-grown adult, of approximately 20 human years old. He was completely healthy, young adulthood in full swing, with all of his memories and personality traits intact. This set him instantly apart as those native to his new home were neither his race and were on average of a much smaller stature than he.

But he was not lost or so very strange as to be unacceptable. Through time travel, the knowledge of the Priori and the detailed data collection of Brough, he would know their language, customs, overall layout of the cities, the species of fish, the weave of their nets and even some names.

It was *good* to have a multiverse connection through one's parents.

The dizzying images of his multiverse education and transition became memory. The orb-looping ceased and the light from the Vencello was gone.

Alvar's human brain was starting to fade quickly beyond its dying hyper firing stage. It was time to go.

Alvar had heard before that if you travel far enough you would meet yourself. Similarly, if you live long enough everything will happen. Through the multiverse he had sensed his own presence was already there, and it was not his G either. Alvar had *died* in that ancient place long ago and had preceded the Vencello to the multiverse. He further knew full well, being connected to the multiverse that really, *he*, his *energy* could *never* die. Delora knew this as soon as she first became aware in her new universe. The non sequitur beauty of the looping of their lives, the conservation of energy through the multiverse, gave them both peace and closure. No goodbyes between son and parents were going to happen as Alvar made his final transition. Such words, while human and polite, made no sense, really. There was no end. They would always be together.

Alvar, because he had shared even the briefest connection to them, necessarily carried the wisdom of Brough and the Vencello with him to his new home and people.

Despite that virtual superhuman power of knowledge he possessed from then on, he would endeavor to be humble, to let the host culture continue in its noteworthy, peaceful development as his own history had revealed it had developed, on its own path. That culture would be on its journey to history and he would let it go on its way unaltered. He would remain, a mere observer, largely anonymous and in the background.

Yeah. *Right*.

*****

From Johnny-G's stance bedside, Alvar-G remained still and appeared quite dead. From his touch, he knew that Alvar had been expelled back in time and place. Alvar had chosen to live among the Cetapiens and he had made it safely. The Gemini replication was complete but Johnny-G still checked a couple of last details. No breath. No pulse. The house was dark and quiet but he could hear someone beginning to open the front door. *Delora*. He felt a surge of sadness for what was coming, but he had his connection to her through the Vencello. The Vencello urged him back to the boat. He had accomplished *everything* and they *loved* him so much.

Johnny-G, basking in appreciation and satisfied he had completed his task, immediately picked up the C-60 model he had brought with him and time traveled back to the boat; skillfully resuming the space where only nanoseconds before, he had stood, model in hand, focusing hard on his time travel journey to Alvar's bedside.

He was having *so* much fun. He felt like a hero. He *was* a hero. He looked out over the water, raised his arms up in the V for victory, lifted his face up into the sun and fought the instinctive protection of his eyes. The sun reminded him of Brough and he would forever more think of him, feel his friendly protective presence, when he looked directly at it. He dropped his gaze back to the controls and began the trip back to land.

Uncle Liam and Delora were not on the boat. They had not

resurfaced. He knew everything.

Now what was he going to tell his mother...

Universe: Sponge

Priori

As per usual, Grandmothers instructions on how to scan for Cetapiens markers in Sponge space-time were spot on. In retrospect I am sure I could have *eventually* found it on my own if she had only let me continue to star loop as I had wished. Instinctively upon arrival, I performed a comprehensive scan of each of the orbs of their celestial system. Cetapiens' home planet orbited a warmly familiar star.

So, my very first memorable experience in Cetapiens was favorable. I really *liked* their star and it liked me. That made sense. It was the Vencello's star-system of origin after all.

As I then turned my scan on the planet of origin, my returning echoes detailed the shockingly fragile and thin layer of organic activity I found myself in. I compared it to the delicate strata of atmosphere above, and the loose-dirt-to-solid-rock matter layered to the very core of planet underneath me. I was truly amazed that Cetapiens could actually survive in such a limited plane, let alone be truly happy, but there they were.

My next experiences, in quick succession: the organic sensual inputs the native species brains processed. There were a plethora of data sources in the area and they were all very interesting but I did not let myself become *too* distracted and honed in on the human physiology. Sensory input was dominated by data collected by eyes and sensitive fingertips; all eight coordinated on task, dexterous and in fortunate reach of familiar and wonderful fully-opposable *thumbs*.

A series of random memories spontaneously surfaced that were not Cetapien but rather my own: a calming sucking of a thumb. They submerged as easily as an exhale and I trained my attention on all before me; the swiftly moving hands, reaching, touching...

There we were, seated in a large loose circle on warm and yielding sand, undoing then retying knots, cleaning and repairing fishing nets, pulling another one out of the heaping mound at our circles center as each was completed.

Netting. It was the center of my focus...*our* focus, important, urgent, through *human* eyes. From one steady vantage point, where my body sat, the objects of our labor had visual depth, thanks to the retinal disparity created from data input from two separate sources. It had texture, structure, shades of light and dark and variations of color. It had a distinctive place relative to my location. That much I could discern and navigate adequately in its context without *scanning* at all. I could *see* it as a human did.

And I could *smell* it. This was a totally new sensation, much different from Liam's wonderful breakfast aromas. A scan would have provided atomic structure and any energy dynamic throughout the object but never *that*.

The feeling of molecules as they rushed over my tongue, down the trachea and through to the alveoli was exquisite. The organic mammalian body was all new sensations and very distracting, at first. Fortunately, my awareness of every minute of new sensation did in fact fade like the rarefaction of the atmosphere above.

These human bodies were fatigued. They were somewhat under stimulated, bored. They communicated their dilemma in a species-inherent grossly limited acoustic range, the characteristic vague, slow, staccato, typically *human* language, amongst each other. Their words did not detail but merely suggested. Priori, such as Grandmother, would have sung a single well-chosen phrase that described the required influx of energy to balance the expenditure and repair cellular damage they had suffered during their recent metabolic activity.

They were tired and hungry but had netting to clean, dry and stage for the next day before they could retire to their meal, entertainment and rest. The moment I had arrived in Cetapiens the older members of our group had decided that the lesson to help pass the time and ease the boredom of the task of net maintenance would be *history*.

Oh, no. *Not* more human history. I had more than my share from Liam. I was preparing to transition to another time, despite Grandmother's instructions, as soon as this became painful. Happily, it turned out the Cetapiens teaching method affected me as completely human. Therefore I did not *relive*, I merely *heard* the story, just like they did. It was virtually painless.

What followed was a pleasing recitation of verbal, very early history of their culture performed in harmony and rhythm, sung in unison by the older Cetapiens, then memorized and repeated by the younger to the satisfaction of the elders. As the bards began I was confused that they did not call themselves Cetapiens in those verses. I wondered if I was in the right place and time. Nevertheless I was drawn into the song and listened.

They called themselves The People, distinguishing only between before and after they came to their current home. Those who lived before were The Broken and those who lived during and after arrival were The People.

So the elders sang first, the young listened and repeated on Que. None questioned or seemed to want to. It was strange that their spoken voices actually evoked an easy acceptance of the truth of what they were retelling within *me*...ME...a time traveler, descended from the mighty Aware Master: Brough and all that followed. Even at my early stage of development I was a firsthand witness to actual events. I had relived enough from Liam to know that every human had a unique vantage point, influencing variation of their concepts, and so on and then the individually obtained memories went on to be changed over time and retelling. I reminded myself that objectivity was in order and wondered what my time travel might actually reveal if I ever decided to undertake a comparison driven journey to the subjects of these Cetapiens songs.

At the end of it, their story was remembered, reinforced and their minds were distracted from their bodily demands. Their work done, their history revisited, the young instructed and only then did the elders excuse the group to disband for the evening.

But their words, they had a power of their own, even more so in music. Their harmony was pleasing and the rhythm almost forced a synchronization of body and mind. I was fascinated. As I processed their song, the First Days of Sekai: Orca, Eagle and Temple, it took on a voice of time which suggested to my mind an accurate account of the People and I accepted it for a shared moment with them, as fact.

I mused that the song itself was a marker: *start here*. It connected Grandmother and me to them with its familiar cadence. In bringing us to them they had closed their loop. Their world history henceforth stabilized within that eternal song.

I recognized the familiar theme that celebrated the beginning of a period in the planet of origins human history that was considered by all multiverse time travelers as its pinnacle. The People sang simply of how they escaped from harsh climate and a cruel society and came to be in the most stable, happiest, healthiest time for any human culture. In fact, it was true by any human, cetacean or even Priori standards before or since them. Their successful transition included many crucial lessons for the Vencello and all Priori who were students as well as teachers.

But I guessed that Grandmother had placed me first at this time because their greatest leap of cultural accomplishment was to happen very soon.

For this group of Homo sapiens, that is the People, were known to the time travelers as Cetapiens for a very good reason. The pinnacle of their culture was not merely their long-maintained peace with each other rather it was their eventual cultural unification with cetaceans. The arrival and integration of a certain *human* time traveler was essential to begin the elevation to that achievement and *mark* them as the singular human-cetacean society.

I wondered what Grandmother was doing that I had to be at this networking early history lesson without her. I figured whatever I was learning at this time and place was too elementary and she was doing fascinating, wonderful things and I was missing them.

I was right.

CHAPTER 10 – AMARANTH AND SOO

Universe: Vencello

Priori and Orca

"You missed a note." Amaranth was a better weaver than Soo and watched not only the progress of her own work but scanned Soo's quality as well.

"No…" Soo *totally* missed it and still couldn't detect her error.

"Yes, back up…right…*there*." Amaranth wasn't annoyed with her friend at all; she remained kind and patient, despite the potentially deforming or even lethal consequences such errors might result in.

Soo was highly skilled and at this point was making virtually no errors, save a very rare few. In the tedium of the task she had forgotten that some of the code that was healthy and normal was to be modified. She checked her own flippers and made the swap with the human digit sequence. "Ah, corrected." Soo conceded as she deftly zapped away the offending weave and sang the modified atoms in their place.

Amaranth and Soo scanned the entire collection once again; pulling back to behold their masterpiece-in-progress and the ever more familiar form it was taking.

"Ok" Amaranth drew in a deep breath and affectionately nudged the orca matriarch at her side as she inquired. "Are you ready to pick up the intensity? My return echo-data indicates that he is ready. We have been doing onesy-twosy and that's the way it's done up to now, but we'll be at it for eons, even outside of the Vencello, at this rate. He can't stay with me forever. I'll have to wake him up eventually…and his poor mother has been waiting for so very long."

Soo only half paid attention but caught the part about forever. She had been more than ready to return to her home, in the Sponge during that time where she would easily find and rejoin her own family.

Amaranth continued, "Now that we have set the numbers, verified the harmonics and functions it's time to make sure they can do it on their own. This is the fun part."

Soo drew in a deep breath, expelled it and just before she took another in preparation for a long held variable polyharmonic, she caught that last bit. "Fun? Amaranth, your idea of fun is not exactly…"

"Here it goes," and with that clear thought Amaranth let peal the first pure notes of the resonance that would reproduce the last of the enzymes and position them in reactive proximity to their substrates.

It was strange to think of Alvar's molecules as substrates and Amaranth *was* in work mode, but her devotion to the task was driven by affection after all.

Akenehi, the second most radiant orb of the Vencello scanned the distant tiny binary with delight. There she clearly detected two of her most beloved, a progeny after her own heart and working in conjunction with her, was the foster matriarch of her daughter Arva'Anati. They had been at it for a long time. The first part was the most tedious, the most meticulous. It would be ease and speed from then on.

Akenehi's hopes were on the singular abilities of Amaranth, Soo and Johnny-G. This was the first and only practice the team would get before they were presented with a far greater challenge: Arva'Anati-G. She anticipated that they could recall and awaken her beloved daughter to her in the Vencello, just as they were about to do with Alvar-G. But first, Akenehi would observe Delora's acceptance of her sons G. A mother knew her own child and if all went well with the human they would advance to an orca. If Delora rejected her son, Akenehi was not sure if her heart could take the risk that Arva'Anati would be lost to her while a confounding replica took her place.

Delora had been beside herself in anticipation in seeing Alvar again throughout the whole procedure. As a human she could not perceive him until he looked and felt...well...like her son Alvar. As a mother Akenehi understood completely and could not fault her for maternal instincts. In fact, she was counting on them.

Akenehi was vigilant and more than ready to join in at the proper moment; a few more lovely slides and adjusted frequencies and...*now*.

Akenehi, Amaranth and Soo sang their combined frequencies so that the tens of thousands of universases they had worked so long at were instantly reproduced. At the correct note, every marked molecule Johnny had successfully recalled to the Vencello began to be worked on by those fabulous enzymes.

They all stopped singing, as the process was self-maintaining after it started. They began to scan the body intently as it slowly took shape from O-O outward.

Brough scanned and was in awe.

At the sight, sound and especially the smell of it, Johnny-G was entranced. He almost lost track of the fresh collection of Alvar-marked energy he had recalled to the Vencello for the next phase and it began to diffuse back to the Sponge. He contained it. He reached out for a tactile experience to add to his other sensory data and for the first time felt Amaranth's wrath. If he hadn't moved back just in time, she would have taken his whole arm off. And he was pretty sure she would not have helped put it back on again.

The Vencello was dense with Priori in witness and appreciation.

Not because it helped. There were drawn because it was fascinating and miraculous and a rare privilege to see life come together in that singular way.

Alvar took much of his prior shape: human, adult, male, etc. He was precious and beautiful to all of them as if he was their own. In a way, he was.

Amaranth loved him so much. She looked down at him, a human, with the part of her memory that would always be human with him and knew that at that stage of formation he could sense her there. He was not as limited by human physiology yet as to be blind and deaf to any them.

CHAPTER 11 – CETAPIENS, SEA

Universe: Sponge

Orca

Soo, the orca matriarch, carefully supervised her young grandson, Yu, as they approached the human boat, surfacing in near unison, keeping physical contact at all times. They were making a special trip together so he would learn some of the rare hazards the clan occasionally encountered. Here were the humans, land stingrays, as she called them. She sang the common objects that he was to avoid; the boats they had passed at a distance of various sizes and differing functions, the land stingrays therein and especially their barbs and nets. This particular boat was somewhat smaller.

Yu momentarily left her side, scanning them at a distance then spyhopped, his much smaller glistening head popping straight up out of the water until his eyes were also clear of the surface, confirming Grandmother Soo's count. One. Two. Yes, he whistled, the boat contained two humans with barbs and net visible.

His matriarch explained how, despite the obvious difficulty the humans had in capturing and keeping the fish, he should always stay very far from them and resist the temptation to help them no matter how poor their skills. After all, his own mother had been cruelly injured by a human barb when she was still young.

A singular disturbance drew their scans. Yoo fearlessly swam toward the source eager to get finer detail from his echoes but

Grandmother Soo whistled out to him to come back.

Dangerous!

It was shockingly obvious that a third human was unexpectedly present. Echo-location made solid barriers transparent to cetaceans. The orcas perceived accurately right through the hull and beyond the boat itself, through flesh and even bone. Grandmother Soo tightened and intensified her scan which confirmed, yes, there were now definitely three. This was very odd in her experience. There was no orca whistle for 'vanish' or 'sudden spontaneous appearance'. It just didn't happen in their experience. Everything came from somewhere, even if by expert orca stealth. If humans had methods of concealment that rendered echolocation useless, she and her grandson might be in danger. She urged Yu back as she cautiously advanced. She echo-scanned the new arrival and noted he was somewhat larger than the other humans but nothing special caught her attention.

What did grab her attention was an unfamiliar orca matriarch greeting call, one who was also seemingly, suddenly and inexplicably close. She turned away from the humans and returned the greeting in her own dialect, but initially there was no orca reply. She scanned while Yu remained silent and still as etiquette required, when matriarchs were identifying each other in ritual. She detected no other orca within range.

Interesting.

She trusted her hearing and reasoning even at her old age. There is was again.

Unmistakable.

Within moments of each other, Soo had experienced two unprecedented events. This one was an invitation to sleep song from an unscannable and unknown orca.

She agreed, out of courtesy as well as curiosity.

Soo relaxed her muscles and adjusted the air in her lungs so she maintained a sleeping posture and fell quickly into light, lucid sleep. She greeted an unfamiliar matriarch in a strange fluid filled orca dreamscape.

It was Akenehi. She sang urgently and clearly, announcing that her daughter, Arva'Anati would be arriving much as she saw the third human appear, but further out to sea. She would need a caring matriarch and could Soo serve? Akenehi shared her daughters horrific existence in solitude and urgent need in length.

Through the comprehensive mental bridge of orca sleep song; that direct connection marked them as sister matriarchs, intimate partners in thought and purpose. Soo understood and anguished with her, only too happy to offer relief to any orca who had suffered so long and so tragically.

Akenehi expressed her deepest thanks and gave assurance that her beloved Arva'Anati would prove an invaluable help to Soo's clan as she had lived for decades as a captive and understood human behavior as no other orca, outside of the Vencello, could.

Soo agreed not only because she felt Akenehi's love for her daughter and it resonated with her own devotion to her family, but an orca with such unprecedented extensive land stingray understanding would be undoubtedly helpful. She had never heard of such survival and mental stamina as the story of Arva'Anati, but was curious to be in the presence of such an orca and learn for herself.

Further, Akenehi was obviously a gifted singer and Soo desired to learn how she and her clan could sleep-sing across such great distances and to unfamiliar orcas.

Their bond slowly faded.

Soo knew upon full awakening she had not been deceived or hallucinating. As soon as she came out of sleep song she guided her grandson around and headed toward the distant vocalizations of their clan. Sure enough, a single female orca called out in a dialect Soo had never heard before, save the greeting call of Akenehi. Knowing it must be Arva'Anati she summoned her clan to join her, as she and Yu swam directly to the orca newcomer even as they in turn were all being approached by the orca Gemini.

The unprecedented arrival and adoption of Arva'Anati-G was an invaluable benefit for the orcas for generations. They had not imagined that awkward and small humans could pose such a strange and dangerous threat. With her help in understanding, they would offer a truce to the humans and provide assistance in hunting in hopes that in exchange they would be granted amnesty from hunt and captivity themselves. What they did not know was that in their time, while more primitive hunting devices did exist, no captivity tank did.

Nonetheless, Arva'Anati-G and Alvar-G, both intra-universe time travelers and children of the Vencello, would very quickly establish the early days of a Cetapien cetacean-human alliance. For her whole long life, Arva'Anati-G led her new clan through the alliance. She lived well into her nineties, having borne a son and a daughter who both survived well into adulthood. It would seem Arva'Anati had paid her dues in misery while in captivity. Her remaining life was so easy and pleasant she sometimes imagined she had lost herself in a permanent sleep-song, that impossible happiest of places under the constant care of the One Mother.

Initially and reluctantly, Soo agreed to loosen the rule on avoiding humans. Rather, the clan would keep close tabs on the human's behavior, study it and pay special attention to nets and spears. Eventually, true friendships between Soo's clan and human developed. However the horrific experience of Arva'Anati at human hands was never lost on any of them and was handed down, along with the history of the alliance, in orca song from generation to generation.

CHAPTER 12 – JOHNNY-G AND ARVA'ANATI

Universe: Sponge

Human and Orca

Johnny-G loved his life as a time traveling hero. Over many years he had taken innumerable opportunities to botch whale hunts, give comfort to dying cetaceans in captivity and the like. He made sure to keep up on current news, especially less read sources, which would likely report paranormal events. If any human suspected he was a time traveler and was in pursuit, he had not been made aware of it, through the news anyway.

Another sad story was about to be rewritten with the happiest of endings. Through the multiverse and Akenehi, Johnny-G learned of Arva'Anati's plight. There was little he could do while she was alive but they had all learned from Alvar that there was a third option. For that choice to be available, rescued from captivity, her organic orca body had to be near death.

Johnny-G had always known that Akenehi and the Vencello kept Arva'Anati company in sleep-song, but still he despaired every day at the sad reality of her waking life. He was between cetacean-saving gigs and having lunch in a pub when he overheard the first few words of a newscast which announced her death. He swallowed a huge bite of his sandwich and went immediately into the men's room without waiting to hear more. He was sad and angry she died alone in captivity but elated he could finally save her. He would waste no time getting on with it.

He crouched into position ready for time travel. He pondered his marker; an orca in a concrete tank, alone, dying. As G he carried Akenehi with him always. Akenehi and Arva'Anati were mother and daughter and so their entangled physiology was very simple to bridge as long as one existed. This was one of his easier threads of multiverse connection to follow.

"Marker…"

He had it all planned out. He knew that Arva'Anati would die of heart failure late in the night and on which particular night it would happen. He would travel *back* in time to her and be in physical contact with her at the instant of her death. It wouldn't be easy to see her in that moment; even knowing he would help her. He would have a very small window of opportunity. Like Alvar, their physical connection would activate Metavoli and she could become duplicated in O-O. Both would be Arva'Anati-G. One G would emerge at Cetapiens in the sea at same moment as Alvar-G, utilizing the same unique pathway through which he transitioned. Akenehi could send her daughter, healed and whole, through to the distant past through that very same uniquely opened passageway.

And just as with Alvar, the other Arva'Anati-G would remain in the Sponge. In her case she would finally be liberated from her prison only because she would be dead, but in appearance only, blissfully unaware of the passage of eons that would flow before she would be recalled and awoken again in the Vencello.

"…set…"

Johnny-G knew there would be record of him on cameras and that meant he would be seen, albeit as a blur, as he would have to move quickly. He didn't really care if he was seen but he did not want to be prevented. His plan required the quickest action.

What he didn't know was that his sudden dive in her tank would *cause* the failure of her sadly, atrophied massive heart.

"…focus…"

He arrived, perceived the time was right, ran from his entrance point and took a running dive head first into her tank within a few strong swim strokes of the startled orca. Her heart seized. As soon as he touched her, the connection with the Vencello was complete and Arva'Anati spent a precious few moments in a most close connection with her mother.

There was no choice to be made, Arva'Anati followed her long-lost matriarch's urge to undergo Metavoli processing without question and, knowing she was so very loved, she became G. At long last Akenehi's daughter would live healthy and free, far away from that forsaken tank.

CHAPTER 13 – ALVAR RESURFACES

Universe: Sponge, Cetapiens

Human

First breath. Get to the surface for that crucial first breath.

Akenehi, urging him as she would her newborn orca, was so close in Alvar's mind he could feel her heartbeat.

And was that Brough or the sun? Was it the Aware Master who he now knew intimately, returning with Alvar from a deep dive, pushing hard for surface?

Sunlight above, go up, toward it.

Disoriented from the transition through the Vencello, Alvar struggled, completely submerged in salt water. He could taste brine and he knew his mouth was gaping. His lungs, desperate to fulfill their function, instinctively did not take any water in. He oriented and looked up to the surface. He made out a small hull above his head. He saw a figure within it leaning over, looking down toward him. Is that *Mom?*

A human hand reached into the water, clearly grabbing for him. It was not his mother's hand. *Father?*

First breath. Surface. Come on, Alvar, you can do it.

He did not take the hand that was offered but instead swam downward to the bottom. The floor was close and easily reached. Other instincts were urging him elsewhere now. Non-mammalian creatures also merged with the Vencello were confounding him. He belonged in the ocean, right? *No.* He began to remember what his legs were and how to use them. They found the sea floor, toes squirming in the sand. He looked up and around. He could make out *fishing net* just hanging suspended near the *hull*. He recognized the *words* as they echoed like a bell in his mind, reminding him that he had words at his disposal.

His lungs were going to burst. He was going to suffocate, not drown, right there in the water. He finally worked out what to do to prevent that. Squatting for spring action, he pushed off strong and with a few skilled strokes he breached, head and arms above the water, just in time for one desperately needed deep breath. Before he could submerge again hands grabbed him and finding their solid grip, struggled to get him out of the water. They barely managed.

Two men pulled Alvar into their boat, excited and cursing in their native language. Although it was not Alvar's, he understood every bit of it. They were exclaiming to him that they thought he was large fish and had thought to catch him. They finally saw he was a man and not a fish and thought one of the fishermen had somehow drowned. They were amazed at first at his being alive and then at his foreign appearance. They had not seen him enter the water, nor noticed a boat around them. Who was he? How did he come to be there?

He was not thinking strategically. He answered in the only phrase that translated. He answered in their native language, "I came from tomorrow".

Startled at first, they laughed and commented that maybe he had taken in some water after all. They asked once again from where he had come.

Alvar, dripping water and looking dazed back toward the ocean horizon, answered absentmindedly, "Everywhere. Nowhere."

They were satisfied he was delirious and started to grab their oars and head back to shore.

Alvar established necessary oxygen flow to his brain and examined both faces. He pointed to each in turn, smiling in genuine amusement, "I know you! I know both of you!"

They rested their oars and gave him their full attention. The three men sat quietly, drifting with the gentle waves as the breeze ceased. It too seemed to have paused to listen. Of course, neither had ever met Alvar or even heard of such a man. Alvar was *different*. Surely if he had appeared in any of the villages it would have been highly discussed and they would have learned of him.

Alvar spoke their names without hesitation. They were taken aback for only a moment. Had they perhaps used each other's names in the struggle to bring him up from the water? They exchanged meaningful glances and then tested Alvar.

"Oh, you've heard of us! Well, you must know then that we're the bravest and most respected among fishermen! Now that we have saved your life you must do whatever we tell you."

Alvar recognized their claims as totally false and laughed, "I'm a great swimmer and I wasn't in danger. Trust me." He continued with confidence and sarcasm that would have been recognized as a mere exaggeration or even a friendly jab in his own culture, "Actually, you guys are *horrible* fishermen! *Your* best trade skill is net weaving but you're not that great at that either, are you?"

Alvar had, unknowingly, just slapped them with a serious insult. They looked at each other. Their word for *horrible* was rarely used and only in regard to the most serious and terrible of tragedies. To exaggerate so much negativity to an essential survival skill was basically saying these men were completely and truly worthless. Their pride wounded, they sought to correct Alvar's impertinence. Their faces dropped and they stiffened.

Alvar imagined his own sandy, wet foot hanging painfully out of his mouth. This was not the first time he had been the new guy in town. Even in his own time, each school had its own distinct cultural differences, nuances in codes of conduct. If he was going to make any friends here he would have to master this cultures' subtleties, which was obviously going to require a mentor. He decided he just wouldn't talk at all until he had found one. He made up his mind fast that he would feign a sudden onset of muteness for the time being.

The men examined his clothing. The men weren't wearing *any*. Alvar was fully outfitted for a day at high school, sans shoes.

Alvar began babbling despite being a mute but couldn't seem to stop, "Sorry, I have a poor sense of humor and I'm not from around here. Please accept my apology." He pulled slightly at his T-shirt to emphasize the truth to his claim. Then looking everywhere but the display of nudity, he pointed to the shore that was mercifully quite close.

"I can swim it, do you mind?" Alvar did a quick evaluation of the vessel he was in and estimated how he would exit while causing the least amount of destabilization. He started to move without waiting for their response. He wanted out of the boat before he said or did anything else to worsen his first impression.

They assured him they would take him directly to shore. They picked up their oars once again and Alvar nodded thanks. As they slowly paddled, they continued to bore a hole in his head with their stares. They accepted, in part, Alvar's explanation. After all, Alvar did have a slight idiosyncratic manner to his speaking they had not come across before. Still, he had spoken their language with relative ease and had correctly identified them. The insult stood. Their expressions hid nothing.

"We're unaccustomed to your *face*. You *speak* as one of us and say you know us but *we* have not met before. There are no *strangers* here. We do *not* know you. Come with us and we'll take you into the settlement."

"Thanks, but no." Alvar couldn't wait. As soon as he saw the water was shallow enough, about knee deep, he sprang out of the boat.

Grinning, waving thanks again and goodbye he appeared even clumsier by his attempt at speed wading. Alvar didn't even consider the possibility that he could get dangerously lost. Instead, he waved one final thanks for their help and turned to the forest tree line. He fled because he feared they were still angry with him over the accidental insult and assumed that men settled their differences much in the same way as he had recently experienced. He had just ended with a fight. He did not want to *start* here with one. They reminded him too much of

Guy, Mike and Johnny, who only hours ago, back in his original time, taught him the danger of isolation and unchecked aggression.

Reaching the beach at last, he pushed off hard with each step through confounding overly yielding sand. He relived the details of the attack he might not have survived had it not been for Johnny. He pondered that those guys wouldn't even exist for thousands of years. Yet, in a sense, they seemed to have followed him.

The soft beach sand transitioned to grassy hardy scrub. Tough and thorny leaves snagged his jeans below the knee and his feet were getting cut right through his socks. Driven by apprehension of the two, who were still within eyesight and although he was still dripping wet, he forced one foot out in front of the other, defying the pricking jabbing pain and choosing not to stop and check his wounds. The forest had looked close enough from the boat but he realized a foot-slashing, leg stabbing gauntlet lay before him.

CHAPTER 14 – THE ACRITUCHI

Universe: Multiverse and Sponge

Human and Priori

It would have been wonderful if the People could have come upon their enlightenment entirely under their own human power, as their early history song suggested. But the Priori were present with the People's early physicians and during that era an elixir catalyst was developed that greatly facilitated their cultural advancement. Through Priori comprehensive understanding of the multiverse, Sponge bio-chemistry and human physiology, the People benefited from an unprecedented chemical communication method to each other and their environment.

It would also have been great if the Priori had the ability to come up with that elixir without help, but that was not the case. They had the assistance of a sentient energy so vast and incomprehensible they could scare perceive it at all.

The entire forest and surrounding ancient jungle that cradled Cetapiens on all land sides was enveloped within a mere nano-section of a most ancient multiverse time traveling sentient; the Acrituchi. It was definitely not cetacean or human-like and had little in common with those organic lifeforms, other than they all thought through energy.

The universe of origin from which the Acrituchi had emerged was very similar to the Sponge. That universe, the Seed of Acrituchi, had long since morphed into the cold inhospitable darkest end spectrum of the multiverse, *died* by analogy, before the Sponge itself had emerged.

The Acrituchi had survived by spreading itself throughout *living*, hospitable, similar-spectrum universes. It was an extremely prolific energy mutualist, a robust quid pro quo benefactor wherever it was hosted. It survived across a plethora of environments within a given universe. Within *those* and upon further compatible worlds, through the common multiverse environment O-O, it engineered essential organic functions pertaining to native organisms so that those were able to access what they needed to adapt and survive in their own harsh environments.

On the Cetapiens home world, this meant a complex and ancient symbiosis existed between the native flora and fauna and the Acrituchi's vast interconnected multiverse parts. Energy shared by both flowed continuously through the food chain and so the Acrituchi was also redistributed throughout the ecosystem. It expanded its mutualistic advantages to plants and then to the animals who consumed the plants.

Importantly, the Acrituchi had a role in redistribution of energy throughout the multiverse itself. This meant, under the proper circumstances, the entire Cetapiens ecosystem could be transitioned in part or whole to any compatible part of the multiverse.

The whole Acrituchi-infused system could time travel connected as one.

The Acrituchi existed as one being and maintained its connection through all of its incredibly vast parts, even as it adapted to each of the universes it called home, simultaneously. It persisted within its own common time frame, as relative uniformly to its collective self. Despite a sometimes huge time differential between itself and the many universes it called home, it was able to survive. This was because in most universes relative to its own time frame, it appeared virtually motionless to organic senses.

Because it moved so slowly in relation to some organisms, the Acrituchi may have seemed vulnerable. This was far from the case. It did not suffer threat of destruction because it was so multi-universal and spread out; nothing except one of its own kind, equal in scope and energy potential, could possibly be a threat. *That* was impossible because anything of the Acrituchi sort was pervasively not predatory or destructive in any sense. Through sheer size alone it was seldom detected by the vast majority of native organic sentients who were limited to much smaller micro-scales. Those who could detect it could only direct a very tiny nano-section of its flow or change the state of a correspondingly tiny amount of energy.

It was so vast and so adaptable, so incredibly regenerative, it was virtually immortal.

The Acrituchi was extremely adaptable, dynamic, multi-phasic and *intelligent*. Those features alone might have easily explained its survivability but there was more to its success. It utilized entanglement between universes in much the same way the Vencello did but those markers of the Acrituchi were so powerful and long used that they required the very center of highest energies. In the Sponge, suitable energy centers were stars.

Through the sun it completely permeated the pristine forest and jungle that enveloped Cetapiens. The Acrituchi thrived at its peak surrounding those humans. As soon as the first Broken had arrived and began breathing the oxygen produced by the forest, drinking elixirs from various plants and eating their leaves and fruit their bio-chemistry had been altered. Distinctive differences manifested in comparison to those early days regarding how they felt about each other, the environment they lived in, how they communicated and so on. It wouldn't take long before Alvar's own bio-chemical uniqueness would be infused with the Acrituchi and adapted with his surroundings. A deeper natural connection to Cetapiens and the time he found himself in would be achieved through botany and chemistry.

Alvar's gauntlet served to provide the Acrituchi with body tissue and fluid samples of his modified human-multiverse time traveler biochemistry and all of its inherent markers required to communicate his arrival and unique survival needs. He could not have survived without the determined help of the Acrituchi. And Alvar couldn't even perceive it, let alone thank it.

*****

Bleeding from several cuts and limping from a thorn that had lodged into his right arch, Alvar pushed through to the boundary that marked the last outer realm of his prickly gauntlet. As he entered an area of expansive trees and rich undergrowth, he perceived a mass of life force breeze right into him. The noticeable change caused by a sharp variation of humidity hit his lungs as he took his first breath of its pristine, unpolluted air. A wonderful chorus of bird, insect and animal sounds greeted him. They were alarmed at his intrusion into their sanctuary but it was fabulous music to *his* ears.

Alvar stopped after several steps forward because the canopy was so dense; the foliage so tight around him that the light difference rendered him unable to see at first. He needed time for eyes to adjust, find a place to sit down, pull the blasted object out of his foot and then remove the multitude of thorns and barbs from his jeans and shirt.

His eyes adapted despite the dimming ocean of plant life. He pushed through with swim like strokes, wishing he had a machete even more than a place to rest. Exerting huge amounts of effort produced little progress. Branches just recoiled and swayed and seemed to spring right back to their place in front of him, like a school of curious fish. This went on until lifting the weight of his arms was almost too much. He closed his eyes as they were doing him little good and were in danger of being jabbed anyway. He stumbled blindly forward, just barely catching himself each time before falling face down. With no sense of direction, he opened his eyes again. There was barely enough sunlight to let him see his hand, let alone beyond it. He suspected he could get lost forever, die right in that forest and no one would know it. He was already buried really, he had only to sit down and let himself be consumed by his surroundings.

What little distance he could see, gave no indication of light change or even the smallest clearing. The forest floor was so dense with plant life that he did not actually walk directly on it. The cushioning was offering a little mercy to his foot pain but he still really needed a suitable place to sit down.

He finally groped what turned out to be a slender tree trunk that felt sturdy enough to support him if he leaned against it. As he pressed the length of his back to it, something very gelatinous and soft plopped out of his way and he jumped away from the trunk in reflex. He groped around and found dry, firm support again, leaned back into it, summoned his nerve, and braced for more slime bags. None came for him. The tree gave just a bit and he hesitated, fearing it might not take his weight. It answered with an adjusting series of diminishing waves that eased away.

Alvar gingerly felt around his body and brushed away a few other smaller creatures he didn't wish to crush or let crawl all over him. He was no longer trying to brush away the leaves that comfortably readjusted until they enveloped him. He was about to give up on the bugs too. If he did die, it wouldn't take long at all to be eaten, he was sure of it. There in the dark, with only the tree for support, he feared this was his last day, after all.

Alvar looked around at the darkness and started talking out loud to his mother for no other reason other than it was strangely comforting to do so. He was exhausted. He couldn't see anything anyway, so just he closed his eyes and told her he was going to sleep now. He rolled over so his side was against the trunk, adjusted an imagined pillow, tucked his hands, palms together, between his ear and tree bark, all the while still standing, and settled in for a nice nap. He wanted water and then he wanted dinner. He asked what she had planned for it. He wanted tuna casserole. He wanted to hear how her day went. What news of Akenehi and the pod? He dozed off.

As he fell asleep he lost his balance and rolled off the trunk. The drop onto the cushion of dense plant life startled him awake. He didn't know how long he had been asleep but it felt like hours. It had only been moments. Now lying prone and completely covered in foliage he was finding it even more difficult to breathe. He fought his way over to supine position, moved a leaf away from his mouth and called out for his mother again, believing he would soon suffocate.

Then he heard a faint call. He called out to her again, "Momma?" "MOMMA?" He listened and the return call got louder. For a moment he thought his travel through time, his ordeal through the thorns and now the suffocation by those blasted plants, it could all be an extremely vivid nightmare. His mother was calling him to wake up, to get up. *Get up.* He could hear her clearly in his mind. The bird songs started to resemble an orca whistle. *Move. GO!*

Coming suddenly awake with a rush of adrenaline, he sprang up and took a fast leaping step toward the command. He ran full smack into his vertical bed, the tree. Smarting but not stopping, he pushed on, hands clearing his line of sight with increased efficiency, invigorated by the occasional whiff of strong botanical scent, and then reaching the end of this brief second wind when he finally found himself in a clearing.

It was very clear in fact, so unnaturally devoid of the botanical overcrowding he had just escaped. The natural dirt floor looked to Alvar like it was well kept up, even smoothed and must therefore have been maintained by humans. Sun beamed like a solid cone shaped spotlight through the humid air, illuminating the very center of the clearing, inviting him to show and warm himself within it. It reminded him of a theatre from his own time, complete with a single dramatic stage light, requiring a player. Effectively it was the most mesmerizing streams of light he had ever seen and he did not resist the urge. He half expected a booming voice to announce his entrance even before he took his first step into it.

"Ladies and gentlemen, please put your hands together for…ALVAR!"

Alvar smiled and waved to the imaginary crowd of fans as he walked one side of the perimeter, as if he were pacing a stage edge. Placing his hands on his hips and resting his full weight on his right leg, he swung around in one graceful swoop and stood with his back to the audience, which consisted in reality of several species of botanical undergrowth, thousands of insects and several other well concealed observing sentients.

He looked carefully into the light beam, examining what appeared as a swarm of miniscule insects as they darted around inside. It looked harmless enough. He cast his gaze around the opening, his personal stage, again. It was just about large enough for three men his size to fit as they lay feet to head. The beam illuminated a path opening apparently cut through the far end, opposite from the point he entered. The remainder of his jungle walk promised to be much easier.

He was relieved to be alive but he was so exhausted, he dropped his play act and merely threw himself down smack dab in the opening center, within the beam, lying on his back and basked in the light stream. His eyes smarted through his closed, still dark-adjusted eyes but the light felt absolutely glorious.

"Welcome home, welcome…you made it Alvar…" he heard the announcer fade low as the words filled his ears, then he heard…singing. Birds? *Akenehi*. Then the distant snapping and popping, like dry kindling underfoot or…echo-location. *Brough* was the last thought that crossed his mind before he fell again into deep, dreamless sleep.

Universe: Sponge, Cetapiens

Human and Priori

Alvar woke up to faces peering over him in the semi-dark. The sunlight was no longer in his eyes but it was still illuminating a portion of the clearing beyond his feet. There was just enough visibility that he could see those faces belonged to the same two he had fled. They had nudged him awake. Again Alvar felt as if he had slept for days. That was not the case. He was merely having difficulty adjusting his time perception.

Alvar was at their mercy. They had him alone and he expected they might beat him, perhaps even kill him. But these were Cetapiens and Alvar's assumptions were based on his culture, not theirs and were entirely incorrect. He was right, in that they were angry over the initial insult and Alvar had yet to make proper amends, but Alvar was a human being and needed their help. They were trying to give it to him.

One of the two men was particularly annoyed with Alvar and began admonishing him about running off to this part of the forest alone. The other urged his friend to lower his voice and remain calm, to show restraint. He emphasized with equally emotional gestures that the strange man they had pulled for the water was obviously confused, perhaps even ill.

Alvar didn't wish to cause them to fight amongst themselves. He rose, leaned over supporting his weight on his knees and took a moment to get blood to his brain. The men offered to support him but Alvar wanted to manage on his own and he did. He followed them onto the open pathway. The lead man held the hand of the second and that man grasped Alvar's. They were friendly but that wasn't the purpose of the gesture. This was how they customarily walked through the forest, especially this part. Even on a familiar path it was better to not only walk with a companion, but to keep a physical connection to each other.

Alvar noted the men had donned loin cloths since their meeting on the boat. Lightheaded from exhaustion, he laughed inwardly to himself because he was so much more comfortable than he would have been; walking through the darkened woods holding the hand of a *naked* person.

Alvar noticed their path had begun to run parallel to an impressively well-constructed aqueduct. He tried to drop the hand holding his so he could venture off the path to it and drink. The hand tightened and he was pulled forward.

"Don't break the bond. Drink, up ahead," was all the lead called back.

As they approached the village, which was mercifully sooner than he had anticipated, Alvar saw the path gradually merged into a very well maintained walkway and he wondered whose job it was to keep it in such good shape. From these few early details, already it struck him this was not the primitive culture he had naively imagined in school.

Alvar's newly acquired knowledge of the people and surroundings was due to his transition through the multiverse but that didn't mean he knew *everything* and he certainly could *not* read minds. He knew their language and their names, yes. He had been exposed to a non-linear detailed experience of their society and behavior patterns, absolutely. But, to isolate dynamic thought within an individual mind or know the full linear detail of what was going to happen at any given moment, was well beyond his ability.

Despite the advantages his brief passage through the multiverse might have taught him, he had much to learn. He continued to calculate that he may well be dead before nightfall if he didn't face the fact that he didn't know everything and sometimes, just every so often, he needed to keep his mouth shut. He assigned the numerous stings and cuts he had just endured as punishment for his stupidity.

Alvar finally encountered people, other than his guides, heading toward them up ahead on the walkway. They were a group of women, six young mothers with their infants in back slings. He stopped dead in his tracks, breaking the hand hold. So did the women. Alvar smartly checked himself, trying hard not to gawk. After a conversation of brief explanation between the guides and the women they resumed walking. He found himself quite speechless, only nodding to them as he moved graciously aside and they slowly passed, examining his bizarre, excessive clothing and tall strange stature.

They were naturally and casually topless. The women, and men for that matter, wore little other than a cotton braid belt with cloth wrapped around and arranged for fit. It was a functional piece that provided a comfort barrier against briars and insects. Sometimes they didn't even wear that, the two men who had pulled Alvar from the water were a case in point.

Very soon after they resumed their walk, they came upon the outer limits of a populated area. Alvar observed women of various ages and childbearing status, were walking not only topless but with bare backsides in full view. Men were dressed, or more appropriately, not dressed in the same way. Aside from the shock of flesh, there were so many fascinating objects of which Alvar could not even begin to imagine their uses, brightly colored accessorized costumes and ornamentations. Faces still and staring at him, frozen in position of the day-to-day activities, people interrupted by his sudden appearance. His multi-verse memory flashed enough matching data up to that point that he recognized this was very early in the cultures history and it was not the best of times *quite* yet.

As he walked, he continued to connect dots. The combination of multiverse, Vencello and his own knowledge from his prior life was his weapon and his defense. He assumed from his own discomfort that he needed both.

He was too fresh from his beating, near death experience and subsequent time travel. He was in survival mode. He failed to work out that no one was lunging at him, laying hands on him or showing aggression of any variety. Still, he planned his immediate strategy. *Go to the constable.* There *had* to be law enforcement of sorts. Tell him what had happened in as few words as possible. Reveal too much and it might also be his undoing.

He badly needed a drink. He was starving too, now that he thought about it again. It had been a real workout through the wilderness. It felt like an eternity since he'd eaten his last meal. He amused himself that it probably had been. He was struck more than ever how his physical body was taking over, pushing back his thoughts of the multiverse and his prior life only hours ago. He was hardwired to stay alive no matter what, simply survive. His body was making demands for water, food, shelter and protection, and Alvar had no choice but surrender to them.

He plopped down on the ground.

"Can I get some water? Water?" Alvar asked to everyone and no one in particular.

His two guides merely moved off a few steps and turned around casually and observed whatever was going to happen next. Alvar was drawing a lot of attention. He looked very foreign, exhausted and rough. He was bruised from his tree bump, bleeding from several cuts and it was all signaling alarm. People didn't know him but through the multiverse he had known them. He should relax, stop and talk, explain himself. Those two, who pulled him out of the water, were perhaps his first friends, even future allies, protection. First things first, he needed water.

He was approached by one of the older men who had observed their emergence from the forest path, his continued movement around people and structures and whose eyes had carefully followed him to his seated position. As soon as Alvar's bottom hit the ground the man came over to where he sat and stared directly down at him. Others were watching intently. Alvar knew as a stranger, it was up to him to make the greeting and put the man, and the growing crowd, at ease. Alvar proceeded this time with few words, carefully selected in humility and respect. The introduction went smoothly. Alvar requested and was provided with the most satisfying refreshment he had ever imbibed—local, plain rain water.

No sooner did he finish and wipe his mouth on his T-shirt, which definitely stuck out like a sore thumb and marked Alvar as unusual among so many undressed people, then his prior two acquaintances addressed the man, and they obviously knew each other. They determined that no one present had seen Alvar before. They told the story of how they pulled him out of the water.

Here was Alvar's second big challenge, what to say with minimal words and do damage control on his obvious oddity so he would in no way be perceived as a threat.

Alvar repeated his initial assertion, the truth, that he was new to the area but he meant no harm. In fact, he hoped for acceptance, an opportunity to prove his value to all the people and a permanent home among them. He was about to ask the man if he was *in charge*.

At that moment, before he could ask his question, an elderly, grey haired woman came into view. She had obviously been close by, watching and listening. She approached Alvar and looked him over carefully. She touched him in familiar and easy fashion. She felt the texture of his hair and pulled gently at sections, examining the smooth and uniform cut. She noted the color of his eyes, the shape of his ears. She took keen interest in his clothing; T-shirt, jeans, socks, the small rips and tears, the sweat pattern and his bloodstains.

Alvar, still seated, blinked up at her. Unlike everything else around him, she evoked *no* memory *whatsoever* from the multiverse or the Vencello. He looked at her again, more carefully. Nope, nothing. He pulled instead on his human experience and knowledge of what he knew of these people. She was definitely kind and he sensed no threat or suspicion from her and he trusted her immediately. The others, still watching, took their cue entirely from her.

The woman asked, "Do you know me?"

She was like a human piñata, fashioned to look like something familiar on the outside but filled with mysterious goodies inside. He couldn't say that though. He thought deeply. Something did start to strike him. She was going to be very important to him, he only knew that much. He couldn't say *that* either. Then one word came to him and he felt sure it was correct. He waited a respectful time of silence when her inspection had paused, lowered his eyes and asked politely, "Grandmother?"

She smiled down at him, "Yes, Grandson".

At those two small words, she nodded to the two men who had pulled him out of the ocean, who then promptly turned and went back to the trail in the direction from which they had just come.

The lead asked without turning around to her, "Tea?"

"Of course!" she called back to them through the darkened door to the forest they had just disappeared through.

The others resumed their activities, albeit still watching them and some gesturing with noticeable excitement. The older man didn't budge but remained staring at Alvar intently but this time with some amusement. He gestured that Alvar should stand. Alvar was exhausted but he sighed in resignation.

As he stood up slowly and with much effort, the elderly woman observed with mild surprise, his relative tall stature, towering over all of them. Grandmother, short but straight and strong, kept her gaze on him all the while. Her happy countenance, eyes dancing above a grin that completely stretched out her wrinkled lips, conveyed all at once her wisdom, inner youth and mature sense of humor. Some of her teeth were missing and those that remained were aged with decades of tea stain.

"Come, you are with me" and she turned and spoke in general to the people, still watching. "We will welcome him."

With very few words exchanged, and just that quickly, Alvar had the support of a most powerful ally. Much more, he also had someone he could call family.

Universe: Sponge, Cetapiens

Human and Priori

Grandmother, as Alvar affectionately called her from that time onward, had the unremarkable appearance of a native woman of the people well into her seventies. She was one of several acting matriarchs of the very early clan; Orcasekai. There were three broadly classified clans at that time and those names reflected the daily work of the people, not their genetic lineage. Orcasekai were the fishermen. Templesekai were the brewers, entertainers and artists. Eaglesekai were the clan of the farmers and were also net and cloth weavers, living further inland close to open fielded areas. Templesekai and Eaglesekai integrated their activities and often supplied workers to each other to satisfy workload demands as needed. The Orcasekai were often out at sea and tended to be more isolated than the other two but they provided the fish. Fish was the staple and the preferred source of protein of all the clans and the Orcasekai were the sole providers of such.

The People differed from The Broken in that their new society was largely matriarchal, primarily because the women commonly lived to their ninetieth year while men died on average at a much younger age, rarely surviving past their forties. It was a natural consequence of human biochemistry interacting with the digested elements of native foods they ate. For whatever reason, males were immune to longevity benefits, females were not. A male who did survive his forties was considered old. Living to old age by *any* individual was considered a most sacred state of being,

Council representation for each of the three, Orcasekai, Templesekai and Eaglesekai, was largely symbolic and honorary. The most aged of the matriarchs and *any* male who could live to old age served on council. Their direction was wise and rational. None were autocratic rulers; rather they were in fact the lionized.

Within a day of Alvar's arrival, Grandmother, who was part of council, called a meeting of the elders for two reasons. One, so the people would have an opportunity to meet the new arrival, Alvar, in person, and assign him to a clan if any were willing to accept him. And two, to discuss the prospects for her granddaughter, Amaranth, and many other Cetapien adults who were eligible and willing to celebrate their sacred fertility ritual.

This meeting was a more formal gathering, meant to be witnessed by large numbers firsthand, and so it took place at one of the Templesekai arenas. There was no signage whatsoever, anywhere to indicate what the arena was called or where to proceed. So Alvar asked Grandmother, who was walking directly in front of him, if it had a name. She did not turn around or acknowledge that she heard him but she sang out two simple notes.

The arena was totally open air, had it been raining and everyone would have been soaked with no shelter readily available. The structure itself was immaculately clean and kept up with no twigs or debris cluttering any of the levels or rolling underfoot.

Instead of circling bleachers or chairs that Alvar would have expected in his time, there were only four simple descending circling levels lined smartly with smoothed, packed stone. Rather than built up, the area had been excavated and dug into the ground. The center was clearly an open smooth floored depression that served on this occasion as the stage. Alvar quickly calculated that, unless there was drainage that he could not see from him viewpoint, the stage area would be subject to flooding. For now it was completely dry and there were many people meandering around on it.

Beautifully woven individual sized cotton mats were in place on the floor of each encircling tier for comfortable seating. *Everyone* seemed to be in charge of offering each other space to sit on the mats and saw to it that the placement of each offered unobstructed viewing. Each level seemed to have been constructed considering the reclining human figure. The floors were just long enough for one person to stretch out with legs fully extended, back supported against the wall, without interference from dangling feet from the next tier.

Alvar mused his mother would have loved the design that completely eliminated the irritation of people kicking the back of one's chair in this arena. He estimated his own legs would be too tall and he would have to sit crossed-legged.

Alvar tapped Grandmother on the shoulder and she startled and turned back at him. He motioned to a nearby unoccupied top level of the structure and she nodded in agreement. 'But come right back' she told him with clear gestures and pointed to where she would be.

A lot of eyes were on him as he maneuvered awkwardly, not thinking to first look around at how others might negotiate one level to another and follow their example. Instead he ascended from the inner lowest level in his own unique way, until he reached the top. From that height he got the panoramic view of an entire section of the exterior and the whole interior the arena. He turned his back on the interest he was causing within and faced the exterior surrounding clearing and the forest beyond. It was green and lush and full of life that he could easily detect because its edge was not too terribly far away from the structure itself. What the arena lacked in above ground height it made up for in magnificent size and perfection in shape and function. He noted the smooth transition of earth that had been pushed up all around the structure. He marveled why they didn't just walk up the outer slopes directly to the top level and descend to lower levels as desired but no one did. He watched as the last few people came in the same single entrance that he and Grandmother had just emerged from.

He took a deep breath. He could *smell* the surrounding forest and *feel* the comfortable warmth of the stone lining the structure radiating the heat it had absorbed back up to him now that the sun was beginning to set. He *listened* to the cacophony of distant bird song, the much closer human vocalizations and wished for home. It was brightly musical, unspoiled and beautiful there. But he missed his mother, his room, his school and his town. None of that existed yet. He longed for the familiar. He wondered where his own ancestors were at that moment. This place was almost certainly different in almost every respect from *their* lives. Even the stars that were beginning to appear were a little off from where he expected them to be.

Then Alvar turned around and saw the moon had just begun to rise over the tops of the trees. Now *that* was still the same.

He cast his gaze back to the overall scene of the inside of the arena, he noticed most of the people were either greeting each other happily or were engaged in some kind of promenade. People were moving in ordered pathways through the center chaos of the arena, a few alone but most holding hands in connected small groups. He imagined this was done so they didn't lose each other in the crowd, but for the most part he was wrong. It was just their way; they liked holding hands. Some were slowly circling the inner perimeter looking up into the raised levels as if searching for someone, others climbing up steps utilizing smaller protrusions for that purpose that Alvar had not noticed until then, and finding places to sit or recline, all friendly and affectionate.

Impressions of the whole environment were not wasted on Alvar; those were of careful timing, order, geometry and unity.

Alvar took it in. He didn't want that scene to be forgotten, ever. He had never witnessed a happier, more energetic gathering of people in his life. It was like one huge joyous family reunion. And the singing! These people seemed to sing more than they spoke.

He noticed the overall patterns of human movement and energy shifted. People were ascending, finding their places at last. The center stage area was quickly emptying except for those heading toward the central group of council elders. Grandmother was staring at Alvar when he caught her gaze, she motioned, and he hurried down to her side.

All fell quiet as Alvar walked over and stood like a tree breaking over the forest canopy, a tower of a human next to the elders who were waiting for him. His name was spoken and then it was sung. It was the first time he had heard it sung and he had to admit he liked the song version better; this was repeated by the council elders, then to his surprise everyone sang it.

Every face was curious if not openly friendly and he didn't detect any animosity. He hadn't expected to be so overcome and he choked up. He clamped his jaw tight and fixed his eyes straight ahead, focusing on the forest tree tops rising over the back of the structure. He had been officially presented to the council and the people. Grandmother explained the clan structure and Alvar nodded politely. She spoke clearly and Alvar was amazed that everyone could actually hear her. Ah, the *arena* structure, he worked out, was acoustic as well. He was already aware of the clan structure and Grandmother knew that he was, but it was part of the ritual.

"You must contribute value as one of the people if you wish to stay among us. What exactly can you provide us we don't already have ourselves?"

There had been no rehearsal and he was caught off guard by the question. Alvar thought fast about his actual work experience because that is what he thought she was after. He could have said, "My devotion to all of you" and if he had spoken it well, that would have sufficed. But he didn't say that.

Alvar was brought up in a different time and culture. There he was educated and beginning to think about what he wanted to do as a career. He did not have actual work experience other than serving as his mother's research assistant. He was a great swimmer, skilled at navigating at sea by the stars at night, at least *his* stars. He knew a thing or two about marine biology, chemistry, limited knowledge of theoretical physics and what he had introduced himself to in the field of quantum biology. He also had knowledge of the multiverse and memories of the Vencello. What couldn't he provide by way of value, assuming they valued knowledge? But there was something that made him special, from which he had stood out from his peers at school.

Alvar spoke directly to the elders, "I have experience with orcas! Do any of your people ever come in contact with orcas out at sea? I hear the word in your clan name but I haven't…I mean, I don't…"

He stopped himself from stating that he had expected to see Orca symbols, well, everywhere. Their clan name reflected knowledge of the existence of orcas but other than hearing the word, he saw no other evidence of them. Alvar remembered what he learned in school. This culture was something of an enigma. There was an unprecedented lack of evidence of who these people had been. There were no symbols, written words or much at all that had given a clue to archeologists about this culture.

Alvar shifted his gears smoothly and proceeded to make his case, "What I mean is, where I come from, I have a very good friend, an orca. Maybe that can somehow be of use."

There was complete silence. Every eye was on him. No one moved.

Alvar shifted his weight and thought he might walk around and determine if he was in some sort of frozen time bubble in which he alone was unaffected.

Two piercing bird calls from the surrounding jungle sliced through the silence in quick succession and broke around the arena. It sent a wave of shifting startled movement through the crowd. Then quiet again. In the immediate moments of stillness that followed it was if everyone was meditating on the meaning of the statement from the jungle. Alvar choked back a sudden burst of laughter as he thought to himself, 'did that bird just yell ''*bullshit*!''?

Grandmother broke out in one of her huge, almost laughing grins and clapped her hands loudly together, in seeming imitation of the bird, "Orcasekai it is then!" The other council members looked at each other with significant doubting looks.

Energy moved through the four levels, evident by bodies suddenly shifting weight again, turning heads and bending in hushed conversation. Alvar observed with some alarm that many people suddenly stood up but then sat down again as if that was a significant gesture in itself. Was that the equivalent of a 'Boo' or applause he wondered? Several of the Eaglesekai elders spoke up and over each other. One in particular was incensed and commanded the council's attention.

"What nonsense! Friends with an orca! He is obviously *lying*. Or he is a *fool*. No, no! Look at the size of him! We need him in the fields! Did you call us to announce your decision, which it seems now has already been made without our consult? Do we not even get a chance to introduce him to our clan? How insulting! Just like an Orcasekai…"

Then a member of Templesekai moved to Alvar's side and gently soothed the Eaglesekai with initial gestures of agreement. "Alvar," The matriarch almost sang her greeting with varied, deliberate tones. "We are all looking forward to introducing you to our clans. It is each of our hope that a young male, strong, brave and as knowledgeable as yourself will refrain from deciding in favor of Orcasekai, who obviously want your value as much as we do, until you have visited us in turn, in fair length of time and with open mind and heart. Then you can decide, not as a desperate lonely stranger, but as a level thinking, welcome contributor to a clan…"

Grandmother cut her off. It was rude but that was just the way she was when she was irritated, "His thinking is level, now as ever."

The Templesekai matriarch in obvious state of insult, moved aside slowly, with the fluid physical grace of a dancer.

"However," Grandmother nodded roughly, a gratuitous gesture of apology in her direction, "I agree that Alvar would indeed benefit from an initial extended visit to the clans. Is it agreed then, that all clans accept him and he is to select from among them, from his desire alone, when the visit is over?"

"Yes", "Agreed", and "Absolutely" were exclaimed all around.

"I am satisfied."

The other matriarchs stated plainly as well, "I am satisfied." The elder men on the council gáve their agreement as well.

Grandmother concluded that segment of the meeting with elevated enthusiasm. "Now, let us get on to *important* matters."

Alvar shrunk away at this but quickly saw only friendly jesting; it was not an insult. He watched and listened from the side, observing that the many people who had left their places on the steps and were heading to the center of the arena were all women. The entire crowd had really perked up and leaned in at the first "I am satisfied" and those that remained on the steps were repositioning themselves. They found their comfort at last and the women on the field were standing in concentric circles around the council, adjusting their heads for a clearer view. They were several women deep. Many eyes lingered on Alvar, all over him, in fact. He couldn't help but smile as he caught their eye contact, which startled him with their easy boldness. These women were not afraid of him, or shy. Their eyes wandered to other males as well and Alvar noted with amusement, a flirt festival had seemingly begun.

At first Alvar wondered if he should leave. This was obviously a very important ritual. He was not on the council, he was unimportant, uninitiated. Then he understood. No one indicated he should leave. *No* one was leaving. All made up a credible body of witnesses who could latter verify proceedings and no one was recording, no writing. There was little if any secrecy in such matters for this culture. Everything was obvious. If you wanted to know, you could probably know. Attend the council meetings, talk to people. Face to face, directly. Many other faces farther away were circling. All were politely quiet so voices could be heard. This was an open broadcast. Those in direct attendance would spread the news and their account could be easily verified by many others in at the meeting. Alvar wondered if anyone would be intentionally excluded. He could perceive no evidence that that was the case.

Alvar took it all in, he felt at ease now that the attention was drawn elsewhere, even as shoulders and thighs jostled and pressed around him, close enough to feel breath and smell bodies, as people positioned for viewing advantage.

The sun was setting, the moon rising. A whole new sound, nocturnal and sensuous, was emitted from the forest. Elegant ornamental torches suddenly were produced and lit. They were carefully passed around and positioned in holders throughout all levels that, again, Alvar had not noticed until their use drew his attention. All were settled when bodies were adjusted so as to not be scorched. The mood was definitely enhanced and many who might have looked plain or ordinary by daylight, looked warm and inviting in the yellow wash of flickering light waves.

This was not a marriage ritual nor was leading up to one. As he was about to learn, marriage as Alvar knew it was unheard of among their culture. Producing children was on the agenda and it was a quite serious, much regulated, huge deal. In contrast, throughout their culture, non-intercourse sex play was casual, friendly and without perversion or aggression. Sexual desire was considered as natural and shameless as eating or sleeping and it was naturally integrated in their daily social function.

They drew little distinction between 'immediate families', as Alvar would have defined 'family', and the extended community. In fact, their word for family was another word for The People. Each new birth was everyone's most cherished concern. It affected them all profoundly. They had their own unique culture of population control. They not only accepted it, they truly appreciated it. The associated rituals were the most eagerly anticipated and participated in. None were coerced into attending and none were admonished for not doing so. They were all family, they all loved each other and this was their way.

Alvar was amazed during his first ritual that everyone would know so openly of everyone else's business. The arena obviously had a huge role in community communication. Maybe his super knowledge would not be such an advantage. They had no need of mass media; the people *were* the mass media.

By the end of the evening Alvar was aware of eligible women, meaning those announcing their readiness and intention to produce a child with a man of mutual choosing. He had seen them with his own eyes, and they had likely all seen him. He learned through ritual groupings by clan, which of the three, Orcasekai, Templesekai, or Eaglesekai, each generally lived with, and therefore which of the matriarchs he would have to negotiate with (the important first step of making his interest, if any, known) for a suitability evaluation, introduction and more. He met many other men, he knew their intentions, which were openly stated, and who was interested in whom.

Many had looked him over if not spoken with him directly. Alvar knew that within days, perhaps even hours, he would be known throughout much of society. Further, he suspected his impending decision of which clan to choose would not be the focus of anyone's discussion for long.

Universe: Sponge, Cetapiens

Human and Priori

Grandmother approached Alvar early the next day and asked if he had noticed a favorite. Alvar made his removal from consideration for a mating match known to Grandmother immediately. He sensed she was disappointed but not at all surprised. When she suggested perhaps next time, Alvar agreed, perhaps.

Grandmother mentioned her granddaughter, Amaranth, had not been among the available women because she had flatly refused to participate. However, she might be persuaded to participate at the *next* festival. The first child is a serious step, especially for a woman, and Amaranth was still relatively young.

Alvar explained that where he came from this step was very serious and he did not fault her granddaughter for delaying. For him, he hoped it would be a lifelong commitment and was not something to decide in one meeting. He was surprised when Grandmother agreed in principle.

Over the next few days he asked questions about daily life and got answers. There was no home ownership. The possessive word descriptors were generally nonexistent. A mated couple did not live together in their own house. The climate was so mild year round and warm enough even at night that structures were all open. No doors and no windows, just tight weave to keep bugs out at night. A mated couple could remain together if they so desired for as long as they wished.

Anyone could sleep anywhere they wanted to, even in a hammock if they wanted to set it up and could stand the bugs, Grandmother described how she frequently slept so herself. Friend groups often slept in the larger communal sleeping huts. Mothers nursing infants tended to support each other and formed temporary groups as long as they were still nursing and similarly slept in larger huts with their friends. But no one sleeping arrangement was encouraged or enforced.

That sounded like a permanent sleepover party to Alvar. He described matter-of-factly how different his culture had been. He and his mother lived alone for years, in the same structure with many things around him. He had his own room and had always slept there by himself.

In fact, he was working up to asking for a space to build his own hut. He guessed this was not the time.

Grandmother looked at him with sad, sympathetic eyes and she looked as if she might be tearing up. She regarded his unconcerned countenance for a few serious moments and then continued.

The smaller simple, usually single room huts, such as those used for sleeping and cooking were built, modified and repaired easily as needed. Hut and building construction was an activity that was not unique to a single value clan. They all learned at an early age and participated in structure and ground maintenance; Orcasekai, Eaglesekai and Templesekai were all builders. One structure was not considered better than another; they simply had different functions and locations. One could enter where they wanted and when.

Alvar was truly shocked. What about locks, safety and security? Surely there were bullies and predators? He referred to the two men who had pulled him from the water. He felt intimidated by them and had fled in fear. There, he insisted, he had already encountered a couple of those in her paradise.

Grandmother continued, already vindicated. And what *had* happened there? Had he been harmed? She recounted the events. They had helped him not once, but twice. They pulled him from the water *and* guided him from the forest density into a safe clearing. People would be curious and make their concerns and requests known. They would be frank and sometimes they may be angry. However, they were civilized People after all. He may have felt threatened but he had never been in danger from those men.

Alvar didn't agree. His mother had taught him the harsh reality of ocean life; Mike, Guy and Johnny the equally harsh lessons of human violence. There were *always* predators and prey. Grandmother acknowledged that as true fact and simply offered the promise of future guidance.

He wondered if he would ever be truly as immaterial, trusting and comfortable among them, as they so obviously were with each other. Probably not.

CHAPTER 18 – A SHARED VISION

Universe: Sponge, Cetapiens

Human and Priori

Grandmother was satisfied that Alvar was to be one of the people and had enough basic knowledge to function as one for the time being. Alvar was a grown man by all of their standards, and she treated him as such. He had choices to make and rituals to honor if he was to remain and be accepted by the People. A certain spiritual journey, a ritual for which there could be no preparation, was in store next for him.

So, the next morning she woke Alvar and did not allow him food or water. She walked him to a nearby Templesekai hut, providing him with an orientation to the ceremony he was about to undergo, along the way. This structure was highly decorated, inviting and suggestive of celebration in exterior detail; very distinctive from the rather plain sleeping shelters. It was also more expansive in that it consisted of several inner chambers.

Alvar tried to look cool and adult, a bit of a swagger in his stride as he passed to the first inner chambers, projecting willingness and readiness. His transition through the multiverse had revealed nothing to instruct him on what he was about to experience. He had studied what very little was known of the Cetapiens as an ancient vanished culture, briefly in high school. That included the assumption that these mysterious people employed vision inducing substances in their spiritual rituals. The ceremonial tea was not comparable to street drugs of his time, which held no appeal to him whatsoever. The tea of Templesekai was meticulously crafted by supremely skilled, practiced and caring hands. It was nothing less than sacred. The ancient tea's enigmatic spiritual base had appealed to his scientific curiosity as well as his spirit of adventure *then* and even more so now. His mother was nowhere to raise an objection or provide counsel. He was a man and this was a rite of passage to his being accepted as such among his new people.

Alvar could hardly contain his enthusiasm.

Arriving in the most inner room they met the same Templesekai matriarch, whose name was Pranaya, and who had addressed Alvar at the council meeting. Pranaya was somewhat younger than Grandmother but of similar stature and appearance. Like Grandmother, Alvar had no memory from the multiverse of *this* woman either. He shrugged the enigma off as a result of his own limited abilities and gave it no further thought.

Grandmother lowered herself easily onto a floor mat, carefully adjusting so that her back and head lightly touched against the wall, crossed her legs and closed her eyes. Both mat and wall reacted to the contact with subtle light and pattern flashes that seemed agitated by the disturbance. She settled in and so did the energy behind and under her. Her lips twitched in silent conversation and Alvar mused she had been plugged into a communication device.

Pranaya motioned to a nearly identical intricately woven mat that she had set down for him and he plopped onto it. The mat flashed bright and Pranaya's eyes narrowed on him. Wearing little, he was not comfortable with her cross leg position and reclined instead with legs stretched out beyond the edge of the mat and crossed at the ankles, but it just didn't work. He became very uncomfortable and agitated.

Pranaya and Grandmother did not react or offer a suggested position.

Finally he settled in, imitating Grandmother's sit after all. He quickly became very comfortable and relaxed, amazingly so. He pulled away from the wall and turned to examine it, he noticed the mat and wall looked to be made of the same smooth organic plant based substance. He reasoned correctly that there had to be something in both of them that worked together to make it so pleasant to be in a particular sitting position. He made sure none of his body touched anything other than the organic surface behind and below him. He kept his eyes open and watched Pranaya, who seemed to have been waiting for something and when he had found his position again this seemed to be her cue.

She very slowly portioned out the contents for a single ceremonial cup. It too exhibited patterned light responses to her touch and variations of pressure as she handled it, and apparently even temperature as she poured. He watched her intently, remaining silent, fascinated by the illumination, anticipating a closer look if she ever got around to finally offering it to him.

She spoke to Alvar at last as she closely observed the small amount of tea she had just poured. He could not perceive if there was evidence of reaction inside the cup that held her gaze so intently, but if he seen into it, *he* would have processed nothing but the tea. "Do you know what this is, Alvar?"

"The cup or the tea?" Alvar asked.

Her eyes pierced his.

He wasn't trying to be funny, he really wasn't sure what the cup was, but he knew the contents were tea. He was very interested in the composition of the container but he wasn't there to investigate the furnishings or the utensils. He caught himself.

"Yes. I think so. Tea used for a spiritual journey…visions…I hope…"

"Yes. Would *you* like to try some?"

"Yes." He didn't hesitate.

"There are some things you should know. It will not go down easily. You may *vomit*, and once you drink it, after a while, you may become *terrified*…"

"Yes, I know." His relaxed calm popped like a bubble. Alvar

couldn't help but blurt it out as he was becoming unexpectedly impatient with what he believed was a delay and felt it was urgent to get on with it. "I come from a very *distant* tomorrow. My home is here and *everywhere*. I *know*."

Pranaya remained quiet and her countenance calm as she contemplated his outburst, narrowed her eyes on the remainder of the pour, and resumed the ritual. She took her good natured time.

Alvar thought his head would pop in frustration as he watched her move at seemingly glacial speed and listened to her long drawn out chanting, waiting for his cue to drink at last. He felt he was already prepared. He was convinced she was definitely stalling. Why, other than for dramatic effect, he had no idea. He was sure he would soon be revisiting the multiverse and hoped that is precisely what would be achieved. Little did he know, he would soon instead become a blabbermouth who would be compelled to blurt out any secret he might have, otherwise felt compelled to keep.

Two grown men entered the room, each handing a variety of dried leaves to Pranaya, and then found their places beside Alvar, one on each side. Alvar did not recognize them at first, but when he took a moment to study their faces he did. Alvar, who still did not know their names, despite their pulling him from the water and saving him in the forest, smiled in familiar greeting but they did not make eye contact with him.

Alvar settled down a bit. There was the reason for the delay; waiting for additional ingredients. Now he was annoyed not with Pranaya, but with the two men at this side. *Slugs*.

"In case you *thrash*," Pranaya explained simply, nodding to the men, as she crumbled a tiny sample of each of the leaves into the cup.

Grandmother started speaking, in evocative and emotional singing tones, to Alvar. "*You* are strange and *uninitiated*, but we are making an exception for you, Alvar. You have been invited to drink *now* and it is no *small* honor. Be *patient*. *We* are here for you and *with* you. You will be safe and protected."

Pranaya peered into the cup one last time, apparently seeing what she needed to see, then into Alvar's eyes, same there, and with both steadied hands, presented him his tea.

Only when he lifted the cup directly under his nose for a first whiff did it hit him. The smell was so offensive Alvar thought he might indeed vomit from the odor alone but did not. It seemed reasonable to him that the main ingredient of the tea was very likely the intestines of one of their deceased. Of course he was wrong but he had no way of knowing that. Nor was he about to back out now. He had been fairly warned after all. He managed to get a good amount down after several gagging sips but could drink no more.

Pranaya observed the remaining contents of the cup and was satisfied. She took it away from him and kept it. No word was spoken.

He looked around at everyone, after a long silence had passed, and wondered when anything might happen. Several more minutes passed but Alvar was losing concept of time and it seemed an unbearable span of boredom.

Alvar tried to make some small talk but no one responded.

Eventually he turned his torso toward the wall he had been leaning against and observed the bioluminescence was fading where his back and head had been pressing it. He reached around and began to write "Alvar" with his finger, on the wall. First a glowing stream for the first letter then…

Pranaya gave a sharp bark. Alvar startled, jerked his head around and stared at her, mouth agape.

He understood he was to stop immediately and he turned back around slowly but not before he watched as the last hint of his initial faded away.

Alvar would learn soon that this culture communicated much in song and movement, both fluid and ever-changing as the singular environment in which they existed. A taboo forbidding written words or pictures had curiously been imposed throughout their society. It tempered the reduction of what they considered sacred and ethereal complexity of their acoustic communication to earthly, low, unmoving, incomplete forms. Written words and pictures were considered conductive to miscommunication at best and malicious deception at worst. One could only really trust a source face to face.

Indeed, there were no written words, anywhere. Further, there were no drawings or carved images of people or animals, in their personal and structure ornamentation. He wondered if they were hiding something, *from* something perhaps. They didn't seem frightened or insecure in any way. Fortunately, he did not offer to teach everyone how to read and write as his contribution. He had no intention of abandoning his long-earned literacy but he would pursue that fascinating quirk in a discussion at a later time.

Grandmother had not moved or opened her eyes since he took his first sip and he noticed an expanding bioluminescent halo starting small around her back and head as she too leaned against the wall. That provided some relief from the dullness as Alvar postulated to himself what was responsible for the illumination but then so much more time seemed to pass in excruciating silence. Even aura-like body halos became uninteresting. It was too quiet.

Alvar started to doze but fought it; afraid he might sleep through his visions and miss them all. He anticipated a weightless dream-like light show with beautiful kaleidoscope happy thoughts, perhaps even a renewed link even to the Vencello and further privileged knowledge, compliments of the multiverse.

Then the room seemed to add a dimension. It slightly skewed and stretched. Alvar steadied himself with deep breathing realizing with his last moments of common sense that the tea was *finally* taking effect, comforting himself that was coming, wasn't *real*. It was a merely a harmless vision.

He looked to the man on his right then to the left; both transformed into a zombie threat, oozing gross eyeballs just staring directly back at him. He couldn't make them go away.

Alvar lost it. He screamed and managed to get himself, scrambling in a crab-like crawl into a corner, not caring a bit that he had left the comfort and any mysterious function of his mat. He balled into a defensive sitting fetal position, tucking his face safely out of zombie feasting range. He peered up over his forearms. Neither of the two men had even flinched in pursuit but their gooey eyes followed him and didn't blink. Alvar hid his eyes again. *Make it go away* he thought to himself, you can do it. It's not *real. Make it go away!* He concentrated hard and looked up again.

No good. Even worse. He saw what he knew in his mind were even *more* dead people, but of a different variety. These new arrivals had *normal* looking faces, to Alvar's perception, of strangers of his own race he might have passed on the streets of home. They were standing just out of his reach in long, white flowing robes that were moving in unison with some otherworldly breeze. These had suddenly appeared in the ceremony room while he had been hiding his face. They hung back at their distance and did not come any closer to him. They observed only.

'What the hell are they all staring at?' He shouted furiously, "and why are they even here?"

Even as he yelled out he hoped in the back of his mind this was only a *vision.* He wanted to remain reasonable and sane. But it was no good...

"Get me out of here!" he screamed. He slipped, speaking in his native language, for the first time since his arrival. Grandmother was clearly there, still looking just like herself, calm, close by. Pranaya, also unaltered in appearance, looked casually around to survey the scene. They didn't seem to notice the language difference and he sure didn't care.

By studying his eyes and gestures Pranaya knew, as part of his journey, he was *seeing* what she and Grandmother could not.

Pranaya offered some comfort, "We are all protecting you and *nothing bad* will happen to you. What do you see?"

Again in his native language, he looked up over his arms and verified they were still there, "I see zombies! Real zombies! And dead people, they're just staring at me!"

"We do not understand what you are saying Alvar. Speak the

149

language of our people if you can."

They had no word for zombie. But he pointed to the two men, "There!" Alvar proceeded to describe the revolting characteristics of long dead, partially and grotesquely decayed, but still animated bodies. They meant him harm, probably to eat him alive.

He started to babble and could not stop. He told them about his mother, their cetacean research, their boat, Akenehi, his school, the fight, his molecule model. He rambled on about how he had chosen the distant past, the Cetapien people rather than die, rather than leave a Gemini in his place to die. He told them in only a few badly chosen words about the Vencello, Brough and the multiverse. Now, he pleaded, he just wanted to go home, back to the boat with his mother in his own time. He wanted to be out on the sea with Hototo and Akenehi and the clan again. He had vivid sporadic visions of them as he spoke and he described very briefly what he was seeing as they passed before his mind's eye.

His story told, Alvar then just…snapped out of it. His mind calmed even though he was not yet done with his first Templesekai spiritual journey.

Pranaya motioned to his mat and Alvar understood he should return to it. He picked it up and positioned it in the center of the room, a spot of his own choosing. He stood in its center, bare feet making skin contact with it and watched without fear as the bioluminescent brilliance of the wall emanating behind Grandmother expanded and filled the room. It appeared to have fluid properties as waves of color pulsed through in beautiful flowing patterns but none of the chambers occupants floated or gasped for air. It enveloped all five of the rooms' occupants in a multi-spectrum light bubble.

He crouched low, and that awkward position offered the best central vantage point to view its stars. Steadying himself with the help of his fingertips spread wide on the mat on each side, he held it. Alvar struggled with explanation; either the walls of the room had seemingly been replaced by a domed astro-theatre or they were transported to another realm in what appeared to be deep space or he had merely fallen asleep and had dreamt all of it. Whatever had happened, they were safe within it.

Stars. That's what his mind rested on at first. The outer limits of the sphere were defined by brilliant tiny points of light. He admired them from his distance, turning and moving slightly until he had observed the entire sphere a few times over.

Then he noticed a definite, perfect pattern to the stars, such that he appeared to be standing in the center of a carbon-60 molecule. He recognized the precise geometric arrangement of vertex's, which defined 20 hexagons and 12 pentagons, no two pentagons sharing an edge. The stars, he concluded, were actually *atoms.* Their apparently orbiting electrons were suggested by zipping cloudy encircling atmospheres which also caused color and brightness variations within the fluid which radiated away from each point and interplayed with the whole.

Alvar had expected a kaleidoscopic vision but this was beyond any beautiful complexity he could have imagined.

Yes, he was home within his beloved carbon-60. No doubt. Although he could not find their exact location in the molecule, his mother and father were unmistakably there. Both Brough and Akenehi were definitely present along with a virtually infinite number of others.

Impossible.

He focused in and could come to no other conclusion. It was then he realized that size, position and number were all non sequitur. Focusing *inward* resulted in the detection of energy patterns and the presence of sentient beings. Focusing *outward* had the exact same result.

This reminded him of a self-similarity concept he learned in school. His fascination with the subject of fractal self-similarity that his instructor had introduced during a recent math class was paying off. He was glad he had paid attention. No matter how or where he focused, the bioluminescent source was life energy itself. The sphere was dense with it, patterns of color pulses and movement, reminiscent of cephalopod flashing neuron-rich skin. Self-similarity taken into account, he was absolutely sure the entire sphere was a single living sentience.

A particularly noticeable bright shape drew his attention as it flagellated through the fluid and he let his focus follow it. It was a gorgeously luminous conical being, cradling within it a vast multitude of glowing living beings. Alvar went in closer. Some of those were familiar to him: cetaceans, cephalopods, fish. Even the tiny plankton were within his perception. They swam in brine from water he knew well, from his own time and home, within that being and their beloved ocean. They were all alive and joyful. They were transporting, adapting.

Alvar knew he was witnessing rebirth, relocation, an evacuation. He was relieved. These beloved beings were saved.

Alvar had stopped describing what he was seeing to the others in the chamber. There were no words for much of it in their language. As he turned his attention to them he noticed that Grandmother and Pranaya appeared to also be examining features of the sphere while the other two men were not. It was if the matriarchs could detect the bubble as well. He could not perceive their thoughts. The *tea*. He had rationalized that this sphere was merely a vision evoked by his consumption of an elixir. But if they could see it too…

What Grandmother and Pranaya could perceive from their vantage point is what Alvar, who was in the center, could not. To them Alvar had appeared as translucent and had positioned his cerebral cortex so precisely that it had easily enveloped the most noticeable and brightest objects at the precise center of the sphere, a quad-star like system within it. There was a single very large quasar-like illumination and around it orbited a somewhat smaller one and then farther out but still within the limits of Alvar's brain, there were two tiny binary stars orbiting those yet maintaining a tight orbit around each other, so close they almost appeared as one.

Both matriarchs had not expected this vision, yet they knew exactly what they were seeing; the Vencello. They had been there before. It was Alvar's connection that was then confirmed to them.

The light started to fade and the sphere was no longer visible. Alvar relieved his burning thighs and aching joints, and the locked support provided in his fingers by sitting down, crossed legged on his mat in the center of the room.

When Alvar began to regain his normal senses, it was decided that he undoubtedly belonged with Orcasekai even though he had not visited either the Templesekai or Eaglesekai yet.

Neither told Alvar what they had seen, it had manifested for their three minds but it included data that was specific and personal to each of them. Grandmother looked at Pranaya and thought out loud, "He comes from a very dangerous place, many horrors, people who do grievous harm."

"Sad for him, but maybe…very good for us." Pranaya looked at Alvar and nodded in affirmation.

"We are sorry for your past Alvar but you are safe now. Some of those were visions you brought with you. They do not come from here and have gone back to where they belong," Grandmother announced. "Others belong to all of us and we cherish them as you do".

The two men escorted Alvar outside the Templesekai ceremonial structure, leaving Grandmother and Pranaya alone in the room. If those two men had witnessed anything other than Alvar's babbling and temporary fear of them, they never let him in on it.

Once alone, Grandmother said simply to Pranaya, "The multiverse is an ever interesting mind. Once you believe you have lived so long to know its thinking, something like this happens."

Pranaya heartily laughed in knowing agreement.

Completing the ritual, the two of them shared the remaining contents of Alvar's ceremonial tea, which to their physiology was not only pleasant it was delicious and nutritious with no visions forthcoming.

As they departed, Grandmother said she would trust Pranaya to explain diplomatically to Eaglesekai why the decision to keep Alvar in Orcasekai had been made without their input.

Universe: Sponge, Cetapiens

Human and Priori

The next day was a make or break for Alvar. Word traveled fast through Cetapiens, powerful dramatic recitations of the vision manifested during the first half of his tea-induced spiritual journey, even faster. The two men were appointed by the people as trusted witnesses and they had performed their duty with enthusiasm. Before an audience of the most skilled orators and singers, each of the two had committed details of Alvar's experience to memory, then rehearsed and perfected a satisfactory verbal and musical account that they all agreed to as most accurate and entertaining.

Those performers then spread out to various platforms and arenas where the accounts of Alvar's vision were repeated many times before the sun came up the next morning. During the night the multitudes gathered, learned the story, repeating as many performances as it took to commit it to their own memory before they gave up their place to another. It was commonly known that the people much preferred a great vision revealing performance to sleep.

Alvar witnessed in horror several different singers perform their retelling of his spiritual journey. Did he really say *all* of that? No doubt they were meticulously consistent and factual, albeit highly melodramatic when put to music. It was true about the orcas, back home at least, but the parts about the zombies were mercifully vague. On stage, in dramatic setup, he sounded more like a magician or a demi-god than a cetacean researcher. It was clear from the audience they were highly entertained but dubious.

Alvar quickly realized he would have to prove the *truth* of his revelations through actual demonstration however, that he was an orca *master* of sorts, or be branded a villain or worse.

So much for assurance of his safety.

Grandmother woke him up early again, out of sound sleep that he was really enjoying and could have desperately used more of. Not only was he sleeping off the prior day's tea drama, he had been out viewing "Alvar Will Tame the Orcas" performances all night. Grandmother had also seen a few and confirmed he would now have to prove himself, that very day no less. She reiterated the importance of what he was up against. She asked him specifically what he intended to do. A group of people had gathered to hopefully witness and be entertained by Alvar's unusual task.

He thought about his learning curve with Akenehi and her clan. He had *never* tamed them. He respected them in their wild state. First on his agenda, he needed to lower expectation of these people. He reminded the growing crowd that the performers had not consulted with him and got a few things wrong. No one seemed disappointed or fussed about what Alvar was clarifying. That relaxed him somewhat.

He had always relied on the modern technology of his time while helping his mother with her research. He would have to come at recreating the bond with a new clan of orcas from a whole new angle. He did not have access to hydrophones, recording equipment or any familiar tools. He didn't even have words that could translate those needs. Sound was all he could think of to cross the chasm separating human and orca.

He recalled an early memory of a device his mother had taught him to build. Then, he was eight years old and she was teaching him to construct a tool designed centuries earlier that she promised would help him hear sounds underwater. Alvar strained his mind and the scene was clear. In vivid recall, they were together, objects and tools spread out on their kitchen table. He looked down on the organized lay-out of the pieces and recognized a long tube. He picked it up in his mind's eye. *Hollow*. He carefully examined the detail of other pieces and then his mother walked back to the table, placed her hand on his shoulder and spoke from behind him. She had handed him a sharpened cutting tool. "You'll need this too, pumpkin, but be careful…here, watch me…"

He had struggled. She let him put most of it together but had helped him with some of the smaller, tighter fittings. She urged him to be patient and not give up. When he began to quit out of clumsy, small-fingered frustration, she persisted and pushed him, "You will need this. This will help you talk to cetaceans someday, maybe even tomorrow."

That was the day he learned that dolphins were *cetaceans*. That was the moment that he believed he *could* talk to them. The next day, his mother took him out in her boat, with the underwater listening horn he had made, called him her assistant for the first time, and his whole world changed.

The memory faded as his concentration turned back to his present and Grandmother's grave concern.

Alvar described the specifics and usefulness of the device to Grandmother and learned no one had heard of or tried to make such a thing. Fortunately, there were suitable materials and substitutes around the community and within easy walk into the forest. He could be in possession of a suitable version relatively quickly. Untested but suitable would have to do. Within an amazingly efficient hour, he had what he needed with the enthusiastic help of many fascinated, eager people who had initially remained merely to watch him work.

A few of the elder men became concerned when they saw the end product.

Anything that could be remotely used as a weapon, save essential gear for fishing, farming, etc., was strictly forbidden. Alvar was pressed to tell them specifically what it would be used for. There was quiet but intense conversation between Grandmother and these men, which all present could easily overhear, and finally one of the men spoke to Alvar. Calling it a *musical* instrument, he requested Alvar surrender the device to Templesekai once he was finished with it.

Alvar agreed. He requested a sampling of any existing musical-type gadgets that could be taken on out to sea and was told in chorus that all of those, of course, would be found at Templesekai.

Alvar, Grandmother, and a following paraded to the nearest entertainment plaza and its adjoining Templesekai costume and instrument storage structure. Pranaya was there, waiting just outside its entrance. She held out her hand, in wordless request for the device he had newly constructed. Nodding to Grandmother to join them, she smoothly ignored it as soon as she had it in her possession, then invited him in and began a walkthrough of the inventory.

What he found inside was an impressive array of sophisticated, beautifully ornate wind, string and percussion instruments. They were organized in groupings that seemed ambiguous to Alvar as he was not yet familiar with the many rituals and performances for which they were used. Some appeared pristine and others were nicked and faded, obviously often used and aged. There were instruments with matching masks and costumes, resplendent with gorgeous feathers and painted colors that were so vibrant they made his eyes swim. Although many were used in *sacred* rituals, he was invited to take *whatever* he needed. Pranaya added smoothly that his task, if he could indeed deliver, would be blessed as a holy one.

Alvar was drawn to the simplicity of a set of small single and double-hole flutes. She nodded permission and he picked one up and blew clumsily into it. Pranaya, who had been closely examining the underwater horn behind his back while he was studying flutes, turned to Alvar with an unnatural grace and ease. In fluid motion she handed the horn off to Grandmother and took possession of the flute gently away from Alvar. She brought forth from it a simple but pleasing tune.

There was a technique to it, to be sure, but Alvar wished to imitate short bursts and slurs of orca-like sounds, which were quite different from what she had just played. Alvar tried again and this time produced a piercing high pitched tone appropriate for his trial. He sounded, at least to his own ears, like an orca emitting an identification call. He knew orcas used an acoustic range much broader than theirs but he worked around that limitation. It was close enough to the very call he had used to identify himself to Akenehi and her clan.

Pranaya winced in apparent discomfort but returned to her examination as she allowed Alvar to continue his instrument selection.

He tried several others with distinctive tones and ranges so he could imitate any number of audible orca calls that he might pick up through the underwater horn. He decided he would use those wind instruments that produced the clearest simple, loud orca-like whistles and a variety of solid objects that when struck appropriately could produce a rhythmic series that sounded to his ears much like echo clicks. If he was successful those acoustic approximations would attract a pod and hopefully hold their attention for an introductory interaction. From there he could try various sounds, watching for responses. He would pay close attention to any auditory signals this new clan might have in common with Akenehi's.

The most important things in establishing trust with an orca were already deeply engrained in him and provided him the most confidence; respect for the orcas physical space and their fierce intelligence, and knowledge of their close and most treasured family structure.

Alvar was genuinely happy he would be meeting a new pod of orcas. He looked forward to being in a familiar element. His privileged bond with Akenehi had made him feel special. He felt as though he had been initiated as adult by her acceptance, perhaps even thought of as a friend. He would sometimes imagine his soul as one of an orca. He called that feeling his *orca-cool*.

He summoned his *orca-cool* and announced he was ready.

He shoved several distinctly different instruments unceremoniously into his satchel.

Grandmother's eyebrows lifted in amused surprise at his gesture.

Pranaya, keeping a cold and steady gaze deep in his eyes, slowly reached in and carefully lifted them out, supporting them with both hands. Her nonverbal behavior told him what he needed to know. They were *ritual* flutes and were not to be treated in such a coarse manner. His action has been interpreted as an insult. She demonstrated how the flutes were to be kept forward of the body and above waist level. Alvar was given a proper ceremonial satchel and Pranaya placed them correctly in position. She closed the purse, then by way of further demonstration, opened it again and showed him the way they should be removed and placed to the mouth for play. Pranaya did not smile at him during the whole stern lesson.

Grandmother and the on looking Cetapiens nodded to Pranaya in solemn agreement.

There went his orca-cool.

Pranaya offered Alvar refreshment before they began the long trek to shore. It might also be a while before a boat would be readied to take him out where orcas were sometimes spotted. Alvar was terrified at the prospect of drinking anything she would offer him after last night. He was a fast learner and he was done with visions, hallucinations and whatever *that* had been. He was reassured this was no ceremonial, vision-inducing drink. It was their daily hydration elixir of water and some fermented fruit juices, for health and rejuvenation only.

As they all drank, she instructed him on a few other polite rituals he should expect once they arrived at Orcasekai. For one thing, the fishermen considered *themselves* masters of the sea and if Alvar assumed a *superior* air over them he might well be immediately thrown overboard. The crowd laughed at that but Alvar suspected she meant it. Then they were underway.

The walk through the forest to the shore was in sharp contrast to his experience only a few days before. The group was in easy conversation quietly canvassing friendly gossip and catching up with each other. Alvar was all but ignored but he wasn't fussed by that. He was enthralled by the incredible shades of green and detailed textures from floor to canopy. They walked and talked and he busily took it all in. They held hands in small groups and kept a connected, friendly human chain throughout the journey. The path was cleared, comfortable and even inviting. The aqueduct, which ran within earshot alongside them most of the way, was as a soothing babbling brook. A brief and gentle rain complete with distant thunder did little to slow them or even provoke their notice of it. The few drops that did reach them on the path were cool and refreshing.

Grateful for the tips on getting along with strangers, Alvar envisioned the subtle greeting ritual to himself. He worried what he might endure by way of social initiation. Worse yet, what if they didn't even see any orcas? If these people had a history of offending them or even just chasing them away, the orcas most definitely could identify a boat and would have associated with it with repulsive behavior. How would he even get close? He was not familiar at all with this new orca clan. He had no idea really what their greeting call would be like. Through the Vencello he knew there was such a thing as sleep-song, but there was no emotional bond with these orcas so he was sure that was out of the question, at least for now. He imagined he might be out on the water for quite some time, *proving* himself.

Sooner than he had estimated and well before he was fatigued from the walk, they arrived at the edge of the forest. The cacophony wafting in from the beach didn't seem right. The sight that greeted Alvar as soon as they broke the forest barrier totally confused him. He had thought they were retracing the same general path he had used only a few short days prior. He recalled a much different shore. Then it was an empty pristine beach full of brambles and thorns between the water and the trees he had just emerged from and there had been only two other human souls in sight. He doubted his orientation. Surely what he was looking upon now was a completely different beach.

He was not mistaken. He *had* retraced his steps. His presence on the shore his first day had caused a temporary temporal paradox which had since self-corrected.

It happened.

Things were *normal*. The beach was heavily populated and bubbling with activity. There were no platforms or temples at Orcasekai. Their realm was water, beach and the immediate surrounding trees. Their structures were boats and the vast network of small huts that seemed to Alvar to have just popped out of nowhere.

There were boats just heading out to sea and others were arriving. Men and women unloaded nets and fresh fish hauls from a number of vessels, children seemingly as young as five and on up to adulthood were working alongside a sprawling multi-generational mass of humanity that spread up the coast as far as his eye could see. People busily boned and laid out large numbers fish for drying, occasionally sampling a raw chunk of fish flesh as they cut. Some women carried napping babies on their backs as they worked, others held the hand of a toddler pushing through the beach sand beside them as they headed to huts closer in toward the tree line. Nets were laid out on the beach and examined for damage. Sharpened cutting tools were obtained from huts and taken to those on the beach who had dulled their current instruments through repetitive, rapid slashes of fish flesh and rope.

It was busy, noisy and fishy. Alvar found it *absolutely* wonderful.

The group veered toward a small lineup of rough huts calling out as they approached. At that, perhaps a hundred people who had heard the greeting turned and cheered, calling out in reciprocal manner. Alvar thought they had heard of his great project and were applauding him, wishing him success. He smiled and raised his hand, waving gratitude at their support. Several approached their group and Alvar realized they were celebrating *Grandmother's* return to them. They indeed knew who Alvar was but had little to say to him except to gawk at this tall stature. His confidence deflated a bit.

They approached the closest structure.

Alvar observed it was filled with gear and its contents, unlike the hut itself, were anything but rough. Like the instruments and costumes of Templesekai, the fishing equipment and nets organized in these huts were immaculately constructed and maintained. Their groupings made more sense to Alvar who was familiar with net fishing and had seen similar gear from his time.

The salted air blowing in from the water, the direct sunlight and warm sand under feet felt familiar, like home. If he hadn't known he had time traveled thousands of years into the past he would have thought he and his mother were vacationing in a tropical paradise somewhere. A breeze picked up, he inhaled the brine and aroma of fresh fish wafting around him with pleasure. His confidence began to swell once again.

A man appeared from within the hut as soon as they came within a few steps of it. Alvar was introduced to him, an elder male, who was also a council member and close friend of Grandmother's. He, like Pranaya, seemed to be waiting for Alvar's arrival that day and knew what Alvar was to ask of him. He was aged and sun-weathered but noticeably more muscular and fit than the men of Templesekai. Everywhere this man looked, he squinted, and his face seemed frozen in a soul piercing countenance. He cast his gaze on Alvar and held it, he didn't blink.

Alvar performed the appropriate greeting. It was not brilliant but sufficient.

The Orcasekai man was extremely blunt and down-to-earth even by Cetapien standards, who all shared those characteristics. He merely grunted approval at Alvar, still scowling a frozen squint but then turned deliberately to Grandmother and smiled. Their affection for each other was as obvious at that greeting as the glisten on mother of pearl. She spoke his common name so Alvar might know it, but it was more a paragraph long description of a great leader and lover. It was lost on Alvar who thought of the man from that moment onward, simply, as the Admiral.

The pleasantries over, Alvar jumped right in and shared his concerns with the Admiral. He preferred a smaller boat carrying a minimal group, rather than a crowded larger one that might be associated with threat to the orcas. Better yet, he suggested, they should take out a vessel that was distinctly different from all others and one that the orcas had never been exposed to before.

Alvar was offered a ceremonial craft of sufficient size that was ready and seaworthy. It was very recently built to be used only once for a unique ritual, and then it was to be destroyed out at sea, never to return to shore. Reading associated negative signals in the crowd's body language, Alvar decided not to ask what the particulars of the ceremony were, guessing it would very likely turn out to be an unpopular, perhaps discouraging story. He did accept its use, however.

The Admiral had only to nod and the entire group wordlessly adjusted their plans. A few purposefully turned and left the gathering but everyone agreed as they chimed in unison, Alvar would need plenty of witnesses.

After his briefing regarding the underwater horn and the intended use of the instruments Alvar had gathered, the Great Leader and Lover broke his squint. His eyes widened as he looked the collection over and nodded thoughtfully to himself. He then grunted an Orcasekai ritual request for a successful catch.

Alvar, taking that as the go ahead, stated simply that he had nothing more to say at that time. No word was spoken by anyone in attendance, a few inquiring glances were exchanged between people but after a few moments it was apparent that it was time to depart. Out they went, exposed to the cloudless sunlight of mid-day; crowded into the ceremonial boat that could just safely contain the small crew, a few respected Orcasekai witnesses including Grandmother, Alvar and the Admiral.

Pranaya, who had been silent and in their company up until that time, did not board with the others as the practice was to never have more than one high council member on a boat at one time and they already had two.

They made good time up and down the coast, men rowing and clanking their oars against the boat in a distinctive rhythm. Alvar asked them to stop the percussion for fear the sound would keep any orcas in the area away, but the crew refused. They protested the orcas were certainly used it, the rhythm increased efficiency, but most importantly kept them alert and happily going all day, otherwise they would be too miserable in their task. They maintained a consistent distance within sight of land and Alvar wondered if the oars sound had other purpose; perhaps to report identification and location to those on shore. For hours they power stroked and clicked from one spot to another at the Admiral's direction, stopping and beginning only when the Admiral gave the signal. It was during those frequent delays, which Alvar had no control over, but the rowers certainly enjoyed, that Alvar could use his nifty new orca detector, which he was certain would prove most effective in locating them.

Whether they rowed or not, Alvar practiced imitating orca calls from the various flutes and his efforts in turn were imitated by the crew. Grandmother passed the time with her eyes closed while she serenely sang very pleasing melodies in time with the oar swishes and thumps, her lyrics describing their task at hand, hopes for success and pleas for the orcas to approach them. She also adapted her tunes and lyrics based when and on whatever notes Alvar played. She was a gifted composer and singer, easily handling any range or pattern. Although no one commented, everyone was obviously enjoying her talent.

The Admiral knew his stuff too. He called out the signal and the rowers immediately ceased mid-stroke. He pointed out over the water and Alvar strained through dancing glints of sunlight to follow the line of sight. Soon he too saw them. There they were, unmistakable orca fins heading straight toward their boat from the open sea.

Everyone was swept up in euphoria. They had all seen orcas before but this was special. Alvar looked around at the rower's faces, sweaty and happy, the detail of the oars they still held, their ergonomic handles and broad end paddles still dripping triumphantly in the sunlight, and the wrinkles of Grandmother's face as she squinted an affectionate smile to him, the Admirals loving gaze that fell on her. This was Alvar's place and time. His whole life had been converging up to this point. He had never felt happier or more belonging. Nothing had really happened yet, other than sighting them at last, but it was as if they all knew it was going to be glorious and wonderful.

Alvar urged everyone to remain quiet and this time he received immediate compliance. As the vessel came to rest, its only movement the bobbing gentle motion caused only by the power of the ocean, Alvar and his helpers positioned the horn, wide end underwater. It was surprisingly difficult to hold it so that he could position the narrowest part near his ear, cupping his hands in a steadying and noise reducing effort to hear any vocalizations that might be picked up as they approached.

Alvar urged everyone except those who were steadying the horn to stay back, while he hovered over the water maintaining his connection with his instrument as far as he dared without fear of losing his balance.

The orcas maintained a straight line approach then they broke out of formation before they reached him.

Underwater, he heard calls that he suspected were strategic and cautious in nature. At the surface, he recognized the curved fin of females, the tall straight fins of males and even a couple of obviously younger, smaller orcas. As some circled closer he saw their markings were different than Akenehi and her clan, and Alvar reminded himself that he was geographically very far away from that place as well as removed from her clan in time. He noted the notches and scars and narrated out loud how to remember individuals, facts they let him know they already knew but appreciated that he did too.

One curved fin looked particularly limp and scarred. He suspected that might be the oldest female, the matriarch, and she might be sick or even near death. He explained, to the fascinated crew and witnesses, orca family structure and the fact that the grandmother, also post-menopausal, usually lived far longer than any of the males and that theirs was a matriarchal culture; very much like that of the People.

Alvar noticed one orca was spyhopping; rising eyes out of the water to get a visual on the boat. He immediately switched from horn-listening to flute-playing. He produced an identification whistle and continued to play it as long as the orca's head was above water. As soon as the orca submerged he stopped. He again positioned the end of his underwater horn against his ear and heard distinct repetitions of his own call mixed in with the clan's communicative whistles and echolocation clicks that were in human hearing range. He was very encouraged. He played his whistle sound again and sure enough, the call was repeated back to him, along with a cacophony of others, the meaning of which, he could not begin to guess. He passed the horn to the Admiral and repeated the trial. The Admiral smiled at Alvar when he clearly heard the unmistakable imitation underwater. It was a very promising start.

He turned to his human audience and continued explaining what the spyhopping behavior was but they were well familiar with that one also. He tried to pique their interest in his lecture by explaining the unique call to the orca might associate his image with his unique sound; it would be his orca name.

The faces of the listeners shone intently and their eyes widened, but not because of his monologue. Alvar turned and saw one of the orcas had spyhopped significantly closer, near enough to see into and at the distinctive markings around the eye. It was looking right at Alvar as he turned around, making direct eye contact. Alvar blew his whistle hoping that it would associate the image of him with his orca name. It slowly submerged and came back up to the surface for breath. It was then that Alvar saw it had been the female with the bent dorsal fin who was serving as the clan's scout. When she remained, so very close to where Alvar was standing, he took a risk and leaned over the water to try and touch her.

One touch was all it took. Alvar, who was a G and had traveled back in time, had made physical contact with Arva'Anati, who was also a G and who had also traveled back in time through the same transition period that he did. That point in space and time where Alvar's finger tips touched Arva'Anati's dorsal fin created a fixed and clearly unique marker that distinguished that moment from all others within several billion galaxies and throughout the time-span of the Sponge. A capable time traveler who had wished to find Alvar or Arva'Anati at that Sponge time and location would forevermore be able to easily do so.

The effect was an immediate influx of multiverse time travelers. The Sponge puffed within a very small limited area of the human and orca catalysts in protective reflex to contain the paradox effect of so many. They were very fortunate. After a few very tense nano-seconds for Grandmother, the Admiral and the Acrituchi (who all were acutely aware of the entire dilemma as it progressed) all time coordinates within the time-puff were successfully stabilized.

Alvar had survived the puff. He looked around and the boat was empty except for Grandmother and the Admiral. The sun's position in the sky looked the same, time had not seemed to pass. The weather had not changed. It looked to be the same day. The number of humans present was greatly altered however. The only orca that remained was Arva'Anati.

As long as they maintained unbroken physical contact, Alvar and Arva'Anati experienced shared temporal and chemical reactions and those established a permanent and instantaneous positive bond between them. It transcended time and species. Alvar gained the heart and mind of an orca and Arva'Anati, the soul and knowledge of a human. They were both large brained mammals and so the effect included an emotional bond of deepest love.

Without explanation to Grandmother or the Admiral, Alvar dropped gently in the water with Arva'Anati and taking only one deep breath, submerged to be with her while he could. The whole series of graceful moves between them were executed while maintaining their physical point of connection. There they engaged in their one and only sleep-song together.

They were both G and so they inherently also shared their knowledge and that of O-O between them. So, both knew a time-puff reflex had occurred and that they had defied incredible odds to have survived. Once the bridge was broken, it would be very dangerous to repeat the events that caused it. After this, they could never touch again. Their single precious moment of O-O connection would have to suffice for their entire lives. While they would live in the same area and undoubtedly approach each other at sea, they would have to remain separated by a lifesaving distance.

They coordinated the break away. Alvar returned to the boat with the help of the Admiral. Arva'Anati hung back at the surface, rolling to a position where she kept Alvar's image in her eye. Alvar steadied himself at the side while he looked down at her. They still had a connection of sorts. He was the closest thing she had to family. Her mother and matriarch, Akenehi, was a presence shared with his human. The same was true for Alvar. Through the Vencello, they were of a kind.

Now they had to figure how to get out of the puff, a sub-universe in and of itself, and get everyone back to way things had been. Alvar had no clue, nor did Arva'Anati. Fortunately, Grandmother and the Admiral had been in worse. They explained it simply to Alvar, they needed to do nothing. Natural balancing forces of the multiverse (unbeknownst to them but in their case, The Acrituchi) would come to their aid eventually, as it usually did and soon all would be back to normal.

Whatever *normal* was.

Eventually Alvar became aware of an increasing volume; the rhythmic banging of oars against the boat. When he looked around he saw everything, indeed, was as it had been. Except now time had somehow jumped forward a bit. The rowing crew was happily dipping and lifting in synchrony with Grandmother, who sat, eyes closed, singing lilting lyrics of her love for orcas and high hopes she had for her Granddaughter's future. The witnesses were intently memorizing and rehearsing their retelling of the day's great success. Their mood was understandably celebratory as they embellished their own past experiences with orcas.

Alvar listened as they told of how just moments ago an understanding, perhaps even an Alliance had been struck between human and orca.

Alvar chimed in as the witnesses consulted each other. Their version of events might have people massing out in jubilation to harass the entire local cetacean population. They were leaving out the utmost importance of respect. Both versions, his and theirs, were consistent in that he had touched the orca but Alvar insisted that had been a serious misstep and he should not have (or so he wanted them to believe). That touch had nothing to do with any Alliance. He promised he would never do it again.

He used the solemn tone his mother had used on him the day he jumped into the water with Akenehi and her clan. It was unnecessary. They assured him they were in full agreement. They would include in their retelling that they would all have to demonstrate humans were harmless and would continue to leave them in peace.

Alvar told them historical accounts of fishermen such as themselves who actually were helped by orcas. Catches could be larger and easier than they could have ever hoped if they could gain the orcas trust and accept their assistance without fear, in return. Alvar's anecdotal stories were incorporated in the performance and quickly spread throughout Cetapiens as the most celebrated and promising part. Those together with the day's reenactment of the orca encounter were performed at Templesekai that same evening, over multiple showings, on various platforms and arenas. It served to announce Alvar's initiation into Orcasekai. It was very favorably received and remained a wildly popular performance. So much so it was replayed, enhanced and evolved into ceremony over the entire history of Cetapiens.

The Admiral had only stood sternly squinting toward the sea, watching Arva'Anati and her new pod swim out to deeper waters. He didn't speak until he and Alvar were together on land. There he gathered a crowd around and announced that the boat from that day onward would be Alvar's for private use. The Admiral welcomed him as a vital family member of Orcasekai. He took Alvar under his protection and taught him what he needed to know to contribute and thrive among them. Eventually, he was as a father to Alvar who never knew his own during his original time.

CHAPTER 20 – THE ORCA ALLIANCE

Universe: Sponge, Cetapiens

Human and Priori

With the help of Grandmother and the Admiral, Alvar made proper cetacean behaviorists out of the Orcasekai. It was easily done; the people were enthusiastic, respectful and fast learners. In little time at all the orcas began doing what they had originally attempted, to provide help during the humans poor attempt at herding fish into the nets. It became a matter of sacred ritual and survival to honor the orcas participation and keep them as part of their extended community. The establishment of that alliance marked the *official* beginning of Cetapiens, as Orcasekai identified so strongly with the resident pod they began to think of their very souls as cetacean *and* human.

To be more accurate, the Cetapiens came to recognize they owed their long reign of easy and prosperous living to no less than three critical circumstances. One, their location in space and time put them in a stable year-round optimal climate with no other humans in competition for resources. Two, the Acrituchi, which they had no firm detail on other than what they all experienced as a profound spiritual connection, provided a continuously regenerated chemically balanced infusion through the surrounding forest ecosystem. It provided unprecedented optimal survival needs based on feedback provided by the biochemical composition of the Cetapiens. Three, the orcas tipped the scale and eliminated the last threat to potential conflict or power play which would have been a limited or reduced supply of fish. An official recognition took hold; a reflection of their three prophetic original realms. Their location on their planet: Eaglesekai, the chemical symbiosis with the Acrituchi: Templesekai, and their eventual alliance with the local pod: Orcasekai. Those became less divisions of living or work and more unifying spiritual aspects shared by each and every one of them.

The transition happened in classic Cetapien manner: without conflict and with speed. Needless to say, many in the Eaglesekai and Templesekai wanted to enjoy the communion with the orcas as well. Soon a work exchange rotation was organized so that those that wished could apprentice for an extended period with any other group. Relic divisions between the three *value* activities that had discouraged crossover were thus unofficially ended. That eventually developed further until it was *required* that all Cetapiens learn trades and live among each of the three. Unless they simply had no physical ability, everyone was required to be a fisherman, a mixer of elixir and entertainer, and a farmer. The early single-group identity and many accompanying stereotypes disappeared and a well-rounded comprehensive education, work and communal living system thrived for millennia.

The fully matured Cetapien culture mirrored the world of Brough and the cetaceans so more than other human society before or since. As many Priori were attracted specifically to the cetacean life experience it attracted those to the Cetapiens human culture for their similarities. The more that was learned of cetaceans and incorporated into their culture, the more time travelers were among them, which resulted in a less traditional human culture (which had almost exclusively included hierarchical, wealth based, warring, destruction of nature and other time traveler repellents) and became more attractive to multiverse travelers and so on.

The Cetapiens developed very much like cetaceans in spirit, if not in body. Both were not only oblivious to the desire to possess objects, they were adamantly opposed to any possession of a living thing. Even eating fish and harvesting food were not considered taking or owning but rather merging. Lifelong friendship and love were extended to all and not restricted by contract, wealth or group identification. They did not keep pets or livestock although they had ongoing friendships and respect for many sentient species that shared their realm. One gender was not favored or deemed superior to another; one value group was not favored or given more than another. Individual favorites and preferences naturally occurred but they were not considered accomplishments or truths and they were rarely permanent.

For those and many other reasons, Multiverse time travelers never stopped visiting the Cetapiens. The Cetapiens were specific to a time span but the time travelers just keep going back to that special era when they lived attractive lives. That was the primary reason such scant evidence of the Cetapiens was available to post-Cetapien humans of Alvar's original time. Their past kept changing; there was no *absolute* events to be discovered; always visited and always in *flux*.

During their entire time there was no shortage of petty bickering and common stupidity. Mistakes were made that sometimes resulted in accidental injury or death. Disease, natural death and weather related disasters provided more than enough despair, grief and adversity. There were problems, to be sure. However, overpopulation, hoarding, famine, theft, murder and war were not among them.

Orca

Alvar was incorrect. The limp fin did not belong to the matriarch. *That* was Arva' Anati.

She had been fresh through the multiverse herself. Like Alvar she was in the first few days of adjusting to her new family, the unfamiliar ocean territory and freedom.

Freedom. That was a human word and there was no cetacean equivalent. At sea, an orca life was lived so that human *free* was to that orca *undefinable* as *droplet* was to *ocean*. It would have been a nonsensical concept had she not been enslaved.

Her heart was repaired but the memory of how to move through the water to turn, spin, breach, tail slap at full orca speed…she was relearning it all.

Through the Vencello she had been with her mother, Akenehi, again. Akenehi, whose desire for revenge on those who held her daughter slave for so long was tempered by Arva'Anati's sincere affection for some of her captors, was regaining balance and able to focus on the clan she left behind in the Sponge. They would always have a connection and Arva'Anati received her greatest assistance in her new time from her mother who never stopped loving her.

She was not near death when Alvar first saw her. Her passage via the C-60 process had restored her to the general health template written in her DNA. Instantly *filling out* from atrophy caused by decades of severe movement restriction would take food intake and exercise and was not included in the travel arrangements. Her dorsal fin simply took a little more time to recover. And recover she did, happily and speedily. She breathed easier in the clear, unpolluted air. She heard better in the water that was free from human sonar, motors and the like. Her scars she kept. Those were deep on many levels and would remain a permanent part of her. Her dorsal fin straightened out eventually, as her fit, natural orca musculature returned.

Because Alvar incorrectly assumed she was the matriarch, she had drawn his attention at that first contact. His respectful behavior toward her and his imitation of orca calls that roughly imitated her own beloved mother's had opened her mind to further interaction with him. Arva'Anati had allowed a human touch, something she was very accustomed to from her captivity. Her subsequent bond with Alvar had been a sacred gift to her, exposing human goodness and courage, purging any bitterness she might have held on to from that long agony.

Through that singular relationship, the other orcas made swift and significant progress toward interspecies communication and cooperation with the Cetapiens.

When it came to contact with the other humans, Arva'Anati was equally at home. She would approach and remain around them with an ease that astounded the pod and Orcasekai alike. Her new family was suspicious of her only at first because she was an unknown with strange familiarity with humans. Eventually they adopted many of her behaviors including allowing close proximity to humans. They developed a deeper trust, then a strong bond through many positive experiences of their own.

Orcas are fiercely intelligent and their memories are exceedingly accurate. Arva'Anati's implausible experience of captivity at the hands of humans was not lost on the pod. They had no way of knowing that the Cetapiens had *no* means to capture and enslave them any more than Akenehi could have known that the humans of her time *could* have done so. Their alliance was indeed a truce on their part. They would help Cetapiens capture fish and in return would not be killed, captured or enslaved.

Eventually, the orcas came to see humans through much interaction over decades as interesting and even comical. Always they felt sorry for the humans who could never really get the knack for life in the water. They especially appreciated the music the humans would play for them after receiving help with a great catch. Using it as a base, they composed their own greater-hearing-range versions they would not have thought to sing had it not been for their musically inclined human counterparts. They even learned the individual human whistles and developed many sincere human-orca friendships that lasted lifetimes.

Arva'Anati was Akenehi's daughter. She had inherited her mother's voice. There was never an orca before or since, so happy to be free, so grateful to her new family and as connected to the Vencello and the multiverse as Arva'Anati. Suffice it to say the joy expressed as she sang of the love for her family, her life, Alvar, and her ocean, was enough to satisfy the most discriminating ear that she was the greatest of all orca kind—ever.

Years later, when Soo eventually passed, they all agreed that

Arva'Anati would be the new matriarch. As matriarch she continued Soo's legacy, which she had initiated, to honor the Cetapien alliance and kept it going for future generations. Sometimes she would be saddened by what she knew the distant future held for cetaceans and her own beloved family, but if one thing was certain about orcas, it was this: they lived in the *now*.

The Cetapien alliance held for over a thousand years. Like feeding the early wild wolves that became docile, the Cetapien humans had become domesticated by the orcas. The orcas never needed help fishing or hunting but they needed humans to leave them to it. When necessary they were willing to help ensure a truce that allowed them to enjoy life and each other. The humans respected and benefited from that truce and an unprecedented peaceful period in human history was the result. Thus stabilized, it was a safe Priori destination, especially beloved by those with cetacean ancestry.

Universe: Sponge

Sperm Whale

It was either orient her massive head immediately toward the surface or be jammed right in the eye by an idiot Deeper. Or so Param thought. At the last moment, Auden-G, that idiot, or Orion, as he would prefer, turned smoothly and gently, and merely gave her a gentle thump on her underside, as close to her skull as he could manage. That small surface area of physical contact was enough to exchange some cells and initiate a reaction. Auden-G pushed away from her and swam immediately away without sound or ceremony.

Auden was Gemini with characteristic Metavoli, Vencello and multiverse physiology. The Metavoli was a progeny of a C-60 Priori hybrid, the descendant of a singular Master of the Ocean: Brough. Inherent in all of that, when Auden-G exchanged even a single molecule with Param it facilitated a conduit for the Metavoli, anchored deep within the ocean floor, to connect to her through O-O. The Metavoli altered her own single function enzymes but hers also worked in turn on the universases. In combination they mutated within her body from a universase into a multiversase. The original simple enzymes in her organic whale body were no longer limited to a single function. In a single leap, they bypassed the universase level and went straight to multiversase functionality. It transformed her dramatically.

And not just her. Param's Sponge genetics, matter and energy connected her to all Masters of the Ocean. The result: every living member of Param's entire species spontaneously self-organized into a multiverse-enhanced super-colony of sperm whales. Their enzymes specificity had been nullified and simultaneously so broadened that each molecule of their anatomy drove fresh complex functions. Each individual whale was compelled to consciously execute clear multiverse purposes mandated at O-O. Each mind was as a holographic map that indicated their function within the new colony species. Not unlike the much simpler slime-mold, the transformed Masters were drawn together from the far reaches of their ocean with single purpose. Environmental triggers had been released, notifying them of mass imminent extinction. Because they were sperm whales, and not mere slime-hold, they all knew where they were going and what they were to accomplish once they got there.

The colonial configuration was new to their new species, but a similar natural behavior had always been a part of their culture even before the transformation. Sometimes they did it to warm the water around one of their young or a sick whale. Sometimes they did it to simply experience soothing body heat from another. Also, any Master that wished to experience a closer bond with another of their kind would physically press together into a contiguous group and echo-click to exchange thought or just float and experience the physical presence of the collected mass.

The similar colonial configuration was triggered and it felt very familiar and natural to them. Param was the nexus for colonial function. She innately compelled her family instantly to her. They arrived and began to take their place around her. The more that arrived, the more the final colony structure took form and the stronger the urge to join in throughout the species.

As they swam to her they arranged themselves near the surface, close enough to touch but loose enough to breathe. Keeping Param at the very center and directly over the Metavoli base, with the most efficient geometry, would offer the most direct route from it at the ocean floor up to Param and then to them.

The subtle change in ocean properties caused by the mass of whale bodies attracted fish and curious dolphins of several species to the unusual event. Sea birds were compelled to join the fray of fish and the temporary 'land mass' of whale bodies near the surface. The result was a steadily increasing concentration of ocean life in the evacuation area.

They remained like that, in formation, for days while more whales arrived. Critical mass was achieved which triggered an unprecedented group behavior. In unison, they orientated head down toward the Metavoli and echolocated in synchronized bursts. At that, a current of C-60 and Metavoli particles stemmed up from the ocean bottom, honed in on the Masters then extended a net-like membrane a mere molecule thick around them. At that point, the whales and the Metavoli became one combined super-organism. It in turn was connected to the Vencello. The evacuation process was well underway.

The requirements had been met to begin expansion of the evacuation membrane. So they radiated straight out in all directions away from Param, who remained where she was, near the surface, at their center.

For the super pod, it was great fun and hilarity. Immediately upon Metavoli transformation and thereafter, when they scanned *anything* at all, they recognized a plethora of micro and macro pattern similarities in everything about their new colony that playfully taunted them. They had scanned woefully inefficiently and underestimated significant information within what they would have called 'meaner creatures'. As they began to radiate outward, swimming apart and spreading the C-60 membrane as they went, they maintained easy communication despite separation over increasingly great distance. That was always natural for their kind but now it was clearer. They clicked to each other new realizations that played off of each prior, quick-evolving concept. Echoes of fitfully laughing whales tickled the ocean. The revelations were as surprising and clever as anything the world had ever known and they easily agreed that the funniest thing of all was that they had always called themselves 'Masters of the Ocean'. How very little they had actually perceived of the multiverse! They exchanged friendly jabs at how different the perception of individuals had become now they were all interconnected. They had all gotten each other, even the most beloved of family members, completely and ridiculously wrong.

But that was all in the past. They were finally together, truly more 'Aware' than any could have imagined, and they were on their way.

On their way to where? None of them inquired. Since the moment of transformation they no longer felt like the ocean was their only home. They were pulled to another realm. They acted as one super-organism 'searching'. Like spawning salmon, their adapted multi-verse physiology calibrated them to a compatible, viable new ocean in another universe.

What would it be like? Well, they didn't know that. But they were as jolly as they had ever been and would certainly love it unconditionally once they got there together.

*****

Over the course of the next several days Param's colony-pod swam away from each other to form a perimeter. The Metavoli membrane was still anchored at the base but expanded, thinned out and intertwined with them, self-organizing into what would be required at the moment of evacuation, right along with them. More whales, also compelled by new instinct that had swum far and fast to meet up with them, joined the pod. They also took up the task at the perimeter, knowing what to do and why.

Param remained at the expanding circles center directly over the Metavoli anchor. Brough's communication never let up; a hum of multi-dimensional detailed information in her mind; a dynamic representation of the status, history and future of their dying ocean world; a continuous mapping and inventory conceptualizing even the most subtle non-linear changes over time.

Brough's conclusion was pretty darn grim. She and her super pod were living in the time when the human population was in the final stages of its burst past critical; the point from which there could be no stopping their consumption of the world's contents. Humans were too like cetaceans, in that they valued the lives of their families and themselves so much more than others of even their own kind, let alone other species. As resources became scarcer, the interspecies competition would drive consumption so complete…

Param understood. The human survival instinct was unstoppable. It would play itself out but only for a short while at the expense of a ghastly number of other sentient beings. No defense could be forthcoming from within their numbers, human or cetacean included, against the damage their world was to endure.

Param was realistic. She understood nature's population mechanisms in fine detail. All of this verified what she had been scanning deep within the ocean floor strata. Extinction was the rule and not the exception. Her home planet had periods of growth and diminishment in repeating, varied cycles. This was merely another one of those finely interconnected iterations.

The cyclical pattern suggested that life would eventually find its way again in whatever forms were possible. Brough's notice from the Priori was that this was so catastrophic an event however, that played out meant there would be no more Masters, no more Orcas, no more cetaceans.

If her whole *planet* died, and she knew now it *eventually* would, other worlds, life containing worlds, would be unaffected and would carry on the *multiverse* sentience in its place.

She grimly digested the concept and the inevitability of all change. She was witness to the last struggling days of many of her most beloved and favorite life forms, especially her own kind.

But it wasn't the end of their linear story. Thanks to her mammalian nature, Param could not give up her family without a fight. Brough was counting on the tremendous maternal instinct of an Aware Grandmother

Master of the Ocean. With her as their nexus they were being *evacuated, relocated* to one of those other worlds. There was no need to have her species vanish from the *multiverse.*

Similarly, there was a need for her *specifically*; her experience, wisdom, detailed memory of the ocean ecosystem and how it all interconnected and balanced. Param had spent decades studying and sharing knowledge of her home ocean and the life it contained. It was not only interesting, she simply loved it so. She cherished her ocean more than her own life. She took care of it. It was more than just a place to swim and eat and raise young. She was *one* with it. Masters of the Ocean would not last long in their new realm without her.

Through the Metavoli and the Vencello she focused in on detail of their new realm, the parameters of the ocean floor and the various species and cetacean individuals that were already there. She rolled her massive eyes back into her skull in a revulsion reflex. There were Auden and Jomei. *Deepers.* They were busy at work in that entirely other universe, doing a wondrous task that would save so many, including her and her family. Those two were expanding the membrane at the *receiving* end of a massive scale evacuation. She got that but she couldn't help feeling repulsed at the same time.

Nothing in the multiverse is perfect. Param's learned prejudiced was one of her persistent flaws.

On her end, the Metavoli was already anchored deep in place, it merely had to be expanded outward at the surface, enclosing as much water, and variety of sea life as they could attract. The Masters were on that. With or without her, the data clicks conveyed to her that some level of evacuation could, and indeed was, going to happen. Auden and Jomei were evidence of that. A larger scale one, including her, was preferred.

She also learned there were already a surprising number of pre-arrival transplants in that other ocean. There were new native species, in the process of evolving and self-organizing, adapting to available energy sources and reproducing at an encouraging rate. Param felt the pull to investigate and work everything into the final balance of the ocean ecosystem. It was tempting; a puzzle that suited her talent and desire for long-term challenging distraction.

She agreed she would assist in *expanding* the Metavoli membrane. She had no scruples there. She was still not convinced she was the only possible nexus. There were many Masters who were heading in from so far away that they would probably not make it to the evacuation perimeter in time. She would be valuable to those left behind. Perhaps a second evacuation could occur.

Unfortunately, the Metavoli was not a permeant resident of the ocean floor. Its ability to remain stable and therefore pliable in Param's universe was limited. Time was of the essence.

That fact only evoked a protective instinct in her for those who remained. She hesitated to evacuate *herself*. Brough pressed her; once the cetaceans and other ocean creatures arrived in their new ocean Param's presence would greatly ensure their survival. An initial imbalance would most definitely occur and her knowledge on achieving and maintaining ocean balance was crucial.

She held the connection to the multiverse in her massive being and begged it that it should not be so, that the ocean would be stripped and polluted and killed off in such an ugly stretch of history.

As she hung suspended in her beloved ocean she recalled her own grandmother's clicks of an ocean filled with life and activity. There were always long stretches of ocean that were relatively devoid of creatures, but now that emptiness had expanded. Param did the click comparison. She increased force and desperate intensity which extended her perceptive range to its utmost species limit. Even those echoes confirmed exactly what the super pod's travel and population counts revealed to all Masters. The ocean's creatures were not just moving off, or *hiding* better. They were critically decreased, being plucked out of the ocean in unimaginable numbers and frequency and many more dying en masse from lack of prey, pollution and other omnipresent factors.

Yes, Brough was right. The mass extinction was coming in faster than any of them could have anticipated. It would soon be a time of starvation and utter desperation. Their established way of being would no longer prevail. They would de-evolve in the end to fearsome, loathsome shadows of their prior greatness.

Param considered which option was worse; losing her ocean if she relocated to a completely different world or losing *herself* as she became what would be necessary to survive the last days and ultimately die despite the struggle. But that was the way of nature in every case. Struggle to survive then die and be recycled. Except there would *be* no acceptable recycling, the ocean would produce slimes and blooms, but the warm blooded sentience that she cherished would be gone.

*****

Param was concerned about the abundance of giant squid in their new home. Night had fallen again and there still didn't seem to be a single one as far as she had detected. The evacuation perimeter was being cast at the surface. She despaired creatures of the deep ocean were being neglected due to priority at the surface and the fact that the anchor at the base was so narrow. They needed squid and she was not willing to adapt to a new food source. They were Masters largely because of what their prey made them. She respected the relationship and considered it a requirement. She expected that it was simply a matter of including enough squid in the evacuation would solve their problem and that was all there was to it.

What she did not expect is what happened next.

While she hung suspended, calculating how many squid would need to be evacuated to feed her family, how she could then stimulate and maintain the squid population spike that would be required, an octopus jetted through the water directly under her. It was unmistakable; the attractive signature turbulence left in the wake of those flowing tentacles stoked her appetite. It had been quite a while since she last fed but she needed to keep this one alive and within the perimeter. It had also been quite some time since she had used an old stun trick that would be useful in this case. With no time to rise to the surface and prepare for a deep extensive hunt, the air in her lungs had to suffice. She dove after it.

The trail of freshly disturbed ocean was still easily scanned with her echolocation and Param followed its trajectory to the morsel itself. The octopus was already too deep, very near the Metavoli anchor. She would not be able to pursue it. It was no use. The octopus was beyond bearable pressure. As she turned to surface, that's when it happened.

The octopus sped straight up out of the depths and attacked her. The sharp beak tore a chunk of flesh away but Param was not in any mortal danger. She was even glad she could now get at it. Still, she could not believe the audacity. Either that octopus was brain damaged and mistaking her for a meal or she had a death wish and desired to be Param's meal.

Param turned to thwack it away with her tail and even stun it if necessary but the octopus intensified its grip and tearing. It was just beginning to get a little annoying when a feast of other octopi joined in.

Unbelievable! Param had never clicked of such a thing! Just when she thought she couldn't be more confounded, but ready to dig in, a giant squid rose from the depth and grasped her tight around the head. She could not open her long jaw. Soon she was covered in a violence of squid and octopi, grasping hard with suctioned tentacles and tearing pieces of flesh off of her. She worked out these idiots were actually trying to kill her, perhaps even eat her. If she didn't do something soon, they would succeed.

In the history of the planet of origin there were many long drawn out grudges. Many were between humans which lasted sometimes for centuries or even thousands of years as Liam's wars taught. But those paled in comparison to those of the ocean. None were so ancient and played out as violently on a daily basis as the hatred that cephalopods felt toward Masters of the Ocean.

Masters did not return the animosity toward cephalopods at all. They felt the utmost affection and respect for their prey.

However, it was the exact opposite in the squid and octopus mind.

Everything that had happened to Param and her pod had also happened to the Cephalopods. They too were now a colony and they were not going to take it anymore from *any* Master of *any* Ocean.

Universe: Sponge

Orion

Jomei-G was desperate to save as many Orion as he could. He had no idea exactly where or even how many there were but he knew precise locations of the Orion realms within and nearest the Metavoli-2 that were likely to contain the most family groups. He also knew, like every adult Orion did, where the closest and largest population spikes of bioluminescent favorites were that season. Find a plentiful collection of favorites and he was sure to come across Orion.

He swam fast through a lot of water. Mercifully, he found most where he had expected, in the depth where no other cetacean could dive, doing what they always did; casually adorning themselves in bioluminescent moving beauty, flirting, feeding and enjoying life in general. He was even able to actually get close enough to touch *some* of them. The Orion didn't trust any stranger, especially sperm whale, orca or human. Even though they trusted a fellow Orion as believing in his own truth, they decided that whatever would be revealed to them was probably bad and warned him to keep his distance. They already had a beautiful, safe haven and it was theirs alone, more or less, so why move on? Many just wouldn't even give him a chance. They let him know they were truly sorry for his distress but they couldn't and wouldn't be bothered. They kept him at a distance while luxuriating in living bling.

Unfortunately, he just didn't have time to argue *ad nauseam* or waste energy chasing them around for a simple nudge.

Those he *did* manage to nudge were sorry because they got real bad news, that mass ocean extinction, especially relevant to cetaceans, was imminent. They learned, however, where they could easily and quickly find the Metavoli-2, be evacuated with other Orion and his own family and be welcomed to a new, unspoiled ocean. Nonetheless, most were firmly convinced of their own selected privilege, existing beyond such *trivia* and felt their place among the stars would be preferable to any new world. Even evidence of their species' certain demise did little to deter their belief in their own safety and superiority.

There was a time for clicks and whistles and there was a time for glowing art. It was time for the latter and Jomei-G was a bling master, even compared to the most suave Orion males. Rather than waste precious oxygen explaining the dire situation he would appeal to their vanity. He dropped the bad news strategy and instead promised them the show of their lifetime which would be only a meager sample in comparison to what the clean ocean would contain. Soon, while his skeptical Orion audience swam above the Metavoli-2 he would demonstrate beyond all doubt that evacuation was in the Orion's bling-demanding interest. Soon after their arrival, *that* ocean would see population explosions, a vast Orion realm teaming with even more beautiful bioluminescent coolness than their current dying ocean contained even at peak season.

A *very* few, after much argument, decided it was at least worth a scan and a look and proceeded to the Metavoli as instructed.

Sadly, Jomei-G had to call it quits with far fewer Orion moving within evacuation range. It was time to return to his family and begin the final phase, spreading light.

Orca

Seasnán *bounced.* This was an idiosyncratic repetitive behavior which indicated she was deep in thought. She surfaced very slowly, felt the sun as it bathed her open blowhole in warmth, then listened to the sound of her breath as it rushed in. She let herself sink slowly; thinking about the automatic response that kept water out and life in. She thought of the absurd positioning of the land squid blowhole and the strange objects that allowed them to continue breathing underwater.

Then she returned to deep thoughts of Akenehi's communication with a series of subtle tail maneuvers that guided her body just beneath the water surface. It was just enough force to submerge her to the very tip of her dorsal fin. She felt the change in temperature as the water cooled it from the glaring rays. *Repeat.* She felt herself slowly rise, then sink again.

Her mother was gone, combined with two such land squid, a long jaw and other small creatures. Seasnán was not sure if she could trust their beloved matriarch as the entire clan always had. Newly responsible for the feeding and safety of her family, she questioned the wisdom of abandoning their ocean home.

She became distracted by the approaching engine of a large land squid vessel. She recognized the sound. These land squid would be taking fish. There were more and more of these vessels, which seemed strange to her, because there were so obviously less and less fish. Fish came from fish, did they not comprehend?

The pod had only just begun to explore their ability, in cooperation with long jaw echolocation, to produce eight fish from one. *That* would solve some of their problems.

The cacophony screaming from the vessel would soon be so close they wouldn't be able to hear each other sing. She called out to the clan and they submerged together and moved clear of its current trajectory.

Seasnán and the pod shared each other's thoughts on Akenehi's desire for their future. Evacuation. A new world. Yes, they had talked about the orca utopia devoid of land squid and dense with clean, healthy prey. Orcas had always honored an ancient truce with humans. For generations, humans had been increasingly in violation of it. On occasion, when orcas realized the humans were hunting fish and failing miserably, they had attempted to help only to be injured, or even killed.

Through Johnny-G, Seasnán learned the horrific truth of her sister's fate; enslavement at the hands of humans. All those moon cycles, while the family had been hunting, singing, playing…Arva'Anati had been suffering, alone. All of those long slow moments, kept from her mother's love and protection; the most heartless act of all.

Seasnán thought back on songs she had been taught of orcas or other cetaceans that had been taken out of the water by humans. She had a clearer idea of what possibly had become of them. Death would have been better, she thought. It seemed obvious the ancient human-orca alliance was no more. And now Akenehi was one with humans and might advocate their species over her own.

She pondered the clans admonition that while Seasnán was in their physical presence as the new matriarch, Akenehi was not *dead* and still communicated strategies to them. Therefore, her family reasoned, Akenehi's desires should still be in full effect.

And so, Seasnán was persuaded to evacuate with her family per Akenehi's instruction to their new realm. She submerged deep and called her clan to her. They gathered around her in tight formation. She announced their priority was no longer the hunt. Instead they would locate the surrounding orca pods and share this: their sacred duty to the enigmatic matriarch and their beloved ocean was one in the same; to unite and sing as never before.

Dolphins and Other Cetaceans

Auden-G fulfilled his mission with Param. She had become a nexus. He wanted to return to Monifa and his family straight away but he had other urgent duties to perform before he could so.

There were many dolphins and other cetacean species that were so critical to the success of the evacuation and he was a catalyst for their participation. As usual, it was easier for Auden-G to approach a dolphin than his own suspicious and elusive species, the Orion. The dolphins had been adequately trusting of the Orion in all rare encounters. Orion avoided everything at the surface as much as possible and spent most of their time in the depths. Yet, dolphins allowed Auden-G to approach and were easily nudged and even friendly in their many reciprocal gestures.

The dolphins were the greatest in number and the most helpful in herding whatever fish were left to be found toward the interior of the perimeter. Auden-G decided that he liked them very much, even if they were pitiful divers. He resolved to pursue friendships with these wonderful little cetaceans in their new realm.

The dolphins were especially fond of sperm whales. They were, after all, universally known as ocean caretakers. Many dolphins owed their lives to those massive friends. When they learned of the nexus and the evacuation, they welcomed a chance to cooperate and even follow them to a much healthier ocean. They were eager to learn what the whales were doing and help if they could.

The dolphins even agreed to temporarily tolerate the presence of menacing orcas. The herds were put at ease partially by the fact that sperm whales would be watching over them and then fully by understanding that orcas would abstain from hunting within the perimeter. Orcas were most critical to the whole process. They alone possessed the acoustic sensitivity and vocal ability required. Without orcas, they were certainly all doomed to die of starvation and illness *en masse* with many other species. Further, orcas were keeping the hugest of the cetacean-threatening sharks out of the perimeter, as only they could. Those were the few ocean creatures that were excluded from evacuation. For that, dolphins were very appreciative.

Having performed his duty, Auden-G took deep dive preparatory breaths at the surface, amidst thousands of cetaceans that he had helped amass. He lost his rhythm for a moment in very pleasant surprise when he detected the nearby distinctive clicks and whistles of a large number of Orion. As he eavesdropped he was stunned that Orion and dolphins were communicating with each other. There was no doubt about it. Orion were mimicking and teaching dolphins and vice versa.

Auden-G dove, glowing within at the prospect of so many potential friendships, to the Metavoli deep in the ocean floor. There he remained, waiting to be reunited with his family who were not where he expected them to be.

He didn't have to wait long. He was soon joined by a very relieved Monifa, his children and his two mothers. They too had been at the surface to breathe, but they had missed each other. Like him, they had stored huge amounts of reserve oxygen utilizing their species unique physiology that let them comfortably do just that. They dove together to continue their vigil for the twins and were beyond joy when they found Auden-G had returned. Being separated was unnatural for the family and they promised each other that whatever happened they would never subject themselves to it again.

Jomei-G soon returned from *his* long absence. A living aura announced his arrival as the faint glow grew into a spectacular frenzy of light the closer he came. He had carefully orchestrated it for their delight and it worked it magic on all of them. They thrilled at his many stories of new Orion with whom they would surely soon befriend and how he persuaded those to join the evacuation to come.

The distant cetacean communication wafting from above slowly became noticeably quieted. None at the depths were alarmed. It was obviously night time and those at the surface were taking turns sleeping and keeping watch. When the Orion felt compelled by the depleted oxygen stores of their bodies to surface, the pod ascended in family formation. Together again, they enjoyed long replenishing deep breaths, quietly admired the moon and the fortunate Orion spirts whose lights twinkled high above them. When their physiology gave the pleasant signal they could maintain extended deep dive once again, the pod moved together into the depths. They passed the time in the usual Orion way until the need for sleep overcame them

They took turns dozing until dawn. It was time to breathe. As they propelled gently upward they whistled how strange it was that this might be the last time they would see their sun rise. They were sorry to find it was shrouded behind cloud cover.

They exchanged many other thoughts at the surface. No one was terribly concerned about short-term survival. They were privileged Orion after all. No other species matched their combined intelligence and depth tolerance and none among cetaceans could match their survival toughness. No other Orion family had a birth survival rate that matched theirs, marking them privileged in even a finer sense. They had everything they needed; their bodies, each other and most importantly their love.

Long-term survival was another issue. They worried somewhat about adapting to an entirely new realm, how the creatures that lived there might change, how they too might be altered, perhaps for the worst. They all understood as any sentient creature of the ocean did, they would live with and adapt to change or perish in short order. It was quite as simple as that. They would deal with whatever came, when it came. The day's events were their pressing concern.

As they lingered at the surface, they synchronized their deep breathing so as to not interfere with their communication. They continued to review what they planned to do and how to stay together as their bodies saturated with oxygen. They waited for their senior mother's signal to dive, as was customary and nudged her out of her reverie when she failed to give it. She had been lost in deep thought and growing sadness. One eye had found the brightest spot in an otherwise uniform grey sky, and it captured her gaze. She observed a few dim rays of sunlight that had managed to filter down on her beloved ocean home. With more than a little regret, she gave the signal and the Orion family dove toward the Metavoli-2 and their privileged deep realm, perhaps for the last time, in unison.

The Orion family took their places, ready for anything. They floated over the Metavoli-2 and waited. They had been affected by their leader's solemn mood. They were all so still and quiet in the dark and preoccupied with their own serious thoughts that they did not notice the bioluminescent brightening that betrayed the approach of one of their favorite bling species, an angler fish. Despite possessing its own guiding glow, the creature skimmed Auden-G's tail at a tangent. Auden twisted and arched unexpectedly, lighting up the water with disturbed organisms. His sudden jolt added to the illuminated swirling fluid patterns from the startled fleeing fish. The commotion resulted in quite the lovely light display.

It certainly wasn't the first time such an embarrassing collision had ever happened to an Orion but the whole family had been intensely anticipating a mysterious 'signal'. In their state of high vigilance, the sudden turbulence and glow set them all violently off. The result was a pleasant pool of light in which they all could temporarily see much of each other.

Monifa thought fast. She bolted away and expertly coaxed the angler back toward them and the Metavoli. At least one of *those* was coming with them, *wherever* they ended up. She charged her young to keep it calm and prevent it from swimming away. She didn't have to coax *them*, they were happy to have an important task to keep them occupied.

Jomei whistled a playful jab to his brother's intelligence and display method. The youngsters quickly imitated it in order to commit the useful vocalization to memory, several times.

The light slowly faded back to black. They resumed their positions and relative quiet. Other than occasional interesting moments of angler control, time passed without further distraction.

Nothing from the Metavoli. Eventually they agreed they should surface again for breath when the youngsters whistled the beginnings of their discomfort. Over the course of the day they took several ascents and dives, some just to break up the monotony more than for fresh air.

It stretched into a long day indeed waiting for a significant change in the Metavoli-2, hoping from one moment to the next that it was coming. Up and down in one column was not natural for Orion and it was wearing on their nerves. They were used to more exercise and empty ocean. They especially missed tranquility. Orion generally took great lengths to avoid others and now with an omnipresent crowd of cetaceans they all appreciated exactly why.

It was all good though. The Metavoli-2 had given cetaceans time to arrive and herd more fish inside the perimeter. However, the growing multitude of dolphins at the surface did not become quiet as they normally would have that night. The incessant excited cacophony could be heard all the way down to the floor. For the first time in their planets' recent history, cetaceans other than Param detected an advanced wave. The zero event was imminent. This particular one was stronger than the Vencello's. Every dolphin and whale within the perimeter perceived it. The Masters certainly felt it and sent out communication clicks accordingly. The orcas became increasingly restless, vigilant and sang so amongst themselves. Dolphins could perceive only a general anticipation but it stimulated them all to chatter anxiously. They all seemed to know that the time was close at flipper.

Universe: Sponge and Multiverse

Cetaceans and Priori

The Metavoli-2 reacted in full force of its agitation. A nexus, Param, was under attack. It no longer mimicked the ocean floor. Instead, it revealed its true characteristics; translucence betrayed its depth and complexity as it franticly pulsed in a spectacular display of multichromatic light. The shades shifted in waves and flashed in synchronized bursts as it assessed and calculated.

Auden-G and Jomei-G nudged each other anxiously. They immediately agreed that the sudden display could mean nothing other than it was time to go. At last! The twins spun around in confused tight circles reviewing in a cacophony of overlapping whistles and clicks what each of them should do, but only for a few moments. Soon, they thought and behaved like privileged Orion again. The family split up according to plan and took their places.

*****

The evacuation mechanism required several key species, serving as the vehicle, an attractor or an activator; all cooperating as an unprecedented unit. It goes without singing that adherence to specific paths was also required.

One was the C-60 Metavoli-2. It was the vehicle. It possessed more than just a talent for organic matter and neural energy Gemini duplication. Johnny-G and the others were all triumphs of that.

It also had evacuation potential, some of which was possible because the Metavoli-2 contained enough essential C-60 molecules that it could act as a multiverse transport. Because the conditions had been right, it was induced to form an extension from its ocean floor anchor to a network of attractors at the surface. Reaching those, it then fanned out to form a membrane as thin as a mere O-O modified molecule thick without diminished connection with its core mass. By analogy, it could extend itself and envelop ocean contents in a way that was remarkably self-similar to an amoeboid feeding mechanism. In doing so, the membrane was primed for the inherent larger-scale adapting and transporting function of the Metavoli-2.

At that point, a harmonic C-60 *transport* similar to that which resulted in the Vencello *universe* could then be completed with sound and light. The expanse of Metavoli-2 membrane defined a boundary that, once activated, protected its contents within a *puff* that existed *within* a universe of suitable color rather than achieving a shade of its own. The evacuation puff was a sub-universe of sorts, like Cetapiens. Time and laws of physics became non-sequitur in relation to any single universe. The C-60 molecules retained their function as quantum organic computers, compatibility between the evacuation and Cetapiens puffs was recognized and the rest was Priori history.

A balancing multiverse quid pro quo reaction could not be avoided. The volume of the C-60 transport was limited only by the swimming speed and endurance of the attractors charged with establishing its perimeter. When the time to shift and balance between universes came, the Metavoli-2 took care of that multiverse computation and all related transport as well. The universes easily self-adapted and so balancing was never an issue.

The attractors were the second required species. Those were of course, multiverse-modified Masters of the Ocean. When Param, as nexus, and the transformed super pod gave the echo signal, it stimulated the Metavoli-2 to orient toward them. Like a reverse lightning strike, C-60 molecules were ejected in a current of multiverse matter and energy upward from the base mass and established a web-like connection between the anchor and the whale colony. As they swam outward in every direction from Param, the membrane self-adjusted and expanded. Masters happily and very deliberately defined an adequate C-60 boundary for the evacuation of the cetaceans and the oceans ecosystem contained within it.

The third species were the orcas. They were activators. They alone had the ability to produce a required organic-sourced pure and perfect harmonic. Their sustained song initiated a chain reaction that unified the whole membrane and its contents to provide data for the Metavoli-2 event. It completed the specific harmonic-dependent phase of the evacuation of all within the conical perimeter.

The narrow path that orca harmonic had to cut across multiple universes, was carefully cleared by none other than the Acrituchi. It was not in any way comparable to an organic species. Nonetheless, without that ancient and vast conduit, no such transport could ever have taken place between any universes, at least none that Priori could access.

The fourth species, also serving as an activator, was Orion, and not just any Orion. The privileged individual who did the honor of *throwing the switch* was none other than Jomei-G. As a G he was also intimately connected to his entangled twins doing their part, one sharing his universe and the other across the multiverse. He could not read their thoughts but could perceive their love for him and their family. It was his ultimate pleasure to create a bioluminescent display that served as the final and most pleasing phase of the activation process. He declared his absolute devotion to his brothers, his mothers, his mate and his children for all to see. Those very same bioluminescent favorites from his own masterful collection provided the sparks that saved them all.

The whole evacuation event also manifested as a clear Priori marker within the Vencello.

Although the cetaceans all knew that if successful, they would be leaving their current ocean, it was a time of incredible excitement and hope. None of them knew what a trans-universe experience would be like, whether they would be able to detect the beginning or even an end of the process. They didn't know whether it was going to be painful, loud, frightening or anything at all. They were very much in the energy and shared optimism of the moment and were all marveling at the dense collection of cetaceans, fish and then...

The orcas detected an unmistakable *acoustic* signal from the flashing and agitated Metavoli-2 at its depth. While they weren't exactly sure if the sudden onset and persistence was the signal they were waiting for, it sounded absolutely gorgeous to their orca ears. They wasted no time and, like the twin Orion, interpreted it as a signal that it was time to sing. If they were wrong, they all agreed, nothing would happen anyway. And sing they certainly did. The orcas found their harmonic and perfected it in polyharmonic tune with the Metavoli. The membrane resonated throughout. The orcas and all the cetaceans then heard what was well within their range, an ethereal resonance that also created a pleasant tickling sensation on cetacean skin.

Auden-G left his brother and rose, hurriedly ushering his family and other curious Orion upward and higher to the center most interior of a broader section of the cone.

Jomei-G remained and delicately corralled his living treasures at the base of the Metavoli.

The stimulated perimeter C-60 transport molecules at that moment existed in O-O and obeyed laws of physics common to many universes. Sharing a physical presence in the Sponge they also disturbed its water in an otherworldly manner. Energy from multiple realms funneled down from the orcas at the ocean surface toward Jomei-G. The Metavoli-2 increased luminosity exponentially so that the cavern below it was bejeweled in light for the first time. Visible energy exchanges manifested from the vertex of the transport cone near the sub-ocean cavern ceiling, pulsing up and throughout the now translucent ocean floor. In a simultaneous flash the membrane molecules crystalized. The result was a multiverse adapted cetacean habitat; a flexible, impenetrable, conical glowing vessel filled with precious brine and so much more.

Jomei-G stirred up his collection of bioluminescent beauties that were Monifa's favorites. They were the very same he and his brother had first used to seal their bond as her mates. They were common enough when at peace but when disturbed they were absolutely gorgeous. Now that they were agitated by all directions and unable to escape they were flashing and displaying in full glory.

Deep in the ocean where the pressure would instantly kill another cetacean species Jomei-G swam comfortably in ever tightening circles within the membrane, choreographing the most dense and complex swirling living light show of his life, reminiscent of his mate's wedding bouquet, his love poem of bioluminescence, into the funneled base. Still not satisfied with his hypnotic seductively pulsing collection he continued to stir the bloom into an even further frenzy, and then he perceived his living masterpiece ignite, a blazing spectrum of multiverse energy surrounding and caressing him as they bolted.

Jomei-G was amazed he could still see despite the brightness, and he watched his lovelies multiply; even Monifa's rarest treasures, exponentially growing in numbers as they flashed. He had not expected *that*. The change in density of living glow leveled as it continued to spread. Soon the entire membrane from floor to surface was full of light beings and the brine became thick with them. It was a bit harder to swim through but the rate of duplication stabilized and ceased before he panicked that they would all be overcome. The glow also stabilized so that the depth of the Orion realm remained illuminated as he never conceived possible. It was no longer the darkest of the ocean. It was transformed through other-worldly light, from the base to the surface, from their Sponge to their new realm.

Full activation had been achieved and transport of everything within the cone occurred instantaneously, without fatality and completely. To those living beings within, their time spent with the Vencello was practically nonexistent. They neither perceived it nor aged much while they were there. Then, without sorrow or regret they all proceeded seamlessly to the next phase. The Metavoli-2 was not oblivious, however. It danced and flashed with sheer joy that it had, impossibly, found its way back.

*****

The humans were kept successfully out of the transport. They did however detect the massive bioluminescent bloom from their space satellites. But they never knew exactly what had caused it.

When Jomei-G spread his light, he really spread it.

Universe: Sponge

Human and Priori

Amaranth refused participation in what would have been her first mating ritual and no one was injured by her decision. She did not wish to be mated to anyone and had made that publically known, simply by being absent from the arena. The people, who had noticed Alvar as an uninitiated observer at the ceremony, worked out that Grandmother was grooming him for Amaranth nonetheless. In that case, they suspected it was Alvar whom she would likely select and who, in turn would choose her. News of his arrival reached Amaranth concurrent with her Grandmother's instructions to not join them until summoned. So their introduction had been delayed. It did not disturb Amaranth at all. She trusted her Grandmother completely. She would find him, when it was time.

Alvar passed from his prior life, thousands of years in their future, while he was in his late teens. The amount of time it took to transition through the multiverse, a process that ensured his survival, adjusted from his natural time, was non sequitur. The effect on his body was not. His time travel journey within two points of time within his own universe necessarily aged him, in his case, corresponding to early in his third decade. That meant he went from a physical teen to fully adult during his tenure in the multiverse. Further, by Cetapien standards, Alvar was therefore expected to sire children, but by their culture and custom, until he was *initiated*, he would not be eligible to do so. Grandmother was eager that he be initiated for Amaranth's sake.

The physical reality of his transition occupied his early days in his new land. He noticed subtle internal differences in sensation. To his human eyes his body limits were evidenced by skin, hair and eyes. To the multiverse the perimeter included radiant heat energy, moisture from breath, etc. So the physical limits of Alvar extended a bit farther away from those layers perceived by overt human senses.

That meant he had transitioned with his clothing duplicated and intact along with a layer of bedding and mattress cover. That had all drifted away unnoticed in the commotion when he was pulled out of the water. He was relieved he had his own clothes at first. They were *cool*, they were his and they respected his modesty. His jeans and T-shirt were, nevertheless, very uncomfortable. They still fit the same. He had not increased or decreased in mass. Externally, the climate was warm everyday and air was dense with humidity. So, his heavy clothing seemed to suffocate him increasingly, until it got so unbearable he gladly overcame his embarrassment and exchanged them for a loin wrap. He had finally and forever handed them over, damp with sweat and reeking of the effects high heat and humidity and overpowered deodorant.

Templesekai had the items burned almost immediately after he surrendered them.

He adjusted comfortably to the freedom of movement the minimal clothing allowed. He appreciated occasional merciful breezes somewhat evaporating his omnipresent perspiration, tickling his bare back, buttocks and down to the back of his legs. He grew accustomed and began to ignore most insects, except for those who too violently demanded his attention or perceptibly sampled his flesh.

Losing his old clothes did little to help him blend in. His racial differences and tall stature drew curious, friendly attention. He had full memory of his old life and that meant he was suspicious and overly-cautious of strangers. He was surrounded by strangers. He was anxious of the crowds of uniformly shorter Cetapiens who wanted to compare their height to his, touch his hair, and so on.

So, he stayed close to Grandmother at first; she obviously and sincerely liked him and had an aura of protection around her. He was happy it was she who served as his particular guide and protector. Soon, he found himself fiercely loyal to her. Alvar noted that strangers in his past and here affected him similarly if they really liked him he couldn't help but naturally return the sentiment. Dislike worked the same way. Fortunately, the people were very likeable. Grandmother was more like family and his affection for her grew quickly. She must have felt the same.

He acclimated more slowly to the common frequent human touch from both sexes that was absent in his own culture. Cetapiens of the same sex held hands as a matter of friendliness. Personal space seemed to be a foreign concept to them. People walked very close together but for some reason, one which Alvar could not fathom, they never bumped clumsily into each other as sometimes he did to them when they got too close. They were all very graceful and aware of their physical position. He began to people watch for the first time in his life and found that contact did occur but it was executed in a longer body stroke with complex nuances varying in contexts, something he had observed similarly in dolphins and whales. Their practiced delicate social *dance* would take time for him to learn.

The shock of females of all ages who casually went topless was not wasted on his hormones. The first few hours within his emergence he had to fight from gawking but it was something he promised himself he would endeavor to get comfortable with quickly. He observed some women wore breast coverings while others did not. It seemed to him it was probably comfort or maybe protection from something they had been carrying, but he was too shy to ask any of them directly.

With so much bare flesh and so little distractive fashion, he noticed whole bodies more and facial features less. Each individual's personal energy level, reflected in their stature and movement, was clearly unique. A beautiful face meant less and less to him as a measure of attractiveness. Energy, grace and communicative movements drew attention and favor. The weight of an individual face lightened into a continuous mass of flesh; torso, arms and fingers. All moved in gracefully choreographed thought and purpose. The entire being used more whole body language in a large part of their communication than his culture.

Alvar obviously took in much detail of bodies and the people were curious about his attention. He offered little in way of explaining himself. He hadn't come up with an alternative to simply blurting out he was from a culture far in the future.

Everything about Alvar fascinated Grandmother, especially his awkward shyness around the females. Even so, Alvar was self-adapting and making extraordinary strides toward complete acceptance and ritual eligibility. He required little overt instruction from anyone on communication in general. Grandmother inquired directly on points she wanted to know. Did he have a mate? She learned he had an interest in his past but he was not suffering greatly at the loss of it. She read his signals and surmised he would nonetheless, quickly form a deep attachment, of a nature very different from the one they had bridged. It was time to introduce him to her granddaughter, Amaranth.

While Amaranth was assigned to one of her favorite occupations, weaving nets with Eaglesekai, Grandmother sent news of his arrival to her. She learned by word of mouth what the others knew firsthand. He was an interesting stranger who had emerged from the water, along with other details of his appearance and behavior. She also knew what only the Master of O-O time travelers did; that although Alvar was human, he was inexplicably like *her* in that they were both out of their usual time-element. She looked forward to comparing their perspectives; they might even be good friends.

When at last she saw Grandmother's messenger coming right toward her, she was seated at the happiest place she could possibly be, under the cool shade of an open huts overhang, singing in a circle of friends, who were composing a new song that made the otherwise meditative repetitive gestures of the task very lively. She hushed their rehearsal with a friendly gesture so they could all hear—she could join Grandmother as soon as she wished.

Finally! The most exciting hub of activity that was going on around Alvar at Templesekai could now include her. New and interesting events had been transpiring and she was getting it all secondhand. It had become as torture to be excluded.

She deftly tied her current knot, signed that her net was incomplete as she passed it smoothly to her friend on the left who had just finished his. She rose and they adjusted their circle. Without words or missing a beat, he smoothly picked up right where she had left off and the remaining weavers began their new composition again. Amaranth grabbed her satchel, made sure the leaves she had collected only hours ago were still within and immediately began the walk alone back to Templesekai.

Before returning to Grandmother, however, she needed to visit the main theatre. She was eager to teach the new song and accompanying movements their weaving group had composed during that day. She rehearsed it over in her mind, as she stepped in rhythm, imagining the choreographed steady weave and tie that had kept them happily entertained as they worked. A wonderful new song that was sure to please and an interesting new human arrival among the people; it was turning out to be a perfect day. Energized, her movements were quickened and seemingly unobstructed as she glided over the forest paths, unscathed through dense foliage.

Even as dusk fell and the woods started to darken Amaranth wasn't worried. She could navigate in pitch dark as safely and as easily as in daylight. Then an unexpected diversion, primal as an instinct to hunt, caught her attention. No great cat of the jungle would threaten her, no Cetapien friend that should happen to cross her path could distract her, and she certainly was not about to allow any time traveler in any universe to undo her actions, not even the Acrituchi.

*****

Alvar, having experienced Cetapiens through the multiverse, was overly confident he could navigate the woods as well as any of the people who had lived there their entire lives.

He was restless and bored. He was used to electronics, motors and a constant omnipresent hum. He heard quiet conversation, birds, insects, some breeze action through the trees. Others were comfortably absorbed in casual tasks and no one was talking to him. They did not notice when he meandered toward the entertainment arena, an easy distance Alvar estimated. He learned a popular performance would commence there that evening. He figured he had plenty of time to sneak a peek at rehearsals and get back to Grandmother before he was missed.

Rather than ask for a guide, he went on his own, an adventure that would include a chance to test the quality of his mind's map and provide him some mental stimulation. As he entered the woods, he searched around and found a long stick with delicate branches off the end. He plucked a few of those away and admired his bug and web-clearing tool. Then he sighed.

"Congratulations. What an accomplishment."

As he slowly walked, he waved it blandly in a wide continuous circular motion in front of his upper body, intent on swiping away any insects or webs that he might otherwise walk into face-first. Grandmother had assured him that most of the spiders weren't as harmful as others but they were all larger than he was accustomed. A soft brush of *something* crawled onto his hand. When he looked down and saw a large multi-legged blot, he violently flung the stick away. He flailed a bit, cursed a lot and then brushed himself over and over until he was sure he was bugless.

He had not been bitten or stung that he could tell. He regained his composure and nerve to continue. He glanced in futility at the darkened forest floor for his clearing stick.

"Idiot" he told himself. Groping through the underbrush to find a substitute would likely produce even more creepers. "Just stay on the path," he said brusquely and clearly in his native tongue to no one but himself. He turned toward the attractive distant sounds of a chorus singing, that at least promised to be interesting. He estimated he was a mere tenth of a kilometer from the theatre from the sound of it and they actually sounded pretty *cool*.

He noticed the sun was setting faster than he anticipated and was having difficulty seeing with what little light made it through the canopy. He hadn't thought to bring a source of substitute light. He paused and reached down to pockets he didn't have, to pull out a light that was back on his nightstand, in another time. With a growing pang of homesickness he mused that somethings, like seeing clearly at night, thanks to that eras technology, were going to be the most sorely missed.

He was getting just a bit disoriented, but it didn't concern him. His strategy was a simple one, he would keep toward the sound of fun and hope rehearsals continued non-stop until he got there. He kept his hands forward and eye-level so he didn't run face-first into anything with more than two legs, or straight into anything that would jab his eyes out. He took one step and heard a twig snap. He was positive it wasn't under *his* feet. He froze and listened.

No mistake, he heard a series of faint snaps and barely audible clicks as something with stealth and speed was coming up right behind him. He spun around toward the source and reached out. The dimming light on his eyes limited his ability to make out only general shapes; *human head, short stature, smooth black hair*. His eyes moved down and in the dark he noticed the familiar features and curves of a topless young female. He withdrew his hands before they found human flesh but she in turn had reached out and touched him first.

With her full palms close together facing him, fingers spread; she pressed both her hands lightly but firmly on his bare abdomen right above the navel. A shiver convulsed him and he sucked in a short breath. For a moment he thought she had some silly prank buzzer in her palms.

He felt lightly electrocuted but it had definitely been friendly, even playful. He liked it. Alvar quivered as the young woman's voice spoke his name, or more accurately, sang it. Still facing him, she began to move her hands up his torso and he reached down and grabbed them to stop her. It was too much. A flood of emotion and images hit him and he involuntarily stumbled back a step.

She didn't falter however. Instead she easily slid her palms out to his forearms and wrapped her fingers around them as she lowered her hands until they were holding his. He was instantly steadied. She knew at approach and confirmed by touch exactly who he was. She had called him by name and now it was her turn to give him hers. It was Amaranth. She told him its meaning, Amaranth, the flower, the color, her favorite, the grain that fed the people...

Alvar interjected what he knew, "Eternal beauty, undying..."

Yes, that too. In the dark he could not see her smile as she dropped one hand but continued to hold his other. She guided him, as they walked together, side by side in the path, at first bumping but very gently and for her part, intentionally. She asked what his name meant but he lied and said he didn't think it had a meaning. It was 'elf warrior' but that sounded stupid somehow and in any event it didn't translate. They had no word for elf. Then he mused, he had never met one but if he did he was sure it would be a lot like her.

She asked where he was going, and wasn't he afraid being new and in the night woods alone.

It was almost totally dark by then and he adapted to her slow steady pace, guided by her constant touch and contact. He answered no, she'd just startled him. Amaranth knew that was an honest answer as Alvar's physical state indicated he was not in the least bit afraid of her. Alvar was aroused. Amaranth knew it and imagined him straining to look down at her. Off to her side and behind her and in so little light, Alvar believed he was cloaked by it, but despite it, Amaranth perceived him fully.

She had been aroused the moment the messenger told her she could finally meet Alvar. Her initial scan confirmed he was a most appealing potential mate.

Alvar asked wasn't *she* afraid, a female alone in the dark woods. She merely answered she was never alone and with a sincere surprised laugh assured him she had no reason to fear him. No truer words had ever been spoken. They talked easily and constantly as they walked, slowing the closer they got to the plaza, both wanting to prolong the conversation. She asked how he found Grandmother to be. He described how kind yet scary she was. They canvassed what they might like to do, the three of them together, the next day.

Even at their deliberately slow pace they arrived much too soon for either of them at the rehearsal, which had just ended as they stepped out of the woods. She only dropped his hand then as they entered the clearing and outermost torchlight. When they entered the plaza they separated at first.

Amaranth went off directly to find those of Templesekai who would commit her weaving group's new piece to memory. She also had well thought out suggestions for those most appropriate to perform it and why.

His boredom completely gone, flushed and happy, Alvar went his own way to introduce himself and talk to others who had collected in small groups about what they were planning on performing. He asked what their masks and costumes meant and if maybe he could participate. He knew he would be expected to eventually in due time as fully as any of them, but he wanted them all to know, right then and there, directly from him, how energized he was at the prospect and that he couldn't wait to get started. No one drew back at his forwardness. To the contrary, they were just as direct. Making Cetapien friends was easy and Alvar felt electric and more alive at that moment than he ever had, multiverse time travel transport included.

Alvar knew the names and stories associated with each face and body he met at Templesekai rehearsals that evening. He still held many details from his multiverse passage but when he had looked at Amaranth he drew a blank. Just like Grandmother and some of the others, she wasn't pre-registered, so to speak. Even so, he was already more at ease with her than anyone he had ever met.

He also started to realize his multiverse memory was being replaced by his daily activity and new sensations. His mental map and impressions that he arrived with were fading as he met actual people in their present and traveled from place to place as each changed daily. The overpowering bodily presence, his physical *now*, was pulling him in like a black hole replacing the Vencello experience as something more vague and dreamlike.

Having made acquaintances and an impression, Alvar walked around seeking Amaranth again. There she was, nearing the forest edge. It was unmistakably her, even with her back to him. She seemed about to leave, without him. He pushed past many shorter bodies, forced to follow a frustratingly inefficient route, as he kept his eye on the black hair in the sea of sameness, which belonged to her. This time it was he who came up behind her, finally moving fast and easily to her side, breaking her eye contact with another. He interrupted without thinking.

"Can I walk you home?" Alvar winced, remembered there was no front door to deliver her to. It was all 'home' in Cetapiens.

Without a word, she took his hand again. She had been aware of his location and desired his company. Had he not perceived and responded to her summons she would have approached him with the same request, to accompany her back to Grandmother.

A small group of Alvar's new friends had followed in his wake as he made his path through the crowd. They casually took position to walk with them. Alvar was disappointed at the unexpected company but grateful for the dark and Amaranth at his side in it. The walk was slow through the newly blackened forest with only a few stars able to pierce the canopy. The lead two held small-flame torches to light the path. Amaranth and Alvar hung back in last position and held hands the whole way. They didn't pull away from each other at any moment. Rather, he often brushed the top of her hand with his thumb as they went, amazed at how much a slight squeeze and stroke of that small appendage could communicate.

Reunited with Grandmother, Amaranth and Alvar stayed with her and talked through the evening meal. She was very animated and lively, more so than Alvar had seen her. Nonetheless, rather than join them, Grandmother announced she was tired and would they mind going on to the evening entertainment without her. Amaranth just blinked at her. On their way, Amaranth stated that Grandmother never missed a show. She was being very obvious, typical Grandmother.

Once there, having watched little except each other, they left, much earlier than most, to continue bonding. They canvassed various subjects for hours, from comically trivial to deep, until finally they could hardly hold their eyes open. They were fortunate to locate a sleeping hut, so late at night as it was, with space enough for two. They fell asleep that very first night they met, face to face, smiling mid-sentence, teasing each other about the shushing from the others in the hut who longed for them to be quiet.

It was the best night of his life.

They spent almost every waking moment together during Alvar's early days among the people, comparing observations and perspectives. As soon as they woke up every morning, they talked. As they toured much of Orcasekai, Eaglesekai, Templesekai and back again they comfortably and naturally maintained their flowing connection.

They were even called brother and sister by the people, mainly because Grandmother called Amaranth *Granddaughter* and Alvar *Grandson*. No one else but these two received this designation from her.

Over days, Alvar watched Amaranth as she in turn observed everything and missed nothing. She had an ethereal knowledge of plants, their effects on and in a human body, and she had many favorites. He was fascinated by her thinly veiled emotional protective behavior toward them, uncomfortable they had to be harvested for nets, clothing and nutrition. She was more than a little sad when she had to eat because, as she complained, she was living at their expense.

Once, Alvar innocently asked why she didn't mind eating *fish* if she was so sensitive to living at another's expense. Fish at least had *brains*. Plants didn't. Her response at first was simply that he was wrong, plants were of a kind that did not require neuroanatomy to think and feel. She knew and loved them and would always know it was so. He said nothing which only provoked her to annoyance. Also, she continued, she didn't like fish they were stupid and ate fish themselves, so why not, and then her energy reached open anger. Why is it he could not sense the Acrituchi, the messages of the plants and had he not been told a story through his tea? It all emanated like a sudden storm right out of her. It blew him away. It was uncharacteristically harsh coming from her.

Alvar didn't know what to say. He just shrugged, "The Acra-*what*?"

Grandmother smoothly explained to Alvar that Amaranth was tending toward plants.

It was Alvar's turn to just blink at her as he had no idea what she meant by that. He figured it was obviously a statement said to him but directed at Amaranth. It hit its mark.

"And why not? None of *this*…" Amaranth waved her arms in graceful sweeping large circles over her head indicating the village and the forest "would be possible if not for them."

Grandmother said nothing else on the subject but Alvar saw Amaranth was already grinning at them and was over it.

*****

Amaranth was a Master of O-O time traveler experiencing extended human form and she had fallen in love with a human, Alvar. As soon as Grandmother gave her consent Amaranth would give him as much information as he was willing and able to absorb.

Alvar was happy and eager to learn whatever she offered.

Once they were comfortably situated on Templesekai ritual mats, it took little more than a tea ceremony without the tea for Alvar and Amaranth to exchange information for which there were no words.

Alvar anticipated concepts of Amaranth and Grandmother that he could relate to humanness; cultural, family and political distinctions. None had fit. To comprehend, he resorted to what he had learned through the Vencello and analogy.

Grandmother translated as a time and space bending catalyst whose purpose, for the time being, was to facilitate maturation and continued growth of Amaranth. Images and urgency suggestive of an eruption and stabilization of a new universe and ensuring Amaranth existed safely within. Exact fit, careful timing, connecting markers across universes.

It felt precipitous.

Amaranth's physiology had translated to Alvar as unrecognizable, unformed, ambiguous, but very close to being ready to phase transition to a permanent, defined state.

Some parts were easier to grasp. Grandmother's and Amaranth's current form, the one that sat on mats and walked on two legs through the village, reflected a mammalian element pervasive in their ancestor's origins and that brought with it behaviors that were familiar to Alvar. Nonetheless, from his view on the mat, he got more a sense of large numbers of cells or perhaps even eggs, conjoined within a membranous realm that could be anything and everything but at a critical moment all other possibilities would be eliminated save one.

It seemed Amaranth came from a generation referred to as Mother which in turn had come from a generation referred to as Grandmother. Neither Grandmother nor Amaranth had been born as he had. They just pinched away from one another. Their shared concepts, introductions to who and what they were, reminded him, remotely, of something he had seen under a microscope. But they were physically with him. They were definitely not microscopic in scale relative to him.

He had only to open his eyes and see her human form to be unconcerned. She was woman enough and he loved her.

The Vencello. They referred to it with a series of harmonics totally different from human language. They came from it, existed very close to it, perhaps even within it. But as soon as he processed what Amaranth was communicating, he recognized the features, the *four bright ancestral orbs;* the pentagon and hexagon molecular arrangement. The whale, the orca and humans, it was all there and it all fit.

He wished he had been able to go to college to study more. To learn about metabolic processes, comparative reproduction among species and diseases. There had been nothing to suggest to him that Grandmother and Amaranth were anything but benign. They were absolutely without malice. They were loving and caring and very intent on not only their own survival but that of their environment as well. It sustained them and they knew it.

Yet he had a gut feeling. Alvar had learned enough during his young educated life to know that it was still a possibility that although they were not aware of it, perhaps they were infecting, causing harm albeit unaware of injury they inflicted, perhaps on the same Vencello they called family.

Nah.

He pushed it right from his mind. Amaranth was his best friend and he loved her. She was all good.

Amaranth and Alvar selected each other as mates.

They approached Grandmother for her consent and proceeded from there.

Alvar had already experienced the multiverse and was therefore pre-initiated. He had proven he could survive transition. He had begun to be desensitized to the strange and unpredictable. If there was an even more interesting experience to be had, he was eager for it. He accepted the risk of transformation to be with Amaranth, the soulmate he loved more than all others.

*****

Of course, Grandmother gave her consent, but first Amaranth and Alvar had to hear her warning to proceed with caution and expect uncertainty. Every mating would have its dangers and unique characteristics, both during and after. Their subsequent creation of a new world would alter their bond with the multiverse and who they were as a result.

Amaranth would return to a form that would enable procreation, confirming what Alvar already knew. Amaranth was not 100 percent human; therefore Alvar was not compatible but could be transformed. Grandmother assured him if he still wished to endure any pain that would likely accompany the change, he would probably survive.

The Vencello universe, defined by its encapsulation within a carbon-60 molecule, would be their breeding ground. The hurricane of genetic variation it naturally generated might be a random hit or miss. On the other hand, Grandmother was not about to leave her beloved Amaranth's survival to random chance. Their kind was very skilled at reading what was to be done and had proven capable enough to keep the Vencello alive as well as their own kind. None could know for sure whether they would be successful or not.

A return to the Vencello! Very desirable. And there it was from Grandmother herself. They had kept the Vencello alive. Alvar concluded that they were benign. His one and only scruple brushed aside, he was ready. Alvar took any warning in her lecture as a mere challenge, as a test of his courage and an attempt to evoke fear, rather than a serious admonition that he could be harmed or worse. Alvar a human male, whose body was aged to its third decade, successful at traveling through the multiverse back in time thousands of years to meet the love of his life, believed in his own immortality.

Amaranth believed in her own power. If she could hold on to him *there*, she could keep him with her. If, for some reason, she couldn't keep him with her, she would return to Cetapiens with him. She would rather live with him to the end of her human life without offspring than have a whole new complete world with some other mate. Believing that her first love was the ultimate and only one possible, she devoted herself to Alvar and proceeded with their plan.

When Amaranth was ready they would go out to sea together. Once submerged, the initial phase of the mating would take place. Grandmother determined through senses, those which Alvar did not possess nor could fathom, that Amaranth was about 12 sunsets from permanent transition.

Amaranth and Alvar probably had two precious weeks.

Alvar did not process the subtleties of that information. He acknowledged Grandmother with polite nods. However, he could hear nothing but the promise of excitement of the ultimate adventure within a fortnight. Alvar even began to convince himself that they would be together in their new forms for all time, similar to his parents in the Vencello.

Their joining was highly anticipated by both of them. Alvar's attachment deepened and he was overcome with grief at the very thought of life without her. He was convinced he could predict all possible futures. In none of those scenarios, could anyone complement his heart and soul as she did.

Amaranth admired and loved Alvar as much as she was capable.

*****

They left Grandmother to walk together, to nowhere in particular. Amaranth stopped and pulled Alvar's arm straight down, signaling they were to sit immediately on the ground. She adjusted their bodies so her knees were resting on top of his and his legs lightly curved behind her. She sat very close but when he went to embrace her, she gently signaled restraint. She moved his face down very close to hers. Alvar assumed he was about to undergo another Cetapien ritual.

"There is something I have to say to you."

Then, for a horrible moment he thought she had a change of heart.

Amaranth gently grasped his face and positioned it until it was parallel to her own, so close their noses almost touched and he could look directly and evenly into her eyes. Hers were so dark he could not distinguish a separation between her pupil and iris. It unnerved him as he searched them for some indication that they were in fact human orbs.

He noticed at that moment that her pupils did not reflect his image. In fact, they weren't reflecting anything at all. At that very close range, he saw she did not have a visible lens or similar cover. The whites of hers eyes were glassy but it wasn't from moisture. He gazed hard from eye to eye, intensified his focus, searching for detail of the single bright light deep within the very center of each of them. The light seemed centrally suspended within the uniform creamy black surrounding void. The space of her eyes where her pupils should have been was the most beautiful creamy black imaginable. He looked directly at one of the center lights, estimating it measured a mere photons width and it did not flicker. The light bridged the distance of their eyes without obstacle. Amaranth's eyes were the most communicative he had ever looked into and their light conveyed wordless deep meaning of their own. He was captured, *entangled*, and could not break his gaze.

Alvar knew she was in a very serious mood and was about to say something that he must listen to with similar focus. This was the most intense those eyes had ever shone into him. His heart dropped noticeably in his chest.

'I love you. It doesn't matter how or why. I do. That's it. What does matter is that I don't want to be separated from you, ever. If something happens, if we are separated and we can no longer find each other, I will never give up.'

She continued without waiting for him to answer, 'If it seems your whole life has been lived and I have not found you, do not be sad. It will be over between us only if you want it to be. But for my part when all that I am ceases to exist, only then will it be possible that I will have forgotten you and I may no longer love you and seek you out.'

Alvar did not speak, but a smile curled the ends of his mouth and it wasn't because he didn't believe her. It was because he did.

She continued.

'If you believe all could ever end, you will know otherwise. But what I am telling you is, no matter what happens tomorrow, know that you and I are already one. I can no more lose you than I could lose myself. The strongest of all of the bonds that you and I share is love. That's all I have to say.'

Alvar didn't doubt her, not for a split nanosecond. His mother's persistence had taught him the possibilities of love.

He fought the urge to kiss her. He had done that once before and she didn't like it at all. The Cetapiens equivalent of a kiss was to tenderly press foreheads together, eyes closed, hands gently covered ears and to focus on each other's living presence.

So, he placed his hands over her ears and closed his eyes. As they pressed foreheads she tenderly kissed his lips, just briefly. Alvar noticed she actually didn't seem to mind so much.

Alvar wouldn't entertain the possibility that she might be correct, that they would lose each other and it would seem hopeless.

But he appreciated advanced planning for a most unlikely event.

'What *should* I do in the event I lose you?' he asked.

'Meet me at our first touch' was all she said.

Alvar was a time traveler, albeit a once only and one-way traveler at that. Nonetheless, he got it.

Alvar responded wordlessly. He took her hands in his, caressed the top of them with his thumbs as he frequently did, and as usual, she noted its corresponding effect; a pleasant wave of tingling diffracting through her body.

*****

Alvar and Amaranth talked, a lot. The only person she talked to as much as Alvar was Grandmother. She never talked much to anyone else, but she sure did sing to them. Amaranth was one of the most beloved songwriters and singers.

Alvar dropped to one knee in front of her, which because of their height difference put them almost eye to eye. He took her hand in his and announced his intention of singing a proposal of marriage to her.

Before he produced the first note, he bobbed his head back and forth, keeping imagined rhythm and humming the first few notes to get the right key.

She looked concerned by his odd head movement but quickly realized it was intentional and he was not playing around. She couldn't hold affectionate laughter and smiled across at him.

Amaranth was serenaded by Alvar's attempt at *A cappella* modern pop from his own beloved music collection, thousands of years in the future. The scale was not Cetapien and the style was nothing she could recognize as romantic or fitting their mood. She absolutely *hated* it.

Alvar didn't falter. He got to the refrain, the mushy stuff, and slowly started to rise as he kept her gaze. He drew her in close to him as he sang and swayed.

She lost it. She laughed and pushed him playfully away but he wasn't hurt a bit by it. He laughed too.

He was *awful*.

But she knew what he meant. She sang it, the only answer; it was seared in their shared being and in the heartbreaking beautiful voice he loved so.

*****

Amaranth's time to finally form came sooner than Grandmother had estimated. An hour before they left for the shore, Grandmother prepared a special tea for the occasion and stated they must both drink it. Alvar trusted Amaranth completely but no so much tea. He raised it to his nose and sniffed. He looked into the cup and it looked green, smooth and it smelled like a mixture of fruit, flowers and grain. So far, so good. Amaranth explained that had she formed during the day it would not have been necessary, but as they would be joined at night, they would both need it. Alvar looked into Amaranth's eyes and raised his glass, "To Amaranth and Alvar! Cheers!" and threw his head back, drinking it all in one go. It was pretty tasty and he nodded in approval. The others just blinked at him. He was going to explain the toast but he just shrugged and it came out as "Never mind".

To Alvar's surprise the Admiral showed up soon after and announced that he was needed and would join them out at sea. Neither Grandmother nor Amaranth looked as if he was unexpected. Alvar didn't mind but wondered why. Then he realized he might not be coming back. Things might not go as planned and then he just quit that train of thought. Nothing was going to hold him back. Grandmother, Alvar, Amaranth and the Admiral took the short walk through the woods together, that lead toward the shore, and then to Alvar's boat. When they arrived at the beach, a crew of rowers was already assembled and solemnly approached them.

Alvar assumed if he ever married that his wedding, he thought of this as that precisely, would be a joyful occasion. These people were behaving as if they might be going to a funeral. What seemed even stranger to him, as he took in the evening, was Cetapiens had celebrations, songs and dances for the *slightest* occasion. He had been to a part of the mating ritual and it was one of the most enjoyable aspects of their culture. But this lack of conviviality was downright bewildering. No matter. He only had to feel Amaranth's hand in his and his happiness was fixed.

The rowers got them quickly underway and modified their usual rhythmic oar bumps to a reduced thud with each stroke. With that sound alone they were hardly traveling in stealth mode but it wasn't the tireless attention-getter he had grown to expect and enjoy.

The sky on the other hand was cloudless and encouraging; the whole sea sparkled, in Alvar's mind, in celebration. Although it was not quite a full moon, it shone bright and it lit up the boundaries between sea and horizon, land and sea. Its path twinkled in star-like dispersion over the tiny peaks and valleys of the waves. Alvar joked that Amaranth had picked a perfect evening to require a boat ride but no one paid attention to the comment. Amaranth merely squeezed her thumb noticeably into his palm as she continued to hold his hand.

Similar to just about every other night, the breeze was comfortable and all they required for warmth was a thin cloth cotton sheet. Amaranth's and Alvar's cloths differed distinctly from the others. The 'bride and groom' had huge fresh supple leaves sewn into the cloth on one side. Soon after the rowers began their percussion he decided to don his. He inadvertently wrapped himself with the verdure side touching skin. He sought to correct but Amaranth gestured to leave them as they were. Without saying a word she picked up her wrap and put it on in the same fashion, greenery against her body. She wrapped it tight around her and motioned to Alvar who mimicked her. She adjusted her wrap so she could continue to hold his hand. She caressed the top of his with her thumb as she did so.

As the leaves began to lightly interact with his skin he felt a physiological transformation begin. It was pleasant. He whispered to Amaranth.

'What is up with these leaves?'

She smiled at him for the first time since the Admiral showed up, "*Love*."

He thought for a moment then recognized the sensation with a simple confirmation. "Huh".

*****

There was no ceremonial or really romantic way to dive into the sea together. They simply dropped their tender cloaks, held hands as they jumped in, feet first and pinched their noses shut, "Alvar style" as Amaranth fondly called it.

No sooner did Alvar open his eyes and let them adjust to the water pressure effect on them than he realized, they were not alone. There were many shadowy dimly flickering masses just out of focus, but Amaranth was not afraid.

He heard her soothing singing voice in his head as clearly as if she had sung, "Don't worry, it's just Grandmother".

"*Just* Grandmother", wondered Alvar. "How could it be Grandmother? We left her at the surface and there are many here." Then he calmed himself with the reminder that he was in the realm of Vencello events, self-similar patterns of multiverse quantum biology where just about anything and everything could happen.

Grandmother(s) took position and began vocalizing, much of it beyond human hearing. They were there to facilitate, to read Alvar's genetic code, deconstruct and rebuild. They would transform him. He only had to let them.

He held his breath and Amaranth's hands. He remained as still as he could without sinking.

Her hand pulled back from his. Instantaneously Amaranth began final transformation. She was still with him but of a scale so large, as a wall before him, he could not make her whole form out.

She was so close to him, all he had to do was reach out and touch her. Before he could, however, Grandmother(s) got to work on *him*. The harmonics needed to produce a large scale C-60 mutation event were immediately achieved. Alvar was instantly transformed into the most likely to survive genetic variation that would be compatible with Amaranth that his multiverse-time-adapted DNA had to offer.

It hurt. He had survived the moment but he wasn't enjoying it. The pain grew exponentially worse with each heartbeat. He began to struggle and happened to bump into Amaranth. She was still there; silky smooth and her mass didn't give. Instead, he literally rebounded off of her. He began to lose consciousness from the agony of every cell in his body's reaction to the shock of molecular modification. Alvar was literally dying of pain.

Amaranth knew that once he was transformed successfully he could no longer survive in the Sponge he would have been adapted to the Vencello. And he would also be there waiting for her. She was astounded that he was still there. And then her massive heart broke when she realized his heart was still beating and he was suffering so much just to be with her.

It was as if she had attempted to push him through a doorway but something on the other side pushed him back out. No matter how Grandmother sang and Amaranth pushed, Alvar was not able to transition between the two phases. Amaranth desperately tried one last maneuver; she pulled instead. She finished her transformation and from the Vencello attempted to force him through from another realm. It simply was not going to happen. Alvar was stuck in the Sponge but he was now made for the Vencello, where she was and could not go back. Alvar was dying. They were separated.

From the surface and under it, Grandmother knew immediately things were going disastrously. Alvar was in mortal danger. She broke a law of genetics as a desperate attempt and intervened. She quickly attempted an infusion, a sacrificial portion of her own physiology to compensate for what his lacked. She was determined to get him through to Amaranth by passing him off as one of their kind.

It was no use. And it costed her, dearly.

In a moment of despair Grandmother believed the multiverse itself had adamantly kept Alvar in his native Sponge, snapping him permanently back to Cetapiens to die as she had foolishly made him. Her beloved Amaranth was in her final form. She had been blocked from returning and even Grandmother, who was at least still in one, albeit diminished piece could not retrieve her.

Then reason found her again. Grandmother had a choice. She could attempt to bring Amaranth back, but if she did Alvar would dissipate before she could complete the action. Grandmother did what she knew Amaranth would have wanted. She saved Alvar.

Her many ocean counterparts surrounded him as he sank and she commenced saving and restoring his human life.

*****

Alvar knew as soon as he broke the surface that Amaranth wouldn't be coming back. He panicked and screamed for help. Refusing to accept it, he immediately dove down again for her, grasping through water in complete vain. Nothing.

Again. He surfaced for another large breath then, in desperation, he dove deeper and further, thrashing and groping until he exhausted himself.

The Admiral grimly watched Alvar come to the surface and then go under again. He waited until sufficient time had passed. Feeling it would not be an insult to Alvar's swimming and survival ability, he dove in to retrieve him.

Back on the boat Alvar came to and took inventory of the faces looking down at him. There were the rowers, the Admiral, Grandmother, and….no Amaranth. She wasn't among them. He looked up into Grandmother's face; she confirmed the worst with her eyes. Alvar dissolved in grief and she couldn't bear to watch. She turned from him and they all perceived a storm in her swell. Screaming out, she seized Alvar by the arm and for a moment Alvar thought she might throw him back over the side of the boat. Grandmother cried out for Amaranth a few last times but they both knew it was no use.

Alvar sat up and reached out for their cloaks still lying where they had dropped them. He selected hers and wrapped himself tight in it. He sobbed and rocked until he realized what was happening. The physiology of her very real love for him was infused throughout the leaves and now did its work directly in him. He calmed as her essence flowed through his veins. Love would never cease to surprise him.

Universe: Multiverse and Orcasekai

Priori

"Grandmother!"

I wanted to be with her again. Because I knew I couldn't be as long as I remained in Cetapiens. I had experienced quite enough. I had followed her markers. I had worked out all that I could bear to. Left on my own to flow where my natural focus would take me next, without her guidance, would put me at the moment of death for one I wished to save from it but would not be able to.

I much preferred the joy and discovery of star looping and was determined to resume it. After all, she promised she would be close and all I had to do is call for her.

But I didn't call out "Grandmother". I used her Cetapiens name instead. I had sung out "Amaranth".

My first action after I realized that I had undergone a drastic transformation was to call out for her again.

She did not answer. However, Soo, the orca matriarch did.

Soo appeared to me in what seemed to be a sleep-song cloaked in an orca-vivid dreamscape. She took me eerily back to a day in the warm dimly lit deep water off of the shore of Cetapiens. As I watched her float before me she looked unnaturally faded. It didn't feel comfortable, like time travel. It seemed as if I were talking to the dead.

We clicked and sang the ritual greeting then she swam right to the chomp. She was not paying me a congratulatory visit. Although she was happy I had formed, she was not surprised at all by it.

No, she had come to me with an urgent purpose. She came in Amaranth's stead to explain what had just happened.

When I called out for my Grandmother as 'Amaranth', I inadvertently also started my O-U-O. Amaranth had made it so the trigger was her name, sung in tones of clear recognition; it was *my own Grandmother* I meant to summon. As a multiverse catalyst of time and space she had carefully selected and marked viable elements across universes so that by specific singing, those constituent parts were woven together, blended in a new multiverse shade, a unique realm. As enzymes manipulated molecules so specifically that improbable reactions essential to life became highly likely, so Amaranth in a self-similar way threaded coordinates of time and space through time travel so I might continue as a fully formed universe.

I had instinctively puffed around the resulting knot of our self-synchronizing markers and kept it safe until it was able to stabilize. Her name continued to resonate around the new universe and when I had called out for her again the second time, a harmonic resulted that sealed the O-U-O loop into perpetual feedback. It was successfully set and as long as it remained, so my universe would too.

It was that simple. It had all happened instantaneously. She had removed virtually all risk of my dissipation. Planning so it would be over before I even knew it began, meant I did not falter in doubt or fear. She made the required execution of that O-U-O song, specific as it had to be on the one and only attempt, so very probable as to be a near certainty.

Just so I knew.

But Amaranth had gone *silent*. Soo could no longer detect her and was increasingly unsettled by it. They were strongly entangled and she could always sense her at some perceptible level.

Soo suggested it might be because Amaranth was trapped in a bad puff.

Soo explained that it was rare but sometimes time travelers were in a puff that could not easily be escaped from or be perceived through. The Cetapiens puff had gone rather bad on several occasions and didn't I know about it? If travelers cannot get out of a puff and it dissipates, well…

Or, I offered, she might be enjoying the amusement of our silliness in doubting her. I had experienced her stealth and she was formidable enough to elude our detection if she so desired.

At that, Soo seemed to have realized something vital but she remained silent.

I wasn't worried. I had complete confidence in my matriarch's ability. She was magnificent, a survivor. She had done something so wonderful for me; she could do even more for herself. I was sure she was in no danger.

What concerned me was *me* and what I contained. I could neither sing nor scan outward let alone echolocate inward. I begged Soo to communicate all to me that she could regarding my new form.

Orcas were patient by nature. Time travelers had no need to rush. Soo was both. She did as I wished. She took her time providing a rambling description based on what she had derived as she had assisted her best friend, Amaranth, with my preparations. She was aware of most of the details of my constituent markers as well as my Grandmothers.

Among other elements, the new universe within was comprised of the entirety of the Cetapiens time-puff, the whole of a completed C-60 membrane transport including brine and teaming with its precious living contents as well as the recycled remains of the dying Vencello. The completion of the O-U-O song triggered universal self-organization. A lot was going on.

That surprised me because, other than Soo, I felt I was alone and perceived little more than a tickle of dynamic activity within. If anything was alive I could not perceive it as I had during my time travels.

In answer, Soo gave me more startling news. Amaranth had known my transition would be perilous and in order to survive, the O-U-O had to occur in the remnant of the near-vacant, dying Vencello shell. In a sense, I had inherited a condemned human family estate that was miraculously saved at the last moment. It had been made just habitable enough with all of Amaranth's mighty ability and my desperate song.

Unfortunately, it also meant I was no longer a time traveler. As if Soo perceived I was concluding that I had indeed been banished, she quickly assured me that it was not that other Priori were unaware of me or averse to me in any way. In fact, Priori would always be with me. My experiences were marked and combined with Amaranth's by her design, which rendered them all so recognizable and easy to follow that other time travelers rushed in immediately, causing the new collection of closely related, *entangled* marks to puff, all paradoxes self-organized and stabilized. In doing so they provided essential time to the new universe, and company.

Amaranth was unsure if I would be able to hear, see or sing after transition. But she knew I would always be able to dream. And so it was a matter of linear time to know whether any of my Priori senses would be restored to me. Other Priori abilities were also limited and time travel was one of those.

Soo assured me that although I might not be able to sense others, I would never be alone. She did not dwell in sadness or regret but moved right along in her description of Orcasekai.

I loved the very sound of that last bit of her vocalization. That was the song I would be called as long as I held form. Soo explained that Amaranth had carefully chosen it for me and it suited. I did not object and let Soo continue.

A reiterated, much-reduced Brough spun at my center. He was no longer a brilliant orb of the Vencello. He had partially dissipated and what was salvaged resembled the single warm sun of his beloved planet of origin. Some of Brough's remaining mass had spun off and provided fodder for three smaller planet-like-beauties that had formed and were orbiting him.

Of those three, two were locked into a binary system. They orbited close to each other so that one appeared to the other as the largest object in its sky, even larger than Brough. Together they orbited close enough to him to receive sustaining warmth and protection. They also benefited from the Acrituchi, which emanated continuously from the multiverse through Brough. It had flowed through all four orbs of the Vencello from the planet of origin and continued throughout their entire existence. The twins both had ocean and land. On each, the land nurtured plants and the plants were infused with the Acrituchi. The cycle was much like the planet of origin and an innate mutualism between multiverse sentient and both native and transplanted species had already self-organized into a viable balance.

Further, I got to keep thumbs, which were expressed through the Cetapiens who were all living happily in their own time-puffed sub-universe on one of the binaries. In the ocean of that same orb, my cherished orca heritage was intact as Akenehi's clan had been spared and transported along with many other orcas. The Cetapiens alliance still thrived.

Brough's super pod and the Orion had been relocated to the other binary. A multitude of Sponge oceanic beings were also there and all were adapting continuously to their new environment. Soo was particularly impressed by that and credited those successes to the new whale colony that was rapidly developing there. With Param as nexus, a sophisticated network of interspecies communication between worlds was sure to manifest from the current early primitive one. The land was home to only three humanoids; Delora, Liam and their still disoriented son, Alvar-G.

A third, completely ocean covered planet-like mass was much farther away from Brough. It was so distant that its surface was frozen solid. Its brine transitioned from life-sustaining at its depths to increasingly inhospitable slushes as it approached the surface, culminating at an uninhabitable thick solid layer. That barrier obscured the dynamic living beauty of its ocean from the Acrituchi and the other worlds of its universe.

It was similar to its twin siblings' seas in that it was alive with a rich diversity. This cold-surfaced ocean world did not have an environment friendly to mammals. Instead, it was perfect for the cephalopods that proliferated within and were the apex predator. With a nexus of their own, they too were successfully adapting to and balancing the energy sources and delicate conditions that would ensure their survival.

Of course, no plants grew there. It followed that none on that orb received the mutualistic benefit obtained through a plant based food-chain inherent from the Acrituchi. Nonetheless its frozen surface was continuously bathed in it and it was available should any system eventually develop that could utilize it.

All was sound so far. I was good with all of it.

What did I need to keep it going?

Sleep. Become dormant. Soo advised the universe would build itself as most multiverse universes did naturally. Later I would begin to require energy from an outside source but for now, the Acrituchi would suffice.

I wasn't ready for dormancy. I was still very curious. Soo's description sounded wonderful to me. I trusted it was truthful. She was an orca after all. Although I might be unaware of any of it, I had the Acrituchi, Brough, Cetapiens, and whatever the transport contained. I would even be infested with pleasure seeking Priori. Best of all I could apparently still sleep-talk to orcas.

I asked Soo to visit me often and she surprised me with her answer.

She would *inhabit* me. And of course, we would share sleep-song again. The other orcas of Cetapiens would also visit me in their vivid-half-sleep way.

Satisfied, I turned my attention back to Soo's worry for my Grandmother. I pressed her why she believed that my mighty catalyst, her dear friend Amaranth, was stuck in a bad puff?

She asked me instead how I recognized that my Priori Grandmother and human Amaranth were one in the same.

That was easy. When she transitioned, I knew her.

Soo settled then gently acknowledged. She was waking up. She was fading and I knew the connection would soon be gone.

Quickly I asked when I would dream with her again and could any other orcas sleep-song with me too and how soon, and what happened to Amaranth's Grandmother...

Soo was gone.

With no one to think with I became dormant. I was not experiencing another's semi-conscious state through time travel. This was very different. I experienced my own first dream-like states, strange, emotional and vivid. All through them there was music, orca song, whale clicks, bioluminescent swirls and patterns and life, but none seemed to know I was there or thought with me directly.

*****

Then I heard the unmistakable Akenehi in all her acoustic perfection. She was singing my O-U-O and my name, Orcasekai, over and over. It gently drew my attention to her.

She pulled me into her sleep-song and I felt her next to me, occasionally giving me an affectionate gentle bump as we glided through warmth and light. She made her thoughts clear in my mind.

'First thing we will do' she soothed, 'is breathe, my beloved Orcasekai.'

GLOSSARY OF FICTIONAL TERMS

Acrituchi – An ancient multiverse survivor. Not a species as much as it was a vast multiverse sentient energy network that thrived through mutualism within universes on any and all compatible worlds of each. Through sheer size and multiverse compatibility, it was virtually immortal. It was analogous to a neural network of the multiverse. The Acrituchi was not the only one of its kind. It found its most efficient relationship with organic beings through direct sharing of its essence.

Bad Puff – A rare event where a puff stabilizes but traps Priori within the boundary. It does not diffuse and the Priori cannot time travel within or escape from it.

Broken – The general designation used by the native Cetapiens humans to refer to their prior culture and time before they arrived in Cetapiens and achieved what they perceived to be utopia.

G – A short cut designation at the end of a name that could be used to remind one that they had undergone Gemini (via Metavoli-2) duplication. For example, Johnny-G

Gemini – A product of Metavoli-2. Rather than result in an original and a copy the Metavoli reproduced sources through O-O. Therefore, *quantum* duplication occurred and each product was as an original and immediately dispersed to a viable universe. A Gemini was one of two quantum O-O products identical in virtually every detail down to memory, personality, genetics and scars.

Marker – Any distinctive characteristic that flags a target destination or coordinates within or between universes. Markers are used by Priori to safely navigate the multiverse. Markers serve as an attractant and have various levels of difficulty in identification and use. A marker can be established through trial and error to a new target but it involves substantial risk to the traveler.

Metavoli – A dynamic sentient progeny of a simple universase that developed the ability to colonize in a self-similar manner to slime molds. As such, they alternated existing between phases of disconnected individual universases that when desired or triggered joined together into a single complex being. When in colonial form its abilities included but were not limited to reading, duplicating, and transferring organic substance and energy between universes through O-O. The Metavoli manifested several types depending on how many copies of an original it could produce at once. A -2 indicated two, a -4 indicated four and so on. A Metavoli-2 was a progeny of the Vencello and began its existence within that universe. The Metavoli delivered their viable-adapted copies instantaneously into suitable universes. Through the Vencello's Metavoli-2, multiverse and time 'travel' for humans and cetaceans became possible.

Multiversase – Self-similar to universase but virtually unlimited and therefore can appear and effect anything, anywhere or any time, in as much of the multiverse, as desired. Rather than collect experiences in a single or small range of universe as in the case of a universase, a multiversase works across all universes to enable multiverse level events.

O-O – The absolute Omni-dimensional-spatial-temporal essence of the multiverse; shared by all universes.

O-U-O – Unique particle-like universe stabilized and existing within a folded protective membrane of the multiverse O-O, a self-similar progeny of the Vencello Universe.

O-U-O song – The required unique harmonics determined individually for each Priori that resulted in enveloping themselves inside a protective resonating O-O membrane which prevented them from dissipating into the multiverse.

Priori – A designation of the broad range of self-similar types of sentient universes. They all were products of species who survived merge and stabilization from their original universe into their own realms. The Vencello Universe was a simple example of one. Some types of Priori, such as Masters of O-O, manifested universase functionality and similarity to Metavoli in that they existed in dual phases; as individuals and a colonial unit.

Puff – An automatic, self-organizing multiverse response to temporal paradox or any other threat at Priori and universe level. Acting as a multiverse-sentient quantum computer, it sets an effected area boundary and enables O-O solutions to work within. It designates a safe zone where Priori and other time traveling beings can come and go without fear of paradox interference.

Seed of Acrituchi – The Acrituchi's long cold and inactive universe of origin.

Sponge Universe (or Sponge for short) – The Vencello's universe of origin.

The People – The general designation used by the native Cetapiens humans to refer to themselves.

Universase – An enzyme-like being, hence the –ase ending. Rather than involving a molecular substrate, they were weavers of *coordinates* in a self-similar mode resembling chemical catalysis but on specific *experiences* across one or a very limited combination of universes. Attracting markers were set and utilized, eventually weaving them together and therein increased from nil to near certainty the likelihood of Priori and universe survival.

Vencello Universe – An offshoot from the Sponge Universe. A product of a successful harmonic driven viable merge of multiple species (mainly sperm whale, orca and human) encapsulated in a carbon-60 molecule.